While he was Away

D0166958

KAREN SCHRECK

sourcebooks
fire

Published by Sourcebooks Fire, an imprint of Sourcebooks, Inc.
P.O. Box 4410, Naperville, Illinois 60567-4410
(630) 961-3900
Fax: (630) 961-2168
teenfire.sourcebooks.com

Library of Congress Cataloging-in-Publication data is on file with the publisher.

Printed and bound in the United States of America.
BG 10 9 8 7 6 5 4 3 2 1

For Teo and Magdalena

One

I won't let the Oklahoma wind whip our words away. They can get lost when David and I fly along like this—him driving his red motorcycle, me holding on tight to him. But tonight, especially tonight, I won't let it happen. Tomorrow is soon enough. Tomorrow is another enforced separation, maybe silence. Only this time it's different. Tomorrow David is really, truly gone.

I lean into the ratcheting wind, into him, and shout, "Say something!"

David's muscled back moves against me. He laughs. I love the sound of his laugh. It's been rare since last March, when he shipped off to OSUT. One Station Unit Training. That's what OSUT stands for. For David and other infantry guys like him, OSUT means basic and advanced individual training slapped into eighteen weeks.

For me, OSUT means Our Separation is Unbelievably Terrible. I never told David this, not in any of our phone conversations during that time. Not at Family Day. Definitely not on the day of his graduation. Positive attitude. That's what I've got to maintain, now that I'm an army girlfriend. At least that's what all the bloggers say. The girls and women in chat rooms. The answers to FAQs on various military-related sites.

Question: *What's the best way to help your soldier?*

Answer: *Keep a positive attitude. Write lots of encouraging letters. Soldiers look forward to daily mail call.*

I wrote lots of encouraging letters while David was at OSUT. David, who wrote letters to me all the time before he left—even when we'd already spent an entire day together, did not write at all. No time, he explained. Phone calls would have to be enough. When I saw his schedule, I understood. Still, there were days when I felt bummed about the lack of encouraging mail for me. On those days I'd pull out his old letters. I'd remember finding them slipped into my locker or book bag or mailbox. I'd read them again.

I'd wait forever to get another letter from David.

"'Say something?'" His voice, echoing mine, is strong against the wind: "Something!"

"You know what I mean!"

But something is better than nothing, so I kiss David's ticklish neck—his brown skin tanned even darker now—until a shudder runs through him and he cries out, "Mercy!"

Now I'm laughing too, laughing like there's no tomorrow. We bank around a sharp curve and bump from two-lane pavement and the outskirts of Killdeer to single-lane, red dirt road and the country. David revs the bike, sending up a cloud of dust. I bury my face in his shoulder to keep from getting an eyeful. My helmet bumps against his shoulder bone. I'm not laughing anymore. Why laugh when I can still breathe him in? Clean, spicy soap. Faint salty tang. And fresh-cut grass, because this afternoon he mowed the yard for his mom and dad. One last time.

David.

When I look up, we've left Killdeer's streetlights far behind. Stars prick the dusky sky. Shapes dart and skitter in the bright headlight—bugs, birds, and bats, trying to clear out of the way. I kiss David's neck again, and we swerve for one wild moment before he swiftly steers us straight.

"Penna! You're distracting me." David casts this over his shoulder like a token. "Stop, or there could be trouble." He flashes his charming, crooked grin and starts singing Elvis Costello's "Accidents Will Happen" at the top of his lungs, all off-key.

"*Don't!*" With such heat in my voice, I hardly sound like myself. "Accidents—not funny. Or victims. Not now. Not ever."

Immediately I'm filled with regret. That was just the old David, *my* David, ready to play the fool for love, for me. Now he's fallen silent. He trains his gaze on the road ahead, our tunnel of light in the gathering dark.

"Hey." I sound like myself again, not the kind of girl who wigs out on her boyfriend, not the kind of girl who panics over stupid things. "Sorry. This is crazy-making. You know. Right?"

He doesn't answer.

I lick my lips, gone dry from the wind. Okay. I'll talk about things we used to talk about before OSUT. All our incredible conversations about important things. All our incredible conversations about unimportant things. I should be able to remember *something* we used to talk about before. I should be able to give us another conversation to remember when we're apart. Never mind if it's just me doing the talking. Right?

Wrong.

Wrong, because tomorrow threatens like an ugly giant just beyond the sunset-orange horizon line. And I can't remember any of our incredible conversations from before. Zero. Zip. Important, unimportant. It doesn't matter. What matters is that in this moment I don't know what to say to David. And David doesn't know what to say to me.

Blackjack oaks flash past, gnarled shapes that anchor the vast fields and the hulking clots there that I know are longhorn cattle. David guns it and we go faster yet. I wrap my arms tighter around his waist. There, where my right elbow presses, is the sickle-shaped scar he showed me the first time we kissed.

(*Golden September day. Oklahoma City Art Museum. Ditched our class field trip to hang out in the sculpture garden. Tucked into the shadows of a gigantic bronze statue of Geronimo—our first kiss.*) David got that scar long before I knew him, when he was just five years old. He was sword-playing with some other kid. Their weapons were sticks. The other kid's stick struck home too hard. David's scar is just the length of my little finger when my little finger bends to a slight curve.

My little finger bends to just the right slight curve now. And there, where my left wrist rests, are the ribs David cracked in eighth grade, playing soccer. I didn't know David then either; I didn't know him when he played soccer like the Tasmanian Devil. That's what he told me once when it was raining, because those ribs still sometimes ache in wet weather.

"When I was a kid, I played soccer like the Tasmanian Devil, totally out of control, always hurting other kids by accident and getting hurt too." That's what he said. (*Stormy February day. Baking cookies in his parents' messy kitchen. The sleety rain drummed against the roof and fell in sheets outside the windows. Checking the oven's temperature, he clutched the sudden ache in his ribs.*) When I first saw David play soccer last fall, he was totally in control, skimming and darting across the field, scoring goal after goal, finishing out his senior season strong. In his royal-blue varsity uniform, he never hurt anyone and he never got hurt. Never. *Never.*

And he never will.

Everywhere beneath the length of my arms, David's familiar warmth reassures me. *Always*, David reassures me. Never mind what we can or can't say, I decide. Never mind deployment. We can hold tight. I tell myself this, holding him tighter. We can hold tight across continents and the oceans in between. We've got the strong arms of love.

"Beauty is truth," I hear myself shout. This kind of stuff—this is what we talked about. Beauty. Truth. Scars. And so much more. Incredible. Never mind the wind, which is getting cooler, almost cold on my skin. David is warm in my arms.

David throws back his head and wolf-whistles twice through his teeth at the bright white fingernail moon. "Beauty is you, Penna."

Us.

Something long, low, and lean flashes across the road in front us, and David gasps. We swerve. He gasps again. He lightens up on the throttle, and we slow down, way down. The thing has vanished into the shadows, but David has gone tense. I can practically feel his nerves jumping against my skin. He leans forward, away from me. The cold air passes between us. The wind whips the back of his T-shirt, grips my throat. David leans farther forward. He wants me to loosen my hold.

I loosen my hold.

"Okay?" I ask.

He nods. "Sorry. Just got a little—" He falters.

"What?"

He shakes his head. Whatever he was going to say, it's been dismissed. "Nothing. Gotta catch my breath. That's all."

I go for the light touch, just enough of a hold to keep me from pitching off the back of the bike, should David decide to gun it again. I peer over his shoulder at the speedometer. We're barely pushing thirty now. Out here in the country, the limit is seventy, and I can't help it: I want it to be months ago, last year again. Him, the senior guy, graduating a semester early. Me, the junior girl, just moved to Killdeer and new to school. I want David to drive away from tomorrow, not toward it. I want him to drive fast.

"I'm wearing my helmet," I say.

But David isn't wearing his. "Don't want any extra weight. Not tonight. I'll be packing it soon enough." That's what he said earlier when I tried to put the helmet on his head.

We ride on, slow and steady, with David silent and watchful. Grassy fields spread around us. Starry sky arcs above. I lift a hand from David, and, what the heck, I reach for the stars. I tell David what I'm doing. He doesn't make me feel like a jerk for being myself, like some guys from my past. He doesn't do worse, like other guys. David loves me.

And he's about to do what he signed up to do, right before I met him.

I reach higher. I will snag a dark but spangled cloak of sky. I will drag it down and drape it over David's shoulders. He will be dressed like a hero. He will be a hero. He will come home from Iraq.

But the stars slip through my fingers, and then the whole sky too.

I wrap my arms lightly around David again.

"Don't go," I whisper.

He doesn't hear, for the wind.

●●●

We turn back toward Killdeer, driving slower yet as David takes a last, long look around town. We cruise past the shopping mall. The big department store stands empty now. There's a string of little stores, all but gutted.

David groans.

"Oh great, just great," he calls back to me. "The Piggly Wiggly's gone under too."

We pass the barren supermarket, and I see the darkened sign—that familiar pig in his funny hat. Once the pig shone bright and jolly. Now in the gloom, he sports a menacing leer.

"This whole town is tanking. I'll never get a job." In despair, David leans back against me.

"You've got a job," I remind David. "Fifteen months, you'll be done. I'll be graduated. We'll be out of here. Together."

"And don't forget my leave." David sits up straight again. "Eighteen days. I'll do my best to bring in the New Year with you. Allocations go first to the guys who have, like, pregnant wives. But if I can get the holidays, I will."

"It won't matter when we're together as long as we're together," I say.

We drive past Killdeer High. (One more year. My new mantra.) Beneath the bright streetlights I glimpse our reflection, flickering along the tinted windows of the cafeteria. David got so dark at OSUT, sweating all day in the sun. Compared to him I'm a ghost. I tell him that.

"So haunt me over there. Promise you will." Then, as the bike slows even more, he says, "Hey. It's Ravi. Hey, Ravi!"

I glimpse a tall, broad-shouldered guy with straight, black hair, trudging along a parallel path past the school, hands stuffed deep in the pockets of a gray hooded sweatshirt. That's Ravi, all right. I've seen him around town. And David has told me about him: how when they were young, they were just about the only brown-skinned kids in school. On bad days David got called "spic" and "beaner." Ravi got called "A-rab" and "towelhead."

In spite of the bullying, or maybe because of it, they played by the rules. They did park district sports—David, soccer, and Ravi, basketball. They joined the lily-white Cub Scout troop. They earned badges, went on campouts, entered pinewood derbies. David, always charming and easy-going, became increasingly popular. Ravi, shyer and more intense, hung in there. They were loyal to each other.

Then in fourth grade 9/11 happened, and things got way worse for Ravi. Kids didn't know exactly where his family came from, but they called him "terrorist" anyway. He got beat up all the time. Year after year he kept getting pounded. David tried to protect him. But as time passed, Ravi hung more and more in the shadows. He just wanted everyone to leave him alone—even David. That's how David remembers it anyway.

Junior year, Ravi dropped out of school. David said he'd heard that Ravi was waxing floors over at the Walmart, graveyard shift. I saw Ravi there once late one evening in the parking lot but never said anything.

"Hey, Ravi! Where you been, man?" David yells.

At the sound of David's voice, Ravi glances up. His striking black eyes widen. He waves.

"That dude is so lost. And what's with the sweatshirt on a July night like this?"

David speaks loudly so I can hear. From the way Ravi's expression hardens, I think he probably heard too. David would feel bad about this, so I don't tell him.

David revs the bike. Ravi watches us drive away. I wave. This time Ravi doesn't raise his hand.

"He's probably on his way to work." I rest my chin on David's shoulder. "The Walmart's always so cold. I bet it's freezing in the middle of the night."

It's weird, defending someone I've never even met. But something about Ravi's eyes got to me.

David shrugs. "Man, shoot me if I ever look that desperate. Okay, Penna? People must just think 'Taliban,' seeing him. They'd probably think that about me too." David shivers. "I'm so over getting hurt."

David could still be talking about Ravi, the bad stuff they endured in grade school. Or he could be talking about soccer, since we're passing the high school's soccer field now. Or he could be talking about OSUT.

Or he could be talking about whatever's next.

I won't think about whatever's next.

I'll think about now, our roundabout ride. David and I know this route like the backs of our hands. We know this route like the life and love lines creasing the palms of our hands. I pressed our hands deep into plaster last week, so we know them really well.

"For keeps," I said when the plaster molds turned out perfect. David agreed.

"When I come back," he said, "we'll add this to your portfolio."

So we know this route like the five-fingered molds we made, which I will fill with honey and flowers soon. Baby's breath for love lines. Purple nettles for life. I'll preserve our hands. Somehow. I'll keep them safe. When David comes home for good, we'll add this to his portfolio too. *Scholarship material. Art Institute, here we come*, we'll say. We'll clap our honey-hands together. *Applause! Cheers! War and high school—over and done!* We'll crack our honey-hands open. *We're heroes for holding on!* We'll spoon honey into steaming cups of tea. We'll swallow ourselves.

Then we'll pick up this roundabout ride where we left off. Country roads. Red dirt. Starry sky. David showed this all to me early last fall, back when we bought Cokes at the Piggly Wiggly for the first time. He showed me Killdeer too, with its moldering, nineteenth-century brick buildings.

"That was a bank once. That was a brothel," David said. "Now they're both just wannabe bed-and-breakfasts, for when Killdeer finally comes into its own again. Ha."

David showed me the oaks, scrub pines, locust trees, red patina bushes, stinging ants and scorpions, brazen sunsets, sulfuric storm clouds, and red clay earth. He showed me abandoned oil rigs. Right here in the center of town by the shuttered train station, David showed me the one rig that's still pumping crude, its derrick seesawing like a giant's teeter-totter. There were tons of rigs here back in the '80s, David said, when oil was busting out all over. Most of those have dried up now, and the towers and pipes have come down.

"But," David told me, "there's still one fat-cat corporation lining its pockets. Some CEO big shot's making some cold, hard cash. Example for us all, I guess."

Even this time of night, that rig is pumping away.

●●●

We jounce over the train tracks. By day, girls perfect cartwheels on the iron rails. Boys set out pennies to be flattened. *Where are their parents? I'd like to know.* That's what I think, seeing those kids.

"My mom would never let me do that," I told David once. This was close to Christmas.

David laughed. "*Let* you? You're eighteen, Penna. Shake off Linda's clutches."

Then David helped me tie my old Barbie dolls to the bitterly cold train tracks. He cast his shadow over their plastic bodies while I snapped photos before the next freight train thundered through town. One blasted by right after David and I unbound the Barbies, but for once I didn't feel like Linda was hovering, afraid for my life.

I've pretty much shaken off Linda's clutches now. But still, I can't help myself. I glance back, checking, and glimpse my house a block away, sagging like the neglected thing it used to be before Linda and I moved in and tried to spiff it up a bit. Four end-of-the-season azalea bushes, planted by the front steps, that just managed to hang on. A new coat of gray house paint on the front and the back. (Linda says we'll get to the sides next year.)

Linda has left the porch light on. The round ring of the kitchen light glows blue too. Otherwise the place is dark.

I see *her* then. I catch my breath.

David must feel the change in me—a sitting-up-straight—because he glances back. "She's home already?"

"No." I shake my head until my helmet wobbles. "It's just that old lady who walks our block. I swear this is her third time today, though. Way late for her." I bite my lip, feeling concerned. "Too late for someone her age."

I watch the lady's frail figure grow smaller as we zip away. Like always, she wears a simple dress—it was pale yellow earlier today, so it probably is now too. She clasps her hands at her thin waist. She picks her way over a broken stretch of sidewalk, lifting her feet in their sandals almost as blind people do, searching for the next safe place to set them down. Her ankles are so narrow that any wrong move might snap them in two. She keeps her eyes fixed on the horizon as she did this morning and afternoon when she passed by. And yesterday morning and afternoon. And mornings and afternoons before that, like clockwork. She looks fairly steady on her feet, even this late. I have to give her that.

We turn a corner and the lady's gone. I lean into David again. "Linda's still at Red Earth."

David nods. No real surprise. More and more in the past few months, Linda seems to have shaken me off too. She's always at the old-time saloon she inherited, along with the house, from her dad. I never met him before he died, but I'd heard that he was a mean drunk who ran my mother out of town when she was about my age. At the very, very end of the day, dead, my grandpa made amends as best he could for his actions.

"Unlike some people," Linda likes to say. Linda's not big into trust.

If Linda were home, it would be way past midnight and our whole house would be ablaze. It takes Linda a while to wind down from work. She's wired like that. Plus, for the first time ever, she cares about her job, so she's got this extra buzz thing going on.

"Adrenaline rush," she says. Ultimately, though, she likes to wait up for me. The last of her clutches, I guess. "I like to know where you've been. I like to know where you're going," she says.

When I glare, Linda glares back.

"I'm entitled. We're the only family we've got," she says.

Until this year, that fact didn't bother me. Linda and I didn't need anyone else. We didn't need people who dumped us, ran off on us, or worse.

Now, in those moments when I feel like Linda is suffocating me, I just breathe in the scent of David, lingering on my skin.

I breathe him in.

What will I do when he's gone?

Two

We pull to a stop at a crumbling viaduct flanked by a U-Store-It warehouse and a boarded-up brick factory. At least the factory was boarded up last time I looked. Someone must be trying to turn it into something else now. There's some kind of neon flaring over there, some kind of noise.

But David and I don't care about neon or noise. Not tonight. The viaduct is where we want to be.

Other kids come here too, especially when some local band sets up its amps in the dry streambed that runs beneath the viaduct. The acoustics are wild. The parties can be fun. But David and I have always liked the viaduct best abandoned.

It's abandoned now. David turns the key in the ignition, pockets the key, and toes down the kickstand. I jump off, whip off my helmet, and hook it on the bike's seat. I lean into David, press my cheek to his hair. His hair is a shadow of its former thick and curly self. But even scalped army style, bristly and prickling, his hair still smells good, like him.

David hugs me fiercely, swiftly.

The bike's engine, cooling, ticks like a tinny watch, tracking the minutes. David seizes my hand. My life and love lines run longer and deeper than his. Even after all the weeks at OSUT, his hands are still soft.

Amazing. These past weeks, when I felt too sorry for myself, I'd go online and watch videos of the boot camp where David was based. I saw what he went through. Some of it at least. He said it was great. Hard, but good. Worth every minute.

But I saw guys in camouflage, clutching guns as they staggered, vomiting, out of the gas chamber. The ropes course, the high walls and fences they scaled, the muddy trenches surrounded by barbed wire through which they crawled, facedown sometimes, other times on their backs. I saw one guy go kill-crazy, screaming and crying like a madman after he got pepper spray shot into his eyes during a training exercise.

"Breathe. Settle down. Go slow. You're good," the drill sergeant kept telling the guy.

"I'm dying," the guy shrieked, blindly swinging his baton.

I stopped watching then, but still I heard him in my dreams. I dreamed it was David screaming and crying like that. David gone blind, his hands blistered and torn from training. David, who never intentionally hurt anyone, not even when he was a little kid. David needs his eyes and hands.

And he's got them. I squeeze David's smooth, perfect hand. We walk into the cool, damp shadows beneath the viaduct. We leave the ticking sound behind.

"I'm glad you won the contest."

I look at David, surprised. By the light of the single streetlight, I can see that his eyes are steady.

I smile. "You never said that before."

"Really? Well, now I have."

We look at what I won nearly a year ago when Linda and I first moved to Killdeer. I'd never done a mural before, but then I'd thought, *What the heck? Might as well try*—and entered Killdeer's Public Art Contest for Teens. I won the viaduct's curved wall. Every morning at dawn, sunlight strikes just there. That's when my work really glows. But even in the gloom I can make it out: six eight-foot-tall killdeer rising from a gigantic, tangled nest up the curved concrete side.

Hyped on winning and on having just met David, who'd entered the contest too, I painted each bird in a different style—every style I could think of except realistic, though I could have done that too if I'd wanted. There's the Impressionist Killdeer, all wavy like it's shaped by gentle light. The dotapalooza Pointillist Killdeer. The Expressionist Killdeer, its feathers great slashes of paint. The What-the-Heck-Is-That? Abstract Killdeer. The Cubist Killdeer, with fragmented beak and wings going every direction. And the soulful Icon Killdeer, with its golden beak and halo.

At the award ceremony, the mayor and other chamber of commerce folks said the mural really made a difference.

"It salvages the place," the mayor said.

"It makes an ugly area pretty," someone else said.

I blushed, happy, but a little embarrassed too. I'd liked the viaduct to begin with, all rough and gritty. But I was glad I'd made a difference. And I hoped—I still hope—the mural might help me get a college scholarship.

"Your manga guys were great too," I remind David.

I can see his sketch of those guys—his entry—even now. With their regal features and supple limbs, they looked a lot like him.

He shrugs. "I deserved what I got."

I bump against him. "Got me."

"Second place: manga. First place: Penna. Far as I'm concerned, that whole competition was about you."

"This whole *year* was about you," I say. "Far as I'm concerned."

David thumps his chest, acting all macho. "Without me, you would have hightailed it back to Chicago. Bright lights. Big city. Lakefront beaches. And let's not forget your snazzy magnetic school. Without me, you would have gone back there in a heartbeat."

I laugh. "*Magnet* school."

David doesn't even blink. "Fascinating teachers. State-of-the-art kiln. Most excellent computer lab. Sophisticated friends. All-around urban chic."

I sigh, pulling a wistful face. "Dingy, small, incredibly expensive apartment. My depressed and unemployed mother. The mistakes I made, going out with guys who weren't you." My throat is suddenly as dry as the streambed beneath our feet. *Don't go*, I want to say.

David stares at his beat-up running shoes. "You would have left Killdeer and gone back if you could have, even after you met me."

I set my hands firmly on his shoulders. "Don't be stupid. We're forever."

To help him remember this, I kiss him hard.

When I pull away, David huffs out a breath. "Okay." He runs a fingertip down my cheek.

I run a fingertip down his. "Can we get to work now?"

"Hold on a minute."

Instantly I know what he's planning. He's his old self again.

"No!" I'm going to be my old self too. I'm going to be the cautious one, on edge whenever he pulls this stunt.

David ducks from my arms. I make a grab for him, but he dodges my grip. He backs up about ten paces. Then he sprints right past me, straight at the viaduct's curved wall. He runs right up it and back-flips off. He lands on his feet.

"Lucky!"

"I'm always lucky." David shakes out his hands and feet, shakes his bones back into place.

"Except for the time you nearly bashed your brains out." I catch my breath as soon as the words escape. But the words hit home. David frowns. His gaze turns anxious.

"It's okay," I tell him. "Everything's going to be okay."

He nods slowly. He keeps his voice quiet. "No tears now, Penna. Please."

I look away.

"I came home from training."

"Training was only training. Training was not Iraq." I realize I sound like a whining idiot. But I can't seem to shut up. "And I was busy while you were at OSUT. I had school. What am I going to do now, this summer?"

"You promised, Penna." David gives me a pleading look. "My last night. No extra weight."

David pulls me close this time. We get all wrapped up in each other.

Finally we come up for air. We agree if we're going to do this thing, we better do it before it's too late. David searches out the two backpacks that we dropped off earlier this evening before our roundabout ride. He lugs the backpacks over to the wall, drops them on the ground. The sound echoes hugely as he kneels in the dust.

He unzips the backpacks and pulls out four quarts of paint, two thick paintbrushes, two thinner paintbrushes, and a screwdriver. He pries open the paint cans with the screwdriver—blue, red, yellow, green. Then he picks up a thick brush and a can of blue. He looks at me.

We've been planning this for a while—our practically last thing before. Part of the prize, the mayor said, was that I can continue to change this wall, as long as I maintain the quality of the work. Well, we're going to make it better tonight. We're going to give ourselves more to remember. More to bring him home.

I stand under the wing of the Icon Killdeer, flat against the wall. David lets the paintbrush sink into the blue paint. Then, hefting the can, he walks over to me. He adjusts my arms against the cool concrete, spreading them wide. He positions my legs too.

"Don't move," he says.

"Don't worry."

David outlines my body in blue, head to toe, on the concrete. He brushes up against me as he does it; he presses close here and there and there, as if he's imprinting the memory of my shape on his hands. It feels good. When he's finished, I step away from the wall. I laugh. I love the shape he's made. Me, big and blue. But something bothers me too.

"Scene of the crime?" I say.

David shakes his head, confused. "What crime?" Then he grins. "Crime of passion?"

I touch David's chest. He drops the paintbrush back in the can and sets the can carefully on the ground. He holds back for a moment, so I do too. Then my hands cup his head—the bristles at the nape of his neck—while his hands tangle in my hair. There's paint in my hair, on my scalp, I can feel it, but I don't care. On and on and on. *Don't stop.*

David stops first. With a ragged sigh, he adjusts his jeans. I try to pull him back, but he shakes his head.

"Now you do me." He smiles. "That's not what I mean. Silly Penelope." He picks up the paintbrush again. "This is what I mean."

So I outline his body in blue under the Icon's other open wing. When I'm finally finished, we stand back and look. We look and look. There we are. Forever.

I brush blue paint across David's cheek. He dabs blue paint on my nose. We could go on from there, make a real mess, but we stop ourselves. We use the rest of the paint to fill in our mural bodies.

It takes hours doing us right. Sometimes we get a little sad and stop. Then we kiss until we can paint again.

It's one in the morning when we're finally finished. Linda will be home soon if she isn't already. I'd better get back.

David presses the lids on the paint cans with the screwdriver's handle.

"Some folks have angels watching over them," he says. "We'll have killdeer."

"We'll have angels too," I say.

From somewhere a few blocks away a car backfires. David jumps as if he's been shot.

●●●

The motorcycle idles beneath us again. We stare at the closed door of my house. We stare at the dark windows of my bedroom.

I clear my throat. "Weird. It's almost one thirty. She's not home yet."

"So should I come in?" David glances around.

I could keep stating the obvious. He could keep asking it, all cautious and nervous. We could carry on like this for twelve more hours, until we have no choice but to stop. Or we could do better things with the little time we have left.

I climb off the bike and walk up the front porch steps. I fish my house key from the pocket of my skirt, unlock the door, and push it open. I turn back to David in the driveway, but he's already by my side. Moonlight spills like milk over him.

●●●

On my bed, between kisses, we remind each other that we won't.

I fumble with the buttons on my shirt, and for a while it feels like maybe we will.

Then David pulls back, drawing in a deep breath. "Something could happen. We can't have something happen. Not now. Not yet. We made a pact."

"What pact was that, exactly?" My shirt is a tangle. My skirt is a knot.

"You know."

David's right. I know exactly.

I sit up, remembering the pact and the past, putting myself back together again. Back in Chicago I got burned so badly, so many times in a row, that I swore off certain things indefinitely. Even with David. And David, well, he's been burned too. Plus, he's had one too many friends get pregnant, or get someone pregnant. And like my mom, his biological parents also had a little trouble on the unwed pregnancy front. That's not going to be us, we've decided. There are too many things we want to do first.

I push my hair from my eyes. I reach for the buttons on David's shirt, intending to do up what I've undone. In the dim light, my fingers graze David's belly.

David sits bolt upright. He grabs our quilt—the quilt that Linda and I found in the closet when we first moved here. Linda said that my grandma, her mother, must have stitched it together.

"Look at all those seams separating!" Linda said. "Such sloppy work—of course it wouldn't hold up over the years. Let's dump it."

Linda held the quilt as far from herself as possible. She held it like it was some kind of dead thing—like it was her mother, actually, my grandma. Linda has made this clear: the only person she likes less than her mean dad is her absentee mother.

But I told Linda that I could fix the quilt, and I did. I've come to love it. David loves it too—all the colors tumbled together out of star-shaped scraps. "Plum Tumble" we call the quilt. As in, "I'm freezing." "Stay put. I'll get Plum Tumble."

"Plum Tumble," I say now, holding out my arms. "Let's just…be together."

"Oh, *be*." David rolls his eyes. "We'll see about that." He shakes out Plum Tumble. He cocoons the quilt around me. "There," he says, tucking the quilt's corners tight beneath my shoulders. "Safe and sound." He smiles at me. "See? I'm perfect for security patrol."

His assignment in Iraq.

He settles down beside me, and I'm thinking what a great dad he'll make someday.

I'm thinking of telling David this. I'm weighing the impact when my bedroom door bangs open. The ceiling light glares against the walls of my bedroom, and Linda strides in, a blur in her black uniform.

"Get dressed," she tells me.

"Get up," she tells David.

I shake off the quilt, straighten my skirt. David is already standing at the bedroom door.

Linda catches his arm, her face softening. "I'm sorry. You're a good guy, David."

David nods.

"It's just—" Linda hesitates, looking at me with such intensity that it feels like she's seeing the future she wants for me.

David nods like he sees it too. He extracts his arm from Linda's grip.

"I'll be thinking of you," she says.

I'm on my knees on the bed now. I fling the quilt against the floor.

Linda won't look at me. I can smell her, even through David's scent lingering on my skin. She smells like Red Earth—food, coffee, beer. She smells like herself too, when she smells like a hot, sweaty restaurant manager. Linda has smelled better, and she knows it. She wants to toss her uniform into the laundry and slip into some soft, comfortable pajamas. She wants a drink, an easy dinner.

Instead of doing any of these things, however, Linda leans against my wall like she's becoming one with it. She takes a deep breath and says, "Good luck, David."

David gives me one last look. Then he slips past Linda and out the door.

"Let us know what we can do," Linda calls. "Anything you need."

David doesn't reply. He's too busy running out of the house. His footsteps rattle the pictures in their frames on the hallway walls—pictures of me at every age, pictures of Linda and me at every holiday. Only me. Only Linda. Only Linda and me, mother and daughter, forever and ever, amen.

I bolt past Linda and down the hallway. I reach the front porch as David jumps on the cycle and starts it.

"Wait!" I shout. "I'll see you again before you go, right? I'll see you tomorrow?"

But David is already driving away, lost in the dark.

And tomorrow is today.

Three

"'*We?*'" I storm back to my bedroom. "'Let us know if there's anything *we* can do?' Like *you* actually give a rip."

"I give a rip." Linda gestures vaguely at my state of disarray.

My room is way too small with Linda in it. I grab Plum Tumble from the bed—avenger's cape, magical shield—and sling it around my shoulders. Through gritted teeth I say, "He's leaving for *Iraq*."

"It's nearly the end, honey." Linda shrugs. "That conflict is all but resolved. He'll be back."

I want to scream. Instead I laugh—a tense bark. "You think?"

Linda sighs her answer.

"So like you to oversimplify," I say. Linda's face twists, but I continue, "In Current Events, our teacher said *that conflict* isn't going anywhere. Even the withdrawal will be bad."

Linda folds her arms. "My point is when someone goes away like David—"

I snort. "When someone goes away like my dad, you mean. Or your mom. Isn't this really all about you?"

"Good Lord." Linda yanks the band from her ponytail. Her hair tumbles in graying, coppery waves around her shoulders, a clash of cool and warm tones. She really needs to break out the Nice 'n Easy. She just never seems to have the time. "Don't you ever give up?"

"Don't you?" I clutch the quilt.

"No." Linda shakes back her hair, triumphant. "That's the point! That's why we have a life. Finally we have a fresh start, a fighting chance." She lets out a breath. "Sometimes you have to let go of people to keep going, Penelope."

"Oh sure," I snarl. "You're the perfect model of rugged individualism."

Linda wavers like there's a strong wind blowing, about ready to push her over. Usually she looks about ten years younger than her forty years. But suddenly she looks about ten years older, shoulders sagging, chest caving in. Linda looks lost. She looks like she needs protecting, and I'm the only one she's got to do just that.

I have to bite my tongue, literally, to keep from apologizing or placating her. *"Forget what I just said." "I know you did the best you could."* I could say those things. But I don't. I say, "When will you get it? I'm not you. The guy I love won't abandon me. I won't get pregnant."

Linda straightens her shoulders. There she is, her fierce self again. I'd know this stance anywhere—stiff as a board, nose in the air. Linda's readying herself to carry on in the face of adversity the way she has always carried on. The way she carried on when her mother left what apparently felt like a sinking ship, casting off two-year-old Linda like some kind of water-soaked wreckage. The way she carried on when her father sank ever deeper into his boozy depths, pissing on the walls of this very house and leaving Red Earth to the care of his employees.

And the way she carried on when she finally fled her father and Killdeer at age eighteen—my age now!—and drifted around the country, trying job after job, squat after squat, guy after guy, but never settling for anything until the age of twenty-two, when she got pregnant with me and that guy ditched her, never to be heard from again—my pops, some hero.

Linda carried on then yet again for me. She carried me in her strong arms. We drifted together—"Flotsam and jetsam," she always said. We drifted through good times and bad until one day we got the call from an old friend of her father's, his executor. And we found ourselves here in Killdeer. Carrying on.

Linda unpins the golden name badge emblazoned in red cursive from her polo shirt: *Linda Weaver, Manager*. She pockets her name.

"I think it might be wise for you to consider letting tonight's good-bye be the last good-bye, Penelope," she says. "It'll just be worse tomorrow."

The *last* good-bye? Did she just say that?

For a moment I think the cries are coming from inside me. They are whirling in the air above our heads—faint, high-pitched pipings, desperate sounds. *I'm terrified*, I realize. *I'm terrified of what's next. I didn't know I felt this frightened. But—listen to that sound—of course, I do. The only guy I've ever loved, who's ever loved me, is going off to war. He feels terrified of what's next too. That's his fear beating against a wall.*

Then I realize my mouth is clenched tight. I'm not making those sounds. Those sounds are coming from something else above. Something trapped in the attic.

• • •

I yank the cord. The narrow trapdoor in the hallway ceiling drops open, just missing Linda's head, and then the rickety ladder to the attic clatters down and strikes the floor at our feet. The sounds in the attic seem even louder and closer now. Whatever it is thuds against wood.

"Sounds kind of big," I say.

Linda nods. "Raccoon, maybe."

"I told you that window is broken."

Linda glowers.

I gesture to the ladder. "Ladies first."

Linda hesitates only a moment. Then—I have to hand it to her—she sets her foot on the bottom rung and slowly, carefully ascends. The ladder sways and creaks beneath her. The frantic cries are louder now.

I clear my throat. "I thought that wasn't much more than a crawl space."

Linda cranes her neck, peering up through the attic opening. "That was just an excuse. I hate attics."

Her head and shoulders disappear into the shadows then. I can only see her from the waist down. Her black pants are wrinkled from work and splashed with something that looks like gravy. Her black clogs are scuffed, and her bare ankles are wobbly with nerves. Any minute, looks like, she could fall.

"Doing good!" I say grimly.

"Thanks." Linda's voice is equally grim. And then, "Oh, crap. What was I thinking? Penelope, find a flashlight. Fast. I can't see a thing up here."

I run around the house searching and finally remember that I was the one who last stuck it on a pantry shelf. It's still dead from when David and I went out on a walk a couple of nights ago. We went swinging at the playground. We went on the teeter-totter too. Just like we used to all last year, even on a couple snowy days. Only this time there wasn't so much laughter or talking. When I asked David what was wrong, he shrugged and said, "Guess I'm not a kid anymore."

As we walked home, the flashlight dimmed, then flickered out. David wanted me to replace the batteries right when I got in the door. "It won't be ready when you need it otherwise," he said, sounding practically middle-aged. I chalked this up to post-OSUT stress.

Now I have to scrounge through three kitchen drawers before I can find two Cs to do the job. I insert them. The bright beam flares in my hands. It bobs and skitters up and down walls as I run back to Linda, who has descended the ladder for her own good.

Linda grabs the flashlight and looks at me with a level stare. "You're going to be right behind me." Then she climbs back up there.

I chew at my lip and watch her disappear.

A moment later, when the thing hits the attic wall again, Linda yelps and I do too.

Silence.

Then Linda laughs.

"Penelope, get up here! And bring a blanket, will you?"

I go for Plum Tumble.

• • •

I blink several times, astonished. But still, yes. There it is.

I state the obvious. "A killdeer. I'd know it anywhere."

"Me too, with all that research you did for that mural," Linda mutters.

We're crouched on the attic floor, staring at a bird that's trying to play injured in the corner. There the black and white wings, the black-capped head, the two black bands encircling the throat. The bird trembles in the flashlight's cone of cold, white light. It flops around, ruffles and puffs its feathers.

"Who'd think something that size could make so much noise?" Linda says. "It's not much bigger than a robin."

"It's in distress, or it's distracting predators from its nest." I must have watched that Internet clip about fifty times, fascinated by the bird's survival efforts—the way it fluttered and flailed away from the nest it had built by the side of a lake, acting all wounded to save its chicks. I gather Plum Tumble to my chest. "You think there are babies too?"

"We would have heard it earlier if it had been setting up housekeeping." Linda nods at the—sure enough—broken window. "I think it got itself trapped tonight. That's all."

Then Linda begs me to do it. "I went up first. It's your turn now."

So I creep across the uneven attic floor, struggling not to snag my feet on the rough wood planks or trip on the quilt. I whack my head against a low roof beam. I get a god-awful mouthful of spider webs, and I let out a scream. Spider eggs string a necklace at my throat. I keep screaming.

"Good grief!" Linda screams, nearly as loudly. "You're going to give me a heart attack!"

I bat at the sticky mess, but it clings to my hands. In the moonlight the eggs look almost like pearls in their silvery casings. I claw at them and cast them to the dusty floor. I creep some more. Finally I'm close enough.

The bird must be paralyzed with fear. It doesn't even move as I throw the quilt over it and carry it to the broken window. No glass on the floor that I can see, but if I could, I would levitate.

"Great job," Linda says.

I hesitate. "I think it's in shock."

"Let it go," Linda says.

I remember what she said earlier about David. "'If you love something, let it go…'" My voice is bitter with the worst of clichés.

"You have to let it go, Penelope," Linda says.

"It must be in shock." I stand there at the window, the ball of quilt and life in my hands. Even through the cotton, I can feel the bird's heat. I can feel its beating heart. David's heart beats hotly when I hold my hand to his chest, though not nearly as fast as a bird's, of course. This fast would mean death for David.

"Penelope!"

"What if it falls? What if it can't remember how to fly?" I sit down hard on the attic floor and cradle the bundled bird in my lap.

"It's a bird, Penelope."

"What if it has a broken wing?"

"It doesn't. It swooped over my head before, right as rain."

"What if—"

Linda is by my side then. She lifts the bundle of quilt from my hands. She funnels the bird out the window. For a moment it drops like a dark ball of lead into the night. Then its wings flare. We watch the little shadow of it, darting away through the honey locust tree.

"See? Right as rain," Linda says. "Just had to let it go. That's all."

I will myself not to look at her. I won't give her that satisfaction.

● ● ●

We're making our hunched way back across the attic to the ladder when I whack my bare toes on a loose floorboard and nearly fall flat on my face.

Linda's the one who lets out a yelp. "You okay?"

I'm hopping on one foot, clutching the other. Linda blinds me with the flashlight, and I go down.

"Sorry!" Linda cries.

I don't answer. Now my tailbone kills too. Wincing, I run my fingers along the end of the floorboard that tripped me up. It's really loose—there are no nails anchoring it in place.

I look up at Linda. "Shine the light down here, will you?"

Linda steadies the beam so I can see. I tug at the floorboard. It lifts away.

And there, lying in the glow of the flashlight and another tangle of cobwebs, is a thin, dusty envelope.

"Look at that," Linda says.

I lean over, pick up the envelope, shake it free of all but the stickiest webs, then leverage the floorboard back into place.

"I can't believe Dad hid something up here," Linda says. "Must have taken some effort on his part. Effort was not his MO."

I look up at her. Her face is strange to me in the flashlight's glow. "I've never heard you call him 'Dad' before. Only 'your grandpa.'"

Linda shrugs. "I didn't just spring from the head of Zeus, you know."

Me either, I think.

Linda's eyes have gone wary now, evaluating me. "Leave it."

My fingers tighten around the envelope. "Why?"

"It's just some stupid old thing that he should have thrown away. But like everything else, he left it for someone else to deal with."

"I *want* to deal with it."

Something in my voice makes Linda draw back. Now she shrugs. "Whatever. Let's just get out of here, okay? Tomorrow's probably going to be a long day."

I remember tomorrow, what it holds.

"Oh, honey." Linda's voice is the gentlest it's been all night. "Here. Let me help you." She pulls me to my feet.

"Thanks," I manage to say.

What I don't tell Linda is that when I took out this envelope, I saw another below.

I'll come back up here and get the other envelope tomorrow. I'll come back late in the day, when it's really sunk in how alone I am. A diversion. I'll need one. I'll come back up here then.

I'll write my first encouraging letter to David, telling him all about it. I'll provide comic relief. *Crazy bird! Tripped on a floorboard! Fell flat on my butt! And get this: I found another family skeleton rattling around in the attic!* I imagine David's face, reading this. He might be dusty and sweaty. He might be putting on a tough-guy act to impress his unit. But reading my letter—all my letters—his face will soften. He'll smile. He'll remember all that's waiting for him here. He'll remember me.

Linda takes the lead. I limp behind. In a clumsy chaos of shadows and light, we stumble from the attic. Linda goes down the ladder first, but before she vanishes with the light, I take a look back, memorizing the exact location of the floorboard that can be lifted away.

●●●

In her deep purple bedroom ("'Smoke on the water,'" I sometimes sing, entering), Linda grabs the envelope from me before I can protest and rips it open. She takes out what's inside: a postcard-sized black-and-white photograph with those old-fashioned scalloped edges.

"Of course." Linda looks at the photograph then lets out a weary sigh. "I might have known."

I press close to see.

A face looks back at me from the photograph—the smiling, heart-shaped face of a young woman. The woman is eerily familiar. I recognize her private smile. Her pert nose and small pointed chin. The widow's peak that defines her forehead and the full sweep of her wavy hair. Of course she's just a picture. But still, I know that I *know* her.

I pluck her from Linda's hand. Linda doesn't say anything as I look and look.

The woman sits at a dressing table before a big, round mirror. She is drawing a silver-backed brush through her hair. She is looking into the mirror at not just me. She is looking at the photographer who must be standing behind her. Her intense gaze holds love and other emotions I also recognize but can't put a name to. Not yet.

I peer closer yet. "Who the heck?"

"Your grandmother." Linda's voice sounds suddenly hoarse. "My mother. Justine."

"Justine," I say, amazed even at the unfamiliar sound of my grandmother's name.

Linda's mouth is a thin, tight line of anger. There's not a hint of a smile on her face. But there, that same nose and chin, surrounded by a few more lines. That same widow's peak and wavy hair, only Linda's hair is going gray.

"She looks like you," I say.

"And you." Linda sounds like she's giving a warning.

I catch my breath, realizing that this is true. I've got that wavy hair too. That's *my* widow's peak.

"And maybe I looked like her twenty years ago," Linda continues. "But not so much anymore." She rubs a tight muscle at the back of her neck.

"She's—" I hesitate, considering. "She looks nice."

Linda snorts. "What have I taught you about appearances?"

I stare at the photograph. I swallow hard, trying to loosen the sudden tightness in my throat. "She sure looks like she loves your dad, though. I mean, then."

"What makes you think that?" With a sharp flick of her hand, Linda pushes back her hair.

"The way she's looking at him. In the mirror, I mean."

Linda's mouth twists. "So you think you see your grandpa somewhere in that picture? My father?"

I nod. "I think so. I mean, I see the tip of a man's shoulder. That's his hand holding that old camera. I *think*. And isn't that a flashbulb—that little pop of light there at the edge of the mirror?" I let out a sigh. "Man, I *love* old photos! So mysterious—I've got to show this to David."

I go quiet then. I might not get to show this to David. I glance at the clock. Really, I've got to get to bed. I've got to grab a couple hours of sleep so I can be halfway coherent tomorrow when I see him again. Because I will see him again.

I feel Linda watching me. If I get worked up, she'll drop this whole conversation. Or it'll takes five times as long as it should take. So I swallow down tomorrow and ask, "What year would this be anyway? Way before you were born, right?"

"Way." Linda forces out a laugh. "Look at her dress. So *not* nineteen sixty-seven."

I study the fitted bodice, the row of pearly buttons. The neatly cuffed sleeves. The simple collar, secured by a little scrolling pin at the throat.

"Very mid-forties," Linda says. "She's probably about eighteen there."

"Wow," I say.

"Wow," Linda mutters.

"Your parents were married a long time before they had you."

Linda shrugs. "If ten years is a long time, then I guess they were. My mother was forty when she had me. She wasn't planning on getting pregnant. I don't think she wanted a child. I don't really know. And guess what? I don't really care."

I've heard most of this before—or pieces of it. But there's something else, something new she's telling me now.

"Then—" I stare at Linda for a moment, open-mouthed. "Then who—"

Linda sighs heavily and plops down on the bed. "Like I said, I don't know anything for sure. Honestly, I couldn't care less about that woman. But...I think probably her first husband took that picture."

I look back at the photograph. Justine seems sadder than ever. "You never told me she was married before!"

"You never asked." Linda sits cross-legged on her bed now and strips off her socks, the better to rub the soles of her aching feet. She rubs and rubs. "Anyway, what's there to say? The past is the past."

"Who was he?" I drop down on the bed too, astonished. "Did they get back together?"

It's terrible, cruel, and I'll never admit it to Linda, but I want my grandmother and this guy to have gotten back together. I want a love that lasts for once. I want that in my family, no matter the cost.

Linda takes a deep breath like it's all she can do to get the words out. "He was a soldier in World War Two."

I gape at her. "A soldier?"

"Oh God. I should have known." Linda presses her hand to her eyes. "He was killed, okay? He was some kind of hero. My mother left me for a *ghost*,

Penelope. That's what your grandpa always said." Linda lowers her voice to a mannish, drunken slur and says, "'Justine left us for a ghost.'"

"She must have really loved him." My voice has turned husky with emotion.

"Oh, sure. That made it all worthwhile."

Linda sounds about as sarcastic as I've ever heard her. I stare at her, too shaken up to speak. She goes back to rubbing her feet, playing for time. When she looks up at me again, she seems sad.

"I'm sorry." She bites her lip. "Penelope, I'm just trying to take care of you. I'm just trying to keep you from getting hurt like I did—like my mother did, for that matter. Justine was eighteen when she married her childhood sweetheart. And one year later she was a widow. That's not a happily-ever-after ending if you ask me."

I hold Justine's photo close to my chest. "You don't really know her side of it, though, do you?"

Linda falls back on her bed, her coppery-gray hair fanning across the purple spread. "Let sleeping dogs lie, all right, honey? Just let sleeping dogs lie."

I don't know if Linda means Justine or the soldier or the past altogether. I don't know if Linda means herself, lying there, eyes closed already, lips parted in utter exhaustion. I only know that it's time to get the heck away from her.

So I do, taking the photograph with me. I'll never tell Linda about the loose floorboard in the attic and, when I know, what's beneath. Never ever.

In my room, I face the clock on my desk. David leaves at one in the afternoon. About ten hours from now.

I prop Justine's picture against the clock. I had a grandmother who loved a soldier too. He died. But maybe she still exists?

I lie down on my bed, willing myself to rest up for the worst day of my life. So far.

Four

When I look at the clock again, it's nearly ten.

David isn't outside waiting in the shade of the honey locust tree. He hasn't left a voice mail or sent a text. No Facebook updates. He hasn't said one last good-bye. I call his cell, but he doesn't answer. His house. No one picks up there either.

On my desk, Justine seems to nod in the flickering sunlight. *Find him*, her expression seems to say. *Now*.

I peek into Linda's room. Still fully dressed in her black work garb, she is sprawled facedown and spread-eagled on her bed. This is the way Linda sleeps when she's really wiped out from work or me, or both. There's no danger that I'll wake her.

I clean up fast. I get on my bike.

Usually I'd wave to the clockwork lady, who is picking her delicate way around the block. But this time I don't think to raise my hand until after I've sailed past her. I don't look back to see whether she hesitates the way she always does when she sees me, whether she unclasps her own hands to wave back—her gesture more question than answer.

Bonnie doesn't know where David is. "He left about an hour ago, I think—about nine. He promised he'd be back for a late breakfast. I went out and got chocolate-chip bagels and cream cheese—his favorite. He was expecting you. And here you are!" Bonnie forces a smile and runs her fingers through her spiky blond hair.

When I pulled up on my bike a few minutes ago, she was standing in the driveway, looking down the street as if David might appear at any moment. She had her hand to her forehead, shielding her blue eyes. She said the sun was hurting them—that's why they were so red and watery. But I could see at once that she'd been crying.

We stand in the O'Dells' kitchen now. It's still a mess from the dinner Bonnie made last night, which was not a culinary success. The lasagna and garlic bread burned. The Fresh Express salad wilted in the bowl. The soda frozen in the freezer. Bonnie, forced to copy umpteen files, had stayed too late at her real-estate office to pull off anything more gourmet. And she had so wanted to pull off something memorable—in a good way. So had Beau. David's dad kept our conversation moving right along, peppering every other sentence with a silly joke or bad pun. Beau wasn't about to let anyone break down. He wanted to remember everyone—especially his son—smiling.

Any assumptions I'd had about adoptive families went out the window the moment I met David, Bonnie, and Beau. They have their differences, sure. But they get over their differences—or if not over, exactly, then *past*. They see each other as individuals, not just extensions of themselves or their history. Like right now, if David is late for breakfast, Bonnie will probably say, "David will be David." She's right. David makes a habit of late. That's one of the many reasons why he decided to enlist.

"I need the structure," he's told me more than once. "I gotta learn some organizational skills."

I seize a suspicious-smelling, damp rag from the O'Dells' notoriously clogged sink and start swiping at the counter.

"Do you think he needed to get something from the store? I mean, he went through his duffel again yesterday, right?" I scrub furiously. Did Justine do this? Did she clean when she got scared?

"I checked the list again this morning." Bonnie is pacing the kitchen. "He's got everything. I don't know why he took off. But he promised he'd be right back, Penna. 'Soon,' he said. So why don't you just wait for him? Sit down. I'll make you a cup of coffee. I'd love to talk for a minute." Her voice falters, and then she continues. "I think—I don't know for sure, but I think...do you think David is having any last-minute regrets? I'm concerned."

I sweep a pile of crumbs into my palm. Once, when he called me from OSUT, something was wrong. Something was very, very wrong. He was barely holding back tears, I could tell. I wonder if Bonnie ever got a call like that.

"Why, Penna!" Bonnie exclaims.

I look up from the solidified splotch of lasagna sauce, dreading what's next. Bonnie must have just realized what nobody else has. She must have realized what I haven't let myself think about too much, or even say. She must have realized that something has happened—is happening—to David, something I don't understand.

But then I see Bonnie's sweet, crooked smile—an expression that David has claimed for his own. Her expression is amused and puzzled. She has grabbed on to some kind of distraction.

"Did you streak your hair blue?"

I touch my hair and the stiff blue paint there. I have to smile too, remembering the best part of last night.

It hits me then. The viaduct.

I fold the rag and drape it over the kitchen faucet.

"I'll be back," I tell Bonnie and tear from the house.

●●●

Luckily the O'Dells live near the center of town too. I zip right over to the viaduct.

But David's not there. Nobody's there but our painted selves, the six-foot-tall killdeer, and, of all people, Ravi, who's practicing tricks on his skateboard. He's wearing that same gray sweatshirt. Maybe this is how he winds down after the night shift. When he sees me, he jumps off his board and propels it into his hands. If Ravi thinks I'm staying, I realize, he will hightail it out of here before I'm able to ask what I need to ask. So I keep my distance, circling on my bike at the viaduct's opening.

"Seen David?" My words come in a rush.

Ravi shakes his head.

"He wasn't here earlier?"

"No."

"You're sure?"

A stormy expression flickers across Ravi's face—he has dramatic features: high cheekbones and forehead, a strong jaw. "Do you want to ask me again? I could lie."

Ravi's voice is deeper than David's, and he speaks more deliberately, like he's putting together a puzzle. He talks the way I've heard other people talk when English isn't their first language. There's a kind of music in his voice that comes with this, a kind of care.

But I want to hear David's voice. I want to hear David say my name.

"I'm not asking you to lie. I'm just—"

I'm just what? Just *who*? I hardly recognize myself, the way I feel, so panicked.

"He's leaving for Iraq today."

The words burst from me, fierce and defensive. Ravi looks surprised, and his expression holds something else too—fear? guilt?—but before he can respond, I turn my bike and head off. Ravi's skateboard clatters as it hits the ground again. The board's wheels grind against the concrete, and then there's a gap in the sound as Ravi gets some air. He lands again. I've put nearly a block between us. Now I glance back. Ravi's banking up the side of the viaduct and swooping back down. Kind of like David liked—*likes, will like*—to do. The way David did only a few hours ago, running up that wall and flipping off it, always a daredevil. Always, always lucky.

I fly down Main Street. There, finally, I spot David's motorcycle, parked in front of a cinder-block building. Tattoo You, the local tattoo and piercing parlor. Open twenty-four hours.

I remember now. Months ago David had said that he wanted to get his first tattoo to commemorate this day. I let my bike fall to the ground and run inside.

The parlor is an open, neon-tinted room. Tattoo art covers the walls— dragons and hieroglyphics and roses catch my eye. The place smells and looks almost as clean as my dentist's office. I hate the dentist. But I love David. And there he is, lying in the last chair at the back of the room. Looks like he's the only one with the guts or desire to get tattooed this early in the day.

He appears almost comfortable, reclining like that before a mirror. But then I see his mouth, a tight line of pain. A mullet-haired, tattooed dude is holding what looks like a gun to David's chest. The whining buzz coming from that instrument sounds like a dentist's drill. The guy is drilling a hole into David's heart.

The tattooed dude curses and yanks back the gun as I throw my arms around David's neck.

"Watch out!" David cries.

But he's hugging me back, not letting go.

The dude has taken himself off to some other part of the room, so we're nearly alone when I look down and see the tattoo transferred onto David's skin—still only outlined in black like a coloring book. It's a circle of barbwire and tumbleweeds around a manga guy. With his curly hair, the manga guy looks a lot like David before OSUT. He's wearing fatigues and jumping around inside that barbed circle like he's kill-crazy, his mouth open in rage. He's packing some heavy artillery, this manga guy.

"Wow." I can't think of what else to say. Plus, I'm out of breath from my bike ride. Not to mention the sight of that tattoo.

"It's great, right? That's what I'm going for, anyway. Color can hurt more, at least that's what Felix says." David nods at the tattoo artist, who's busily cleaning his needle. "So I'm not going to do as much red as I was planning to."

"It's still great."

He grins. "So you *do* like it?"

"Yes." What's the point of saying anything else? Now that he's gone this far, there's no turning back. And besides, I do like it. I always will. I kiss the skin around what hurts on David's chest until he eases me away.

I call Felix over. I tell Felix the other thing I have to do with David before he leaves. David and I talked about it earlier this summer, and he wanted to do it too. For us.

"Tattoo us some rings, matching braids around our right ring fingers," I say. "Don't worry." I pull out my driver's license. "I'm eighteen."

• • •

Four and a half hours, one chest tattoo, two ring tattoos, and a whole bunch of chocolate-chip bagels, cream cheese, and coffee later, Beau, Bonnie, and I drive David to the Will Rogers World Airport in Oklahoma City. David and I sit in the backseat of the O'Dells' massive pickup truck. The heavy smell of antibiotic ointment overpowers the smell of the coffee that both Bonnie and Beau are drinking. David and I are hesitant to hold hands—even left hands—in case we bump the right ones somehow.

Our right ring fingers will kill for a while, Felix said, but David said that's okay. He'll have some downtime. His flight is about twenty-four hours long, with stops in Newfoundland and Germany for refueling. And then David has two weeks in Kuwait before he heads to Iraq. Kuwait won't exactly be downtime, of course. Far from it. David said he'll be learning specific in-country stuff. He'll finally get to try out the special vehicles he'll be using for security patrol. He'll be working up a sweat, getting even darker out there in the Kuwaiti desert, where the heat reaches 120 degrees by day this time of year and drops to a cool 90 by night.

And then there's Iraq.

"By the time I get to Iraq," David said over bagels this morning, "I'll be healed up great. For a while I'll probably just be cleaning out latrines anyway. If something goes weird with my tat, I can always hold a toilet brush—or whatever—with my left hand."

You can't hold a gun with only your left hand, I realize now, way too late. We should never have gotten them.

David is staring out the truck window, as distracted by his thoughts as I am.

"Are you sure we can't drive you all the way to Iraq?" Beau asks this for about the millionth time—a feeble joke. Beau would stay in a motel in Iraq for the duration of David's deployment too if he could. If they even have motels in Iraq anymore. If they're not all blown to bits.

"*Dad*," David says.

For a few minutes, we ride in silence.

Then, because Bonnie is crying softly now and I can't stand to hear her cry, I ask David again how long before we'll be able to email or talk.

Again, he says, "They said a few hours after we land. Remember? I won't be able to get my own cell and SIM card until I get to Iraq. But of course they'll have phone providers in Kuwait. You know me. I'll get through to you." He leans his head against his window. He looks tired all of a sudden.

"At training, one guy told me that in Iraq we'll have to earn privileges to talk on the phone, though other guys said he was just pulling my leg. Or maybe he had a really tough unit. But they all agreed that reception can still be bad over there, even around big cities. Even Baghdad. Phone lines and the Internet can still go down. Depending."

Depending on what?

I don't want to ask. Not with Bonnie crying like that.

Carefully, I take hold of David's tattooed hand. The gauze looks whiter and cleaner against his dark skin than it does mine. In the tattoo parlor I couldn't help but think *war wound*, looking at the bandage on his chest. *Survivor*, I make myself think now. I make myself believe. As we pull into the airport's entrance, I trace a heart in the air just over the barbwire on David's chest. I am careful not even to skim his jacket, for fear of hurting the tender part beneath.

We park in the parking garage. Bonnie, sobbing now, doesn't want to leave the truck. Or rather, she doesn't want to leave the truck because David doesn't want her to leave the truck. He warned us a week earlier, when he first came back from training, that he didn't want any of us to go into the airport with him.

"I can't deal with it." That's how he explained it. "I can deal with the TSA hassles, but I can't deal with saying good-bye in front of everyone. I'm sorry. I know it's not fair. It's not right. But please. You've been asking what you can do? Say good-bye to me in private."

David leans over Bonnie now and hugs her for a long time in the pseudo-privacy of the parking garage. He flinches in pain as her head rests on his chest, right where the tattoo is, but he doesn't pull away. He whispers something into Bonnie's ear. *I love you*, he's probably saying. *Don't worry. I'll be home on leave before you know it.* Finally he looks up and checks the clock on the dashboard. I see the realization flash across his face. It's time. He has to say good-bye.

Beau and I walk with him to the elevator that will carry him up into the airport, where he will meet his brigade and fly away. I thought it was bad when he left for OSUT. It was nothing compared to this.

We stand in our small huddle of three. Fluorescent tubes of light hum and buzz above us—a lethal sound. Cars sail past, probably filled with happy families and couples going on fun vacations. Or coming home.

I draw David's arm around my shoulder. I try to melt into him. Blend, merge, meld, blur. Stay or take me with you, I want to say.

"You okay?" My voice breaks.

David smiles reassuringly. "Be cool. Atta girl."

I pull a new book of manga from my bag. I give it to David. "For the flight. For inspiration too. You've got to work on your portfolio over there, okay? We've got to get into art school."

David looks skeptical. "You know I don't get much done without an assignment."

"I'll assign you stuff then," I say.

"I'll hold you to that."

"Hold me to anything."

Beau takes our picture holding each other. Then he takes David's picture alone. David stands at attention. He looks strong. He is strong. Army strong. Hero strong. I take David's picture with Beau. David leans his head on Beau's shoulder, and Beau cups his hand over David's head like something might fall on his skull and shatter it.

David throws his arms around Beau then, like it's just hit him, what's happening.

"This is just something I have to do, okay?" I hear David say. "Something for me. Something for our country." He looks over Beau's shoulder at me. "The right thing."

David steps away from Beau. He comes over to me. He cradles my face in his hands. He kisses me hard. Lets go. Turns away.

He's gone.

I drag myself out of the humming, buzzing light. I follow Beau back to Bonnie in the truck. We make the long drive back to Killdeer, sudden rain battering the windows.

David would call this a real Oklahoma summer storm. The wind nearly tips us over.

● ● ●

Late that night, after the long ride home with Bonnie and Beau, after cold cereal for dinner and a couple of hours watching I don't even remember what, I sit down at my desk and pick up the photograph of Justine. Just that simple act—picking up a photograph—and pain radiates through my right ring finger. The feeling makes me so jittery that my hands start to shake. Last fall, after David and I kissed for the first time and we were officially "a couple," my hands shook like this. They shook like this when he first told me that he'd signed on to join the army. We were standing under the honey locust tree right outside my bedroom window.

"I joined before you even moved here," he told me, as the leaves rustled above. "Maybe if I'd known you, I wouldn't have done it. But I believe it was the right decision." Then he'd kissed my hands until they were steady again.

My hands are anything but steady now. Justine's photo tumbles to the desktop. And that's when I see it, there on the back, penciled faintly in looping cursive: *Justine Blue, 1945.*

World War II ended in 1945. If Justine's soldier took this picture, he must have gone over to fight right at what they hoped was the end. Like David is now.

Justine must have waited and hoped like me.

Linda is working late again, but I wouldn't ask her about ancient family history—or any family history—even if she were home. And there's nobody else to ask.

There's nobody but Justine Blue. Or Justine Weaver. Or Justine Whatever-Her-Name-Is-Now.

I prop her photograph back against my clock. Then I search out seven Justine Blues online. She lives in Australia. No, she lives in Maine. She lives all over the world, or she has. She's in a rock band. No, she's a lawyer. She's a kindergarten teacher, plumber, porn star, pastor.

She *is*?

More likely, she was. I do quick calculations. If she was eighteen in 1945, she'd be eighty now, or thereabouts. She'd have to be retired. Or dead.

Considering this, I carefully lift the gauze from my finger. It's been almost twelve hours, and the tat looks worse now than when I had it done. I wonder what David's look like. I imagine him flying high over wherever, peeking beneath his bandages too, maybe freaking out on the inside but definitely playing it cool on the outside.

I can feel Justine watching me from the black-and-white mirror in her photograph.

She loved a soldier once.

If nothing else, finding Justine could help pass some time until David comes home.

Five

I wake up to my ringing cell. Squinting against bright morning light, I roll across my bed. My elbow knocks a full glass of water from the nightstand and then a framed photograph of David and me, taken the night we first realized each other existed, the night of the Teen Community Art Awards ceremony.

In the photograph there are people all around us, but we only have eyes for each other. David's hair is thick and curly, not by-the-book stubble. My hair has been whipped into the elaborate, coppery confection that the stylist at the salon I visited earlier that day assured me would be a simple updo. David and I are laughing.

I find the phone and flick it on. *David*, I'm thinking. *Already he's found a way to call.* I blurt out, "Hello."

"Oh, Penna. It's so good to hear your voice."

Not David. His mom.

"Did I wake you? It's nine o'clock." Bonnie laughs nervously. "Can you believe it? He hasn't been gone a day, and I've already forgotten how late you kids like to sleep."

I lie down again and mumble something reassuring about how I needed to get out of bed anyway. Then I sit bolt upright again. "Did he call?"

Bonnie sighs. "I wish. No such luck, though. He's not even there yet."

I sink back onto my pillow. "Oh yeah."

"Thank God for work. I've never wanted to go into the office as much as I did this morning. Never." Something that sounds like cellophane crinkles in the background. Then the distinct sound of Bonnie chewing. "And Fig Newtons. Thank God for Fig Newtons. I don't even like Fig Newtons, but they're what the vending machine has to offer, so they'll do the trick." More crinkling, chewing. "I'm not too worried yet, Penna. Honestly. Not really. I mean, he hasn't even touched ground yet, right? So what could happen?"

Plenty, I think. I roll over on my stomach, let my right hand dangle over the edge of the bed for tat safety, nestle deeper under Plum Tumble, and close my eyes. I want to sleep.

"It's just so *good* to hear your voice, Penna. You mind if I give you a call like this sometimes? Maybe we could help each other get through this. Plus, David asked me to check in on you."

"He did?" I can't help but smile.

"Yep. One of his last requests." Bonnie draws a sharp breath. "I didn't mean that the way it sounded."

I nod and then remember Bonnie can't see this. "Sure. Please, call any time. I'd like that too," I say.

Truth be told, just the sound of Bonnie's voice makes my heart ache. No one could sound more like David, the way she inflects her sentences and punches certain words. It's almost like he's on the other end of the line. Only not.

"Good. I'm glad you feel the same way." Bonnie crinkles more cellophane. "Kind of a nice thing happened this morning. Took me completely by surprise. It's the kind of thing I'd tell David." She's talking fast, like she's afraid I might have to go. Something catches in her throat—Fig Newton crumbs, no doubt. She coughs, then says, "I *will* tell David, of course. But you know me. I'm not the most patient person. So I thought maybe I'd tell you."

She doesn't wait for me to say, Sure go ahead. She says, "Just as I was walking out the door for work, I got this phone call from this kid I haven't heard from in forever. The time was when a phone call from him would have been an everyday occurrence. When he was little, he sometimes called me Mom by mistake.

"Anyway, it only took a few sentences before I knew exactly who he was. He's the shyest, sweetest boy. His voice may have changed, but his spirit still comes through. I think you know him. Ravi Sharma. Or maybe you don't know him? You haven't lived here long enough, I guess. Come to think of it, you never were in school with Ravi, were you?"

I stifle a yawn. *This is David's mother*, I remind myself. *I should care that she cares about Ravi.* But all I really want to talk about is David—especially if I'm going to have to wake up to have the conversation.

I rub sleep from my eyes. "David's mentioned him."

"Then you must know what good buds they were. They lost touch, of course, but I don't blame either of them. I truly loved that kid. So anyway, Ravi called because he'd heard about David's deployment. He was pretty upset, I could tell. He's hard to read, if you know what I mean. But I could tell. So I suggested he talk to you."

Lesson learned: don't talk to strangers, even if the stranger is your boyfriend's old friend. A groan escapes me.

"I know," Bonnie quickly says. "I should have asked you first. But Ravi seemed like he wants to support David. I told Ravi that David will need letters, and Ravi said, sure, yes, he'll do that. He'll write. I gave him David's address, and that's when I thought of you. Like I said earlier, *support*. We all need it."

"Did you give him my number?" My voice is a wee bit terse. Bonnie knows David, who is *the* exception in my experience with guys. And I guess she knows Ravi. But I don't know Ravi. I don't know anybody, really, in

Killdeer besides David—this year was *about* David. I don't need another guy. There's such a thing as loyalty.

"*Of course* I didn't give Ravi your number." Bonnie vigorously crinkles cellophane. "I'm not that clueless. I did get his number for you, though."

"Well." I sigh. "Okay. I guess."

"Penna, he really seems like he needs to talk to someone. I'm thinking *not* an ancient crone like me. So if you need to talk to someone—and *not* an ancient crone like me—you might think about giving him a call. Okay?"

Wrapped in Plum Tumble, I sit up in bed, open the nightstand drawer, and locate a pen and scrap of paper with my left, versus my right, hand.

For Bonnie's sake, I say, "Give me his number."

●●●

The last thing I want to do right now is be strong for someone else. Why should Ravi care about David anyway? He's got his skateboard. His night shift. His own reasons for being in this town he must hate. He could move somewhere else if he wanted. He could start over. He could worry about his own life.

Like I've been sprung from a trap, I sit straight up.

He could worry about his own life.

I sound a lot like Linda.

I get out of bed. I go to the kitchen, stumble and fumble around, make breakfast. I stand at the window, eating toast, drinking coffee, and watching for the clockwork lady. She's nowhere to be seen. That's what I get for sleeping this late. I missed her.

Maybe that's kind of what Ravi's thinking about David. *That's what I get for waiting this long. I missed him.*

The bright day stretches endlessly before me.

Bonnie said Ravi seems like he really needs to talk to someone. Maybe if I listen, Ravi will tell me something about David I don't know. Maybe he could give me a little bit of David back—maybe even a part of David I've never known before.

Maybe.

I look at the clock. It's that time of day again.

I get dressed. Get on my bike. Head toward the viaduct.

● ● ●

Sure enough, he's here.

He must know I'm here too, but he doesn't look at me. He doesn't stop skateboarding. He's executing tight figure eights, one after another.

I lean my bike against the Icon Killdeer. The wheels are like shields, protecting David and me, big and blue.

I turn to Ravi.

He is very good at ignoring people. I guess it's a skill he's had to learn over the years.

I watch him carefully, the way I'd watch a skittish animal or a shy kid.

Clearly he's been skating for a while. His plain white T-shirt is wet down the back and at the neck. Wet, it shows a lot of detail. Given his usual baggy sweatshirt, I'd never have known that Ravi is at least as muscular as David—maybe more so. Ravi's a bigger guy, less wiry. Also like David, Ravi's got great balance. Maybe this is another skill you can learn when you grow up bullied: staying stable. Ravi and his skateboard seem to be one fluid creature, the way David always seems on his motorcycle. Mythical, kind of. Like a centaur or satyr.

I've been counting. Ravi's executed twenty figure eights just since my arrival. He shows no sign of stopping. His black hair is long enough that his bangs keep falling in his eyes, but even when he impatiently shoves them aside, clearing his line of vision, he doesn't waver.

It's getting a little old, just standing here watching. I take a step forward. Another. Still no acknowledgment. Suddenly I'm pissed. I could be sleeping. I'm doing this for me, sure, but I'm also doing this for *him*.

Turns out I'm not so impressed with Ravi's skills. I mean, you've seen one figure eight, you've seen 'em all. An infinity of infinity symbols.

"To infinity and beyond." My voice is as dry as the red dust that suddenly billows around us, stirred by the wind.

Something flickers across Ravi's face—a smile?—before he can loop away again. He loops, showing me only his back.

I cross my arms. I don't need this guy. I'll write David a letter and ask him to tell me every little thing he can remember about himself from when he was a kid. I'm giving Ravi one more minute, tops.

He turns back toward me.

"You going for the *Guinness Book of World Records*? Or what?"

He shrugs, banking another tight curve.

That's it. I'm done. Sensitivity is overrated. I've got a letter to write.

I turn to my bike. The skateboard abruptly stops. I get on my bike. Only now, ready to go, do I look at Ravi. He's got one foot planted on the board, the other on the ground. I'd leave in a red-hot minute if it weren't for his expression. It's like something's cracked open there. Ravi looks like he might cry.

Or be sick.

He says, "I was going to sign up too. Enlist. I went down there and everything. I got the talk, all the forms. I filled them out. Then I didn't do it."

"Why not?" I sound cold. Good.

"I don't know."

I can't help myself. "Scared?"

"Maybe." Like someone's hit him across the back of his knees, Ravi sits down on his board. He wobbles, then steadies himself. "Or I didn't know what I was trying to prove. Or I realized I wouldn't prove anything."

I get off my bike. I go over to him and stand there, looking down at the top of his head. His hair is as glossy as a blackbird's wing.

I shift my weight, feeling suddenly, horribly awkward.

Ravi looks up at me. The circles under his black eyes are such an angry, dark purple that for a moment I think he might have been beaten up again. Then I realize he probably just hasn't slept in twenty-four hours. Or more.

"When we were kids, David and I used to play together all the time. You know this? Yeah, I thought so." Ravi swallows hard. "Our favorite games were make-believe. We pretended we were robbers—good robbers, like Robin Hood. Or buccaneers running blockades during the Civil War. We were all kinds of superheroes."

This—*this*—is what I came for.

I imagine David running wild and free around his backyard, his now aging, very cranky and creaky German shepherd, Mars, trotting along spryly behind him. Ravi is there too, somewhere in the shadows. David was such a beautiful boy. Still is. I'd smile if my jaw weren't clenched so tight, if I didn't feel so awkward standing beside Ravi.

"We pretended we were knights in shining armor," he continues. "We used sticks for swords. Once I accidentally stabbed David in the side."

"I know that scar." My voice comes out in a croak.

"I always wondered if it was still there. I felt terrible about it." Ravi shakes his head. "I suppose I still do."

"What else?" I say. "About David."

Ravi picks up a stone, weighs it in his hand. "He really looked out for me. He took it hard for me more than once." Ravi gives a low laugh. "And he taught me how to belch the alphabet. That was about the closest I ever came to being cool as a kid. Got me through a whole year of recess, probably. I've always wanted to thank him for that."

"You still can."

Ravi looks at me. "I did. I wrote him a letter last night, after work. I had some time to kill."

I go cold. Someone did it before me. Wrote David.

"I've got to go."

I'm on my bike. I'm out of here.

Ravi calls out to me. "I've got some great pictures of David if you ever want to see them."

"Sure," I call back to him. "Someday."

"I was thinking of sending the pictures to him, but—"

But *what* I don't know, because I'm too far gone to hear.

•••

I sit at my desk and write a letter on the thin, blue international paper that I stocked up on at the post office last week with David standing by my side.

> *Dear David,*
>
> *I haven't stopped thinking about you. I miss you so much.*
>
> *Don't forget to let your tats get some air so they can heal. But only when it's safe, okay? Play it safe. I've bumped my ring a couple of times, and it hasn't been fun. And a ring is one thing, a finger is one thing, but your chest—you've got to take care of that.*
>
> *Have I mentioned I love your chest?*
>
> *I love your chest.*
>
> *Not much has happened here. Well, except you know my grand-mother—the star quilter, Plum Tumble maker? I'm going to find her. Linda isn't happy about it, but, oh well.*

I chew on my pencil. Bad habit. I decide not to tell David yet why I feel so drawn to searching for Justine. No need to mention anything about a heroic soldier who died in battle. Nope. Don't think so. Positive, encouraging things. That's what I need to write.

> *It's pretty here today! Bright blue sky. Hot and windy, but what else*

is new, right? I went for a bike ride. I needed to burn off some energy now that you're not around to help me do it. If you know what I mean.

I talked to your mom this morning. She sounds so much like you, on the phone especially. Made me want to talk to you in the worst way. Will you please call as often as you can?

Nagging, I know. I thought only thirty-year-olds and up did that!

Take care of yourself, okay? Eat everything in sight. Drink bottled water. Keep under cover.

Nagging again! Sorry!

I love you.

Penna

I type something similar into an email sent care of the U.S. Army (same address he had at OSUT, which is somehow comforting) and send that off too, so it'll be waiting in his inbox.

Then I carefully write the address he gave me on the outside of the letter (David was told if his mail was addressed even the slightest bit incorrectly, he'd pay with sit-ups or chin-ups or worse) and walk it over to the nearest mailbox.

By the time I'm home again, I'm starving. I wolf a sandwich standing up in the kitchen. The sandwich settles like a brick in the pit of my stomach. I sink down on a kitchen chair.

I'm losing it. I'd better do something. Fast.

I push myself out of the chair. I go to my bedroom and start searching for Justine.

Six

By late afternoon I've found all of the older Justine Weavers that the Internet's White Pages can reveal.

At eighty-six, she's living in Baltimore, Maryland.

At eighty-nine, here's another one, making her home in Eustace, Florida.

Ultimately, I compile a list of five age-appropriate Weaver candidates.

I check my email. Nothing from David, though he's surely landed by now. I check his Facebook page. Status unchanged. No surprise there. But it's nice to see his profile picture: the photograph we took of our hands set in plaster. I press my hand to those hands, then I turn away from my computer. I turn up the ring volume on my cell. I sit there for a moment feeling horrible. Then I get back to work on finding more Justines.

Hours later my neck aches. I rub the sore spot as I've seen Linda do after coming home from Red Earth, which helps a little.

I eat two bowls of cereal, down a few glasses of milk, gnaw on some stale cookies. I think about watching TV. Sleeping. Staring at the towering prep pile of worksheets and readings for senior year that I've barely even dented. Just staring. That's all. Doodling awkward, sloppy portraits of David in my sketchbook, pretending I'm building up my college portfolio when anyone can see my drawings are confused and flat, his features all wrong. At least the ones were that I drew this afternoon, taking a break from Internet searches. So much for beauty and truth and all that. I don't know light from shadow.

I stand in the middle of the kitchen, tearing out one stupid portrait of David after another, crumpling them up and throwing them on the floor.

He's been gone twenty-four hours, and I'm really, truly freaking out.

I can't remember his face.

In our eleven-month relationship, we've been apart eighteen weeks already. We're about to be apart for another fifteen months. Minus the three-week leave. Which equals what?

What are our odds?

I've successfully ruined every single drawing I made this afternoon. I stare at the crumpled pile at my feet. Easy come, easy go.

Easy go, far away to war.

I fell in love with David, I remind myself. I didn't fall in love with a soldier.

So why can't I draw a decent portrait of his face, the face I first loved, with the thick, curly hair and crazy crooked grin and deep brown eyes?

Freak out, make lists. That's what Linda always does.

I kick aside the crumpled portraits, turn to a blank page in my sketchbook, and begin.

WHY I FELL IN LOVE WITH DAVID
AND WHY IT'S A GOOD THING I DID

1. Linda and I have moved around a lot.
    A lot, a lot. From central Ohio to the boondocks of Michigan at the beginning of middle school. (Bad, bad experience.) Then from Michigan to Chicago in the middle of freshman year. I was a dork. Lonely. (Sniff.) And misunderstood. (Sniff, sniff.)

2. Previous boyfriend choices have been not so good.

    Sophomore year I figured out how to look less like a dork—no braces, good skin, all that stuff. Guys took notice. The wrong kind of guys, who were good at making me feel a little less lonely and only slightly less misunderstood. One in particular got drunk and got me drunk. Not just once, but several times.

    The last time, he tried to rape me. I showed him who was stronger. But still. No one would listen to me when I tried to explain. Only Linda. And so…we moved.

3. Once again I was new to town.

    I was lonely. (Sniff.) And misunderstood. (Sniff, sniff.)

    Also, I was not going to make any more stupid mistakes.

4. I made a teen community art mural instead.

    And there was David.

5. David was, *is*, different.

    He got—*gets*—the art thing. He wants to make art too. He understood me. *Understands* me. David was—*is*—safe. David was—*is*—home. David was—*is*—David.

6. And he always will be.

7. Enough. I'm a believer. Again.

I rip the list from my sketchbook. But I don't crumple it up and throw it on the floor. I take it up to my bedroom and put it under my pillow.

I'm freezing. My room is icily gusty. We've only got window air-conditioners, which mostly just stir around the warm air. But once in a while my unit kicks into high gear, and then there's this arctic wind. I turn off my unit. After it gurgles to a stop, I realize how much noise it makes doing what

Check Out Receipt

Town Hall Library
262-966-2933
www.townhalllibrary.org

Saturday, January 23, 2016 11:34:02 AM

Item: 30966001234042
Title: While he was away
Due: 02/13/2016

Total items: 1

Thank You!

it does. My room is now horribly quiet. I can hear my thoughts. The list helped while I was writing it, but now I'm right back where I started.

I turn the air conditioner back on. I pull the storage box of winter clothes from under my bed. I put on a wool sweater. I put on my fleece. I pull my fleece's hood over my head. Doing this, I think of Ravi in his sweatshirt. I don't want to think about Ravi in his sweatshirt. I suck in an icy breath, blow it out. *Breathe in, breathe out.* That's what the drill sergeant kept saying to the poor guy who went kill-crazy in that online video of OSUT. I should have never watched that. *Breathe in. Breathe out.*

I'd put on a pair of mittens, but of course I can't because of my tattoo. I breathe on my hands instead. I start pacing. I stalk past my dresser, then stop short and backtrack to it. I stand for a long moment there, staring down at my little white jewelry box.

I keep the photograph of my father in the bottom drawer of this box with all the old butterfly, dolphin, and peace sign necklaces and rings from my early elementary school years, when I lived in places like Orlando, Pittsburgh, and Syracuse. When I was little, I used to pull out the photo all the time.

Now I open the shallow drawer. I pull out the photo—one Linda says she took just before she got pregnant with me. My father is standing on a beach, feeding Fritos to seagulls. His eyes are wide open—*joyful*, I thought in fifth grade, but now I think *wild*. Too wild to trust. Almost manic, maybe. His tawny hair stirs in the wind. He's wearing a peacoat and a blue-striped sailor's shirt. He looks like an ad for Fritos gone all wrong.

I pluck him from my drawer and dangle him between the thumb and forefinger of my left hand. Then I march into Linda's room, and I stick him underneath the tall stack of shoeboxes at the back of her closet.

I'll show him who's stronger. And her too. Let her find him next time she makes me move.

Warmer now, I walk back to my room. In the blink of an eye, I can rid myself of jerks.

Not David.

My head is swimming.

All I want to do, all I can do, is sleep.

●●●

Morning sunlight pours over my desk. But the brightest sun can't outshine the fact that there's still no news from David. It's been twelve days. He said it would be a few hours. I keep telling myself the phone lines are down, the Internet too. Bonnie's made calls, and that's the case. Bad weather. Still. I can't help but wonder. I can't help but freak out once in a while.

I've written him twelve positive and encouraging letters that basically say the same thing: *Weather is wonderful! Wish you were here!* I've given him updates on my tattoo and asked him about his. I've thrown in other stuff as well, details about all the things I miss about him, all the things I want him to take good care of so he can bring them home to me.

I've avoided Linda. That's the only other thing I've successfully done in the past twelve days, besides freaking out, making my list, sticking Dad in a closet, seeing a few matinees, and watching my tattoo heal. I haven't continued my search for Justine. I can't try to make contact with one other person, only to fail. When Linda's around I keep my bedroom door shut and stay inside my room. I sleep, read magazines and mysteries, try to draw, and do some of the prep work I'm supposed to do for senior year, or check on Facebook "friends" who are really acquaintances (or sometimes not even that).

Once I even clicked from David's (un-updated) page to Ravi's, which was, of course, blocked to me because I'm not his friend. Which is fine. I don't want to be. Not really. Not even after studying his profile picture. I expected it to be some kind of skateboarding shot—him flying off a jump, maybe, with the sun blowing out the sky behind him. But no.

The picture surprised me, the way it showed Ravi sitting across a picnic table from a man—his dad, maybe. In the picture, Ravi and the man are playing chess, intently focused on the board between them. Ravi's hand is poised above a white piece, a queen, I think. I tried to figure out who was winning until I realized how much time had passed, me lingering there, and then I left Ravi's page, and I never went back.

One day Linda passed me in the hall and told me that she thought I was depressed. If I didn't snap out of it soon, she was taking me to a psychologist.

I don't need a psychologist. I need the school year to start.

For now, I take a deep breath and try again to find my way to David—another message in a bottle flung out to where I believe he is, in care of the U.S. Army.

> Hey there,
>
> Here's what hurts for a *good* cause:
>
> 1. Every part of me, missing you. How are you? How's Kuwait treating you? Only a couple more days and you'll be on your way to Iraq. I try to imagine you where you are now. Since I don't really know what you're doing, I imagine you doing things I've seen you do. Sleeping. Reading. Drawing. Listening to music. Making friends the way you so easily do. Unlike me.
>
> 2. My tattoo doesn't hurt anymore. It doesn't itch anymore either, which means it's healed, I guess. Hope yours are too.
>
> 3. Linda still sometimes goes ballistic, seeing my tattoo. Okay, yeah, whatever, I guess that kind of hurts. I mean, I wish she'd just accept it, you know? When I remind her of the belly-button piercing that she has but I don't, she usually calms down a bit. I mean, I could have done something way worse than a discreet tat. For instance, I could sport a neon-green domino stud in my belly button like she sometimes does.

She's at work now, domino stud-less. She left with a warning: "It's been quite a week, and I know you've had a lot on your mind, but I've got something I need to discuss with you, pronto. I'm coming home early, soon as I can, so we can discuss it. You better be here." I hate the word "discuss." It never means what it's supposed to mean.

4. My head hurts from carrying around all the things I want to tell you that I'll never be able to fit into an email. When will you be able to Skype? I want to see you, over there.

5. I'm trying to write a letter to my long-lost grandmother, but I can't seem to get started. Painful.

6. It hurts to look at my drawings. They're that bad. I can't believe it's only a month until school starts. I'm supposed to have done stuff this summer, right? Worksheets and journals and readings and drawings? Well, I've made a dent. But I've still got a long way to go, which should be driving me crazy, except guess what? Except for the drawing part, I don't care.

I love you, and that doesn't hurt at all—or only in a good way.

Write already, okay?

Penna

I press *Send*.

● ● ●

But still I want to hear David's voice.

So I do what I've been doing for the past twelve days when I feel like this. I pull out the letters he wrote me all last year. I start from the bottom of the stack. The first one is written on the drawing paper that he loved best—which isn't cheap stuff. It's written with his Rapidograph pen.

Penna—

*Can't sleep. Keep thinking about today, the sculpture garden, you.
Geronimo!*

I'm in. I'm totally in. Hope you're in too.

*I never had this happen before, the way it's happened with you. We
met because we're doing something we both love to do. I like it that I saw
your painting before I saw you, before I knew anything about you, and I
thought, I've got to meet the person who painted that. You were Painter of
Awesome Killdeer first. Friend second. And now—now...*

*I can't wait to see you tomorrow. I'm going to put this in your locker
before you even get to school. Find me between classes, or I'll find you.
Have lunch with me. We can eat outside. The weather's supposed to be
great. Oh, that's right—this is your first Oklahoma fall. It's the best
time of year here, I think, and in the spring. Let's eat outside every day
we can.*

David

*P.S. If you have to stay after school for any reason, I can give you a ride
home on my bike after soccer practice.*

There was always a study session or an art project to work on. I found lots
of reasons to stay after school.

●●●

I call Bonnie, but she's not home yet from work.

I need to see David at any age. I break down and call Ravi to ask about
those photographs.

Ravi doesn't answer.

Probably skateboarding. Or sleeping the day away. Or doing something I
don't want to do right now, or probably ever. Like playing chess.

I don't leave a message for Ravi. Holding my cell in my tattooed hand, I will it, I will it, I will it to ring.

Nothing happens.

I set the phone on my desk. I'm in the kitchen getting something to eat when I hear it ring.

I race back to my room, flip it on.

"Hello?" I gasp, leaning against the bedroom wall.

"Penna."

I *willed* him.

"David!"

"Can you hear me?"

"Perfectly!" I slide down the wall onto the floor. "This is perfect."

"Good." I hear the smile in his voice. "You doing okay?"

"Yeah. Missing you, that's all. Did you get my emails? My letters?"

"Not with what's been going on. The only way I could have gotten a letter is if you'd written one way before I left."

I swallow down my guilt. "Oh."

"I'm sorry I haven't called," David continues. "It's been crazy here, connection-wise, all-kinds-of-wise. There was this wild, once-in-a-million-years sandstorm that started just after we landed. It screwed everything up. It settled down about a week ago. But then another one came. And we'd just gotten our lines up and running again. Now I just hope we make it to Iraq before another one hits."

"You're okay, though?"

"Yep."

"I'm just so glad you're okay!" This is the truth. Just this. Nothing else matters.

He laughs. "I *am*. I'm hot. Real hot, all the time. But okay." David coughs. Clears his throat. "Hear that? That's me hacking out sand. Can you believe

WHILE HE WAS AWAY

it? I'm still coughing out sand. My eyes and ears are gritty with it. It's a killer, I'll tell you."

My eyes sting as if I'm the one who braved a sandstorm. Then I realize I'm about to cry. No time for that. I wipe my eyes. "Where are you staying?"

He laughs. "We call them circus tents. Cute, right? They're these big white tents with air conditioning and cots and a wood floor. There are about fifty guys in my tent. No privacy. When me and the guy next to me happen to stretch our arms at the same time, we bang elbows."

"Wow."

"Yeah. But it's better than sleeping outside, that's for sure. That would be deadly. Now that the sandstorm's done, we're going to have to work really hard. We had our first real drills these last couple days. It was good to get started."

"I'll bet."

"Listen," David says. "There are a whole bunch of guys lined up here, waiting. I already called Mom and Dad. I've really got to let someone else take a turn."

I can't speak. Tears are stinging again.

"I love you," David says. "If something weird happens again, just know I'll get in touch as soon as I can. No news is good news."

"Okay," I manage to say. "I love you too."

"You're my hero," he says.

And hangs up.

I call Bonnie. She's crying, right there at her desk at work. In the background, someone is making sympathetic sounds that Bonnie is totally ignoring. "He's safe," she tells me through her sobs. "David's safe." I let her say that for a while.

Then we agree that we can't let the waiting get to us like this. Because it's going to go on and on.

— 63 —

Seven

The next morning there's a knock at the front door.

No one ever knocks at our front door now that David is gone.

I consider not answering it. But the knock sounds again, and suddenly my life—my empty life—overwhelms me.

My robe is flannel, too hot for July. So I throw on one of David's old cotton shirts and a pair of shorts. Then, tugging my hair up into a sloppy ponytail, I answer the door.

Ravi stands on our porch, a manila envelope in his hands.

All I can think is maybe that envelope is the color of the sand where David is. Manila sand.

"Hi." Ravi nervously turns the envelope in his hands. He's wearing a plain white T-shirt and black jeans. He's got his sweatshirt tied around his waist. His skateboard is propped against the porch steps. He must be just off work.

"Hi."

The muscles in Ravi's forearms ripple as he turns and turns the envelope.

"I brought you those pictures," he says. "Actually, *copies* of those pictures. I kept the originals for David."

"Oh." I remember Bonnie's description of him—*the shyest, sweetest boy.* Maybe not so shy anymore. But the other thing. Yeah. I guess he's that.

"There's a color copier at work. So...here." He thrusts the envelope into my hands.

"Thanks." I push my hair from my eyes. I probably look like I just got out of bed. Because I just got out of bed. I shift awkwardly on my feet, then notice that I should have buttoned one more button on David's shirt. Plus, there's the issue of a bra, or lack thereof. I press the manila envelope to my chest. "You want some coffee?"

Ravi shrugs. "I wouldn't say no."

We go to the kitchen. I put a pot of coffee on. Ravi waits for me to sit down at the kitchen table, and then he does too.

Together we look at his pictures of David.

There they are, maybe six years old, wading in a stream that is pure Oklahoma—the water rust-red from the clay. David is holding up a dripping turtle. They're both laughing hysterically.

Here they sit at Bonnie's counter, eating peanut butter and jelly sandwiches. There are jelly handprints all over the napkins. David's hands. I'd know them even then, so little.

Now they're marching in the Fourth of July parade, wearing their Boy Scout uniforms and proudly carrying the banner for Troop 27.

And here they are as older boys, maybe around the time of 9/11. Ravi looks miserable. He's averting his face from the camera. But even so I can see he's got a nasty-looking bruise on his cheek, a cut on his lip. David's not smiling either. But he's got his arm around Ravi, and he's looking right out of the photograph, right at me. His gaze says, *This isn't right, what they did to my friend. This is wrong.*

That's it. That's all the pictures. But that's more than enough. Getting this glimpse into David's life, I feel like someone's turned on a light inside me.

Smiling, I look up at Ravi. I start to thank him again. But something in my expression makes him catch his breath and draw back in his chair.

"I've got a bunch of stuff to do before work. Like get some sleep. I've got to go." He shoves back his chair and practically sprints from the house.

I listen to the sound of his skateboard skimming away over the street.

Only when the sound has completely faded do I realize that I never gave him that cup of coffee.

●●●

That afternoon I stand in the kitchen staring down into a pot of gold. Or a bowlful of sunlight. At least that's what it looks like—this big glass vat of honey that sits on the sheet of plastic that I've spread across the table.

Ravi's visit helped me. At least it made me want to do something—really do something. Something meaningful.

I set the four molds of our hands beside the honey bowl. I stare at them, remembering how David and I laughed as we pressed our hands into the plaster, how we cheered when they came out perfect. We kissed, careful not to get plaster all over the place. At first. Then we didn't care.

I take a funnel from a drawer. How am I going to hold a funnel and pour a big bowl of honey all alone? *David should be here to help me.*

No point in thinking things like that.

I put the funnel back in the drawer.

I heft the honey bowl and balance it on my hip. Using my hip as a fulcrum and my left hand as the main support, I tip the bowl forward. Honey spills slowly into a plaster hand—"spills" being the operative word. The honey glops into that plaster hand, the one beside it, and the one beside that until finally I just empty the bowl haphazardly over the four hands, hoping for the best.

"What a fricking mess," Linda would say if she were here instead of at Red Earth.

"Creative chaos," I'd say back.

From the kitchen window I see her then, the clockwork lady, walking past. I watch as the lady moves out of sight. At least she's making progress. If she can, so can I.

I lift the sticky honey hands and set them on a wax-paper-covered cookie sheet. I've sprinkled a little flour on the wax paper too, because I've read flour keeps honey-coated things from sticking. To say the molds are now coated with honey would be an understatement. Honey on the inside, honey on the outside. Honey, honey everywhere, and not a drop to eat. Gingerly, I throw away the glopped-up sheet of plastic, and then I bring a pot of water to boiling. Careful not to burn myself, I use the hot water to clean up my creative chaos.

When the table is clean, and the floor too, I study my flesh-and-blood palms, and I remember his. I trail thick and thin lines of nettles and baby's breath into our honeyed palms. I press two small, blue-green wax braids into the right ring fingers.

It feels good, making something.

I clear more space in the nearly empty freezer and slide the cookie sheet and our honey hands inside. I shut the freezer door, then open it again, take out a lonely freezer-burned pizza, and heat it up. I eat a couple slices and leave the rest for Linda. I watch a movie that isn't about war or love. It's supposed to be funny, a comedy of errors, a laugh riot. Small-town Southern girl becomes president's assistant, starts an international conflict, and then stops it with the single gift of her mama's banana-cream pie? Ha-ha.

I need sleep. I go to my room. I pull the shades and lie down under Plum Tumble.

● ● ●

Next day, I get more prep work done for school. I tackle math. Science. I do not tackle history—those essays we have to read about the Vietnam War.

Still, Linda would probably feel reassured that I seem to be getting my act together. If she were around to notice.

Maybe tomorrow I'll get up early to catch Linda in the morning. I want her to see how well I'm doing now. How love can be stronger than war.

● ● ●

My cell phone rings. I roll over and grab it from my nightstand. It must be early morning, because there's the sunlight, making honey-locust-leaf shadows on my bedroom wall.

It's the fourteenth day. He's on his way there. The call is probably from Bonnie, waking me up to remind me of this fact.

I mumble a distracted hello into the phone.

Static fills my head—a sound like an animal scratching at a screen door. Without thinking, I hold the phone away from my ear. Then I realize I've forgotten about the time difference. Baghdad is eight hours ahead of Killdeer. I glance at the clock. It's 8:00 a.m. here. So it's 4:00 p.m. there.

He could be there already.

I press the phone close to my ear again. Forget how much the static hurts. I want to hear.

I hear my heartbeat pounding through my ear against the static.

I'm right.

"I'm here," he says. "In Baghdad. I've already got my own cell phone—an Iraqi one—from this crazy little kiosk. Support the local business, right? We're staying in these—"

The static covers his words.

"What? I couldn't hear you! David? What did you say?"

"—okay. Really. Like I told Mom, I'm doing okay."

"Where are you staying?"

Again, he says something I can't hear for the noise.

I want to scream in frustration. I press the cell so hard to my ear that my cartilage crackles. I can feel the heat radiating from the cell, probably the same stuff that the scientists say is wiping out all the honey bees. I press harder.

"Did you get any of my letters yet?" My voice is very loud. "I've written a lot. I know it's probably too early for snail mail, but I've sent email too."

"We got in early, early this morning. We're in the city right now. I'm standing outside an Internet café. I'm going to try—"

His words get garbled.

"David! Don't hang up!"

I hear him then, as perfectly as before. "I love you, Penna."

There's a beep. Then dead silence.

I didn't get a chance to tell him that I love him too.

● ● ●

Again I call Bonnie.

But this time something seems to have shifted in her. This time she's not crying. She sounds completely composed, even grim, like now that he's finally there, she's thinking *marathon*, not *sprint*. She's readying herself for a long haul.

I ask her if she knows what it's like where he's staying.

"A camp just outside Baghdad. He said he'd send some pictures as soon as he is able. Maybe even today."

We remind each other that this is a good thing, just hearing his voice. It's the best we can hope for. It's the *best*, we tell each other just before we say good-bye.

Who are we kidding? The best would be if he were here.

But then when I go to my computer, he *is* here.

There he is. There he really is.

A short message, no doubt sent from that Internet café: "For you, because of you." And a photograph attached.

He's sent me a picture of himself lying in the middle of a gigantic heart he's traced in the dark yellow dust of Iraq.

I make the photograph my screen saver.

Then I climb back into bed. I let myself just lie there, thinking of him, the sound of his voice, that lucky dust against his skin. I close my eyes.

• • •

Linda stands over me, holding a steaming cup of coffee. She's made it just the way I like it. I can smell the cream and sugar.

"Rise and shine," Linda says. She's in her work uniform, her hair twisted up into a French knot. She looks all business.

I snarl something unrepeatable into Plum Tumble. Rubbing sleep from my eyes, I glance at my clock: 11:30 a.m. It's only been a few hours since David's phone call, but already it feels like a lifetime.

"Let's try again." Linda sits on my bed. She holds out the coffee. I have to sit up to take it. I take a sip of coffee and burn my tongue.

"It's nice outside," Linda says. "You should get out there and enjoy it."

I touch my tender tongue to my upper lip. "I didn't get enough sleep last night."

Linda arches an eyebrow. "Or the night before that or the night before that or the night before that. I've been waiting for you to snap out of this, Penelope, but I can't wait any longer. We're going to have to make some changes around here."

"Oh." My bad-ass voice. "Are *we* finally about to *discuss* things?"

Linda stands, brushes the wrinkles from her black pants, and goes to my bedroom window. Swiftly, she raises the blinds.

"Yes. *We are*," Linda says. "Things are different now. *We* have to face that."

"Huh." I take another drink. The coffee tastes burned, though maybe that's just my tongue. I know Linda's got her brew down to a science. I watch as she takes in the picture of Justine above my desk. She really regards it. Then she walks over to it and puts it facedown on the shelf.

"Hey!"

"Justine was about forty when she left me." Linda's voice is calm, as if she's picking up a reasonable conversation that we just left off. "It was the nineteen sixties. Nineteen sixty-nine to be exact. Vietnam. Hippie movement. Women's movement. Civil rights. You name it. Everyone was escaping everything to find themselves, even in podunk towns like Killdeer." Linda shrugs.

"Justine probably had lots of reasons to go, lots of excuses. But as a forty-year-old mother myself, I can't imagine leaving my child. I'd never do something like that to you. Just like I'm not going to stand by and watch you fall to pieces now. Over a boy. Or for any reason."

"Put her back up!"

Linda shakes her head. "She nearly ruined me, Penelope. You know that. She surely ruined my dad."

"You can't blame everything on your mother," I say. "I'd think you'd want me to remember that."

Linda opens her mouth, but for a moment—oh, joy—she can't seem to speak.

I set my coffee cup on my nightstand and stride across the room to where Linda is standing. I right Justine on the shelf. Then I turn back to Linda, fists on my hips. We stand there, staring each other down. I can feel heat coming off her. She probably can feel it coming off me. I look away first. I look at Justine, who doesn't give me any answers.

Linda clears her throat. "Here's the deal, Penelope. You're going to start working for me. It'll be a little hard because you'll be plunging into the thick of things. But I know you can do it."

I stare at her. "Come again?"

"The night girl quit yesterday. I have to find another server, pronto. And you have to find a way out of your funk. You need to keep busy. When David was at training, you really threw yourself into your studies—which made me proud. When school first got out, you got a lot of baby-sitting gigs. You mowed lawns. Did some housecleaning. But once he came home, you just kind of ground to a halt. You need to start making some cash for college, pronto."

I throw myself on the bed. "You have *got* to be kidding me."

Linda frowns, then forces a smile. "I don't like that kind of tone unless I'm using it."

"And I don't like having a mother who's also my boss!"

"As long as you're living under my roof, you'll do as I say."

"I could leave," I say. "I might do that. I might drop out of high school too, just like you did. Plus, I know someone else who did that and he's doing okay."

So I'm elaborating a little on Ravi's situation. So what?

Anyway, Linda doesn't take the bait.

We glare.

I repeat the bit about my mother, my boss. But it comes out all whiny this time. Linda has won. She knows it. I'm not going to leave or drop out of anything. I want to go to art school too much. I want to go there with David.

"Think of it as a great opportunity," Linda says. "You have to have some work experience, kiddo, if you want to get anywhere in life. Not to mention— *again*—the benefits of a regular paycheck." Linda straightens her shoulders. "You start tonight. Drink your coffee. We're out of here in two hours. Got to get you there early so you can get oriented."

I feel panicky. "I'm supposed to be building up my art portfolio this summer, remember?"

"I haven't seen you doing that much. Anyway, working will clear your head, get your creative juices flowing."

"Give me a chance, will you?" I'm pleading. I hate pleading.

"You'll have the daytime. That should give you plenty of time to get things done. And nice light, which you also need." Linda walks out of the room like everything is all decided.

I pull up my screen saver. There he is. I could sit here all day, just looking at him. Okay, so maybe that *is* a little troubling, but I just about could.

"Shower, Penelope!" Linda calls from the kitchen. "I've almost got your work apron pressed, and if I find you in your room when I'm done, I'm canceling your cell service for as long as it takes to get you playing for the team again. I'll cancel cable if that's what it takes, honey. And you know that means no email."

I bitch. I moan. But I head for the shower.

And standing there, warm water rinsing suds from my hair, I suddenly remember the loose floorboard and the envelope tucked beneath, holding something I want to see.

Maybe I am falling to pieces. Before, I never would have forgotten about something like this.

As soon as I escape from Red Earth, I'm going up there, alone in the dark this time without Linda hovering.

Eight

I stare at the fake yellow Gerbera daisy permanently enshrined in the dashboard vase of Linda's yellow VW. I'm hypnotized by the flower's bobbing. We are bobbing along, the daisy, Linda, and me. Our first official commute to Red Earth.

I plant my beat-up, black Doc Martens on the dashboard—"All black, all the time, that's the uniform!" Linda said, as she handed me one of her polo shirts to go with my old black jeans—and then I slump down in my seat. I lean against the window, trying to spot places where David and I have gone together. They are everywhere. The train tracks with Barbies. Sonic for limeades. The bowling alley to make fools of ourselves throwing gutter balls.

"First I'll show you around, introduce you," Linda is saying. "New girl. Of course, everyone knows who you are. I talk about you all the time. 'My daughter, the artist!' Oh, I don't know what the specials are today. We'll have to figure that out. Listen, here's how you cope if, let's say, five four-tops and three deuces come in all at once—"

"Please!" I clap my hands over my ears. I feel like the top of my head is going to blow off. "I'll cope exactly how I'm coping now. Just barely."

On the way home—how many hours from now?—Linda will probably debrief me in exactly this manner. Only I'll be even more tired. I'll probably have to guzzle caffeine to get my butt up into that attic, and then I'll be up all night and trying to sleep all day again, and Linda will really let me have it tomorrow.

We stop at a red light. There's the park with the playground.

And there's Ravi, balancing at the top of the slide on his skateboard.

That feeling comes over me—that panicky feeling I get whenever David does something like back-flip off a viaduct wall. I roll down the window and shout, "Are you crazy?"

Ravi shades his eyes with his hand. He must realize it's me, because he calls back, "Nope. Just a superhero."

Linda peers over my shoulder. "Who's that?"

"Some guy," I mutter. And shout, "Don't kill yourself!"

The light turns green. Ravi sails down the slide and into the air. He makes his landing, steady and sure. The momentum sends him hurtling toward us. Linda kicks the car into gear quickly and drives on. As if he might dent her VW.

"Crazy," Linda says.

"No." I sound mad. I am mad. About a lot of things. "Not really."

Linda smirks. "Gotta love the 'really.'"

I scowl out the window. Enough about Ravi. I'll think about Justine, that letter in the attic. What will it tell me? Will it tell me if Justine ever walked these streets like David and I used to do? Was there a playground here way back then? Did Justine and her soldier ever swing on the swings together or kiss there in the dark?

More important, did Justine ever spend time at Red Earth?

I drop my feet on the car's floor, registering *yes*. Of course she spent time at Red Earth. My grandpa owned the place, after all.

I glance at Linda, wondering if she's still trying to get inside my business, inside my head, but she's tapping her fingers on the steering wheel to a song that's playing in *her* head. She's smiling. She might as well be the one who's half a world away. I look out my window again. The houses, apartment buildings, and occasional fast-food joints are dwindling into strip malls, gas stations, and lots of fast-food joints. And up ahead the neon sign for Red Earth flares—a red horizon line and a brown tumbleweed flashing on and off, rolling, rolling, and going nowhere in the neon wind.

We drive around to the back of the two-story brick building and park by the garbage bins. We get out of the VW, and I follow Linda through Red Earth's back door. Linda calls a cheery hello to Isaac, the ebony-skinned chef, who comes equipped with full mustache and trademark green bandanna covering his dreadlocks. Isaac is tending his griddle—the sizzling sausage there. He salutes Linda with his tongs, ignores me, and goes back to flipping links. He's all business, that Isaac.

Linda plucks two gray time cards from the metal rack beside the time clock. She hands one to me.

"After you," she says.

I punch the clock.

Linda gives me a swift hug. "You're officially one of us now."

"Yippee," I say.

Everything happens fast then. Linda introduces me in my professional capacity to Caitlin, the waif-like cocktail waitress with the stick-straight, shoulder-length, pink-streaked blond hair and fake Irish brogue. ("Caitlin tries on lots of different accents," Linda whispers to me, "but mostly she's all Irish, to go with her name, I guess.") I remember Caitlin from school last year. She was a senior. (Apparently she was a hanger-on as well, too old for high school, since she can serve drinks already.) She was all into theater. I saw her play Eliza Doolittle in the fall production of *My Fair Lady*.

"I don't remember you," Caitlin says bluntly when I tell her this.

Linda whisks me off to say hi to Tom, the sixty-something, bald-as-a-cue-ball bartender with American eagles tattooed on his forearms. He gives me a quick appraising glance, grunts hello, and then turns away.

How welcoming.

While Linda checks the table settings, I restock the salad bar. Fill the water pitchers. Make fresh coffee. With Linda's help I gradually start hustling around the dimly lit dining room like I actually belong here—only once banging my head on the low-hanging, faux-wagon-wheel lamps that hang over the heavy oak tables. Only twice bruising my shins on the chairs. Only three times tripping over the cold stone fireplace's raised hearth. And in between all this, checking my cell phone to make sure it's not on silent, in case David has a chance to call.

The rest of the décor is pretty minimal, thank God. There are a few old photographs of Killdeer on the walls that I've never seen before. I want to check them out, but I have too many other things to think about right now.

I go into the kitchen to get some fresh ketchup bottles. Isaac evaluates me from his griddle.

"Wonder what that'll look like when you're eighty-five," he says, looking pointedly at my tattooed finger.

I shrug. I never think about when I'm eighty-five. Before Justine, I'd never thought much above Linda's age, actually. Forty was my cutoff.

"I can always get it removed if it starts looking bad," I say. "But it won't. I won't. I love it."

And I do.

Shaking his head, Isaac turns back to whatever he's frying now.

At 4:15, when everything seems ready, Caitlin stuffs her iPod into her apron and pops a CD into Red Earth's player. An Irish band blares, penny whistles shrilling. Linda rolls her eyes, but the band plays on. Stripped of her earbuds, Caitlin wants to chat. She grabs my arm and steers me over to a table near the bar. She pats the back of a chair, and—what the heck—I drop down into it. These Doc Martens feel too heavy. Guess my feet are used to flip-flops and sandals.

"Two Cokes, pretty please," Caitlin calls to Tom. She seems to have forgotten her brogue for the moment. She's just a regular Okie now.

Tom fills two glasses and pushes them across the bar to Caitlin. Caitlin hands me one and plops down in a chair beside me. I take a long drink; I didn't realize I was so thirsty. Over the rim of my glass, I watch Tom, who's methodically cutting limes into neat little wedges. Tom moves like molasses, tending bar. But Linda knew him when she was a little girl—apparently Tom was an old friend of the family and lived with them for a while—and when he came looking for work because he couldn't make it on his pension, she immediately hired him.

"Tom's a *fixture*," Linda told me one night. "He was like a little brother to my dad."

Now I'm thinking, *Brother to Grandpa, uncle to Linda, great-uncle to me?* And then, *He knew Justine maybe?*

"So you think you're ready?"

I start at Caitlin's voice. I'd almost forgotten she was sitting beside me. I look at her. She's watching me as closely as I was watching Tom, her glossy lips pursed around her straw.

I give a little shiver, pull myself back into now. "Ready or not." I take in the empty restaurant—fifteen tables, plus the one Caitlin and I are sitting in!—and my stomach lurches.

"It'll be slow till five-ish, then it'll be crazy till nine thirty–ish, and then it'll slow down again till closing. I'll help you during the worst of the rush, and I know your ma will too. But basically I'm all about the alcohol. If there's a bunch of folks boozing it up at one table, I'll be there. I make real money, see, on tips from sloppy drinkers. I don't have a sugar mama at home like you do. I've got parents who make me pay rent. So I'm fixin' to make some cold, hard cash. Got it? Someday I'll make my million doing voice-overs in LA, but until then this is it."

I grip my glass more tightly. "I'm not asking you to carry me."

"Oh, *right*." Caitlin rolls her eyes. "Listen. You got clout. Talk your mom into hiring another night person, why don't you? Someone with a little experience? I mean, sometimes I can barely keep up. This place is hopping lately. I don't know how you're going to manage."

"When Red Earth gets really established, we'll hire more help." I push my glass away. My stomach's suddenly too jittery even for a Coke. "That's what Linda says at least." I glance around again. "Where is she anyway?"

Caitlin laughs. "Oh, it's *Linda*, is it?"

Of course I'm not going to tell Caitlin that I didn't start calling Linda by her first name until after I got together with David. Saying Linda's name, and Bonnie's and Beau's too, bound David and me even closer. It gave us access to knowledge and perspective, the way passwords and codes work for spies. Say *Linda*, and *Open sesame!* a kind of door unlocked, and David and I'd find ourselves in a secret place—an interior space, far from all that confined and defined us. Our parents, sure, but Killdeer too. We could do what we wanted there. Talk for hours. Break petty rules. Make out. Whatever. It always felt good.

But he's called them Mom and Dad, I suddenly realize, every time he's spoken about them on the phone.

"*Linda's* in the kitchen, where she so often is these days." Caitlin flicks her pale eyebrows. "Seems the other new member of the crew needs lots of attention."

"Isaac?"

"Yeah. *Linda* took a big risk hiring him. I heard *Linda*—"

"Will you stop with the *Linda*!"

Caitlin laughs. "Cute." She chucks me under the chin. "Anyway, I heard *her* telling Tom. Isaac said he wouldn't work here unless he got a bigger salary than any of the previous cooks. He actually *has* decent restaurant experience. She was worried at first, but now it seems like the risk might be paying off." Caitlin polishes off her drink. "Isaac's food will turn this place into a high-class joint, mark my words. What with the Southern-Down-Home-Cooking-Meets-Tex-Mex-Meets-Cajun-Meets-Irish-Fare thing he's got going on."

"A true kitchen god." I'm a little less queasy. It feels good to joke with someone a little.

"Just make sure you don't rub Isaac the wrong way, or we'll all suffer. He can be a real—"

"Bastard!" Tom shouts.

Startled, Caitlin and I both look at him.

But Tom's not talking about Isaac. He's shaking his fist at the TV above the bar. "They did it again!"

Caitlin claps her hands to her chest. "Watch the volume, Tom, why don't you?"

"Just look at this." Tom stares up at the TV. "*Iraq.*"

He's watching the news—a special report. A hazy video flickers across the screen. It shows a Hummer, on its side and twisted. Bodies litter the dusty road.

So far I've successfully avoided the news. The special reports.

"A resurgence in violence," the reporter says.

Caitlin snorts. "Who *are* these assholes, anyway? Can somebody tell me? Tom? You were in Vietnam. You know everything."

Tom doesn't answer or look away from the TV.

"Penna?" Caitlin asks.

Numbly, I shake my head. There had to be a war. That's all I know. There was evil out there, and we had to defeat it. That's what David always said before OSUT. That's one of the reasons he told me he enlisted.

Tom is gripping the bar so tightly that the eagles on his forearms bulge. He looks back up at the TV. "*Listen* to the man, will you?"

Caitlin ignores him. "And what is an EID exactly? Every day, it's war this, war that."

"Show a little respect, and maybe I'll fill you in," Tom mutters.

Caitlin shrugs, then glances at me and clucks her tongue. "Uh-oh. Now look what you did to the boss's daughter. Doesn't look like she likes that show either. You're nearly as white as the driven snow, Penna." Caitlin slings her arm around my shoulder. "Come on, now. They're there. We're here. It's okay. Look. It's not even us hurt. Those are *them*."

Now there's another clip playing across the TV screen. U.S. soldiers are moving through rubble that was a marketplace, the reporter is saying. One of the soldiers carries a limp, black-haired boy. The rest carry guns.

The boy makes me think of a young David or Ravi.

"Help me out here, Tom. She looks like she might faint or something. Don't hurl, kid, okay?" Caitlin gives me a brisk pat. "Just another day in Baghdad. Come on now."

"An IED is an improvised explosive device." I hear myself saying this. My voice is flat and dull. "A homemade bomb."

"That's right." Tom considers me.

Caitlin claps her hands together, falsely enthusiastic. "Aren't you the G.I. Jane!"

"I took Current Events." I shiver. What I don't say is that before OSUT, David talked about stuff like this. He liked gaming, and a lot of times the games he played were about war. Sometimes I sat down with him at his computer and watched him go at it. I took a few shots myself, popped off a few of the virtual bad guys. I learned some things that way—lots more than I ever learned in Current Events.

Once David and I even shot paintballs at an Iraqi artist through his website. "Shoot the Kaffiyeh," the website was called. It was anti-war, I know. But David and I didn't talk about that. We just thought the site was interesting. Cool. At first. The artist was wearing one of those patterned, fringed scarves a lot of Muslim men wear—a kaffiyeh. He was sitting on a low couch in front of a coffee table in what looked like a simple little living room—other than the fact that everything, including the artist, was splattered with red paint, and there was a paintball gun mounted in one corner.

As we watched, the artist picked up a newspaper and started to read. The newspaper was printed in strange script. The artist took a drink from a glass of water. Then David clicked on something and, *wham*, fired a paintball. The paintball struck the edge of the newspaper, ripped the newspaper from the artist's hands, and exploded in red against a wall.

"Holy crap," David said. He laughed nervously. He said it was my turn. "Come on," David said. "Just think about 9/11. Shoot him."

The artist was bent over, collecting the messy shreds of newspaper when I took my shot. I aimed off to the side, but even when the paintball just burst bloodily against the floor, I practically hyperventilated.

"I don't like this," I said.

David stuttered around for a little bit—9/11 this, 9/11 that. Finally he said he didn't really like this either. Not really. The guy reminded him too much of Ravi. David rolled his eyes then. "Total stereotyping, right? Seen one, you seen 'em all. God. I sound like my worst enemy." We left that site then and went somewhere else where we shot droids, not humans.

"You kids learn a little history then, over at the high school?" Tom is asking. "You got something out of that class. What did you call it?"

"Current Events. I didn't really like it, just took it for the credit."

There's a commercial on the TV now. A butterfly flits across the screen, advertising a sleep aid. *Check with your doctor for possible side effects.*

Caitlin points her straw at the door. "First customers. Or as *Linda* likes to say, 'guests.'"

A family has entered Red Earth—four bickering kids, probably under the age of ten, and a mom and dad who look less than happy.

"Good luck." Caitlin gnaws at her straw as she watches the kids barrel toward a table. "It's a war out there."

● ● ●

Two hours later I'm hiding in a stall. The bathroom is the only place that's halfway quiet. Red Earth is packed—every table full and a line at the door. Caitlin's given up on her cold, hard cash. She and Linda have spent the night covering my butt.

I can't do anything right. I mix up orders or forget them entirely. I spill drinks and tip plates. I don't clear tables fast enough. I'm not working the register or the credit-card machine or making change correctly.

I suck at this.

Tips are next to nothing. Free meals by way of apology to disgruntled "guests" are one too many.

Caitlin and Tom made do okay the first hour or so, just giving Linda these looks like *What were you thinking?* Then they started to let me know they were a little ticked. "First night and everything, but get a brain, kid," Tom said, and somehow I think he's not just talking about my service-with-a-smile skills; he's also talking about my understanding of Current Events.

Isaac's pissed too. He glowers across his gleaming stainless-steel *Order up!* counter. He's practically broken his little silver bell, slamming his palm down on it and trying to get someone's attention so the food won't go cold.

Minutes ago I splashed hot coffee on a man. *A few drops.* Linda over-reacted, I think, maybe just a little. After she swaddled the man's wrist in a bag of ice, she told me to "go to the bathroom and come out a different person."

So here I am, perched on the closed toilet lid, breathing into my cupped hands. Trying not to cry. Trying not to think about the twisted Hummer, the bodies in the road, the soldier carrying the limp boy, and all the others with guns. Trying not to think about David—or at least the space all around me where he once was. Trying to become a different person.

Time passes. I know it's passing. I'm just trying not to think how long it's been since David's been gone—how short it's been since he's been gone, really. *Remember?* I make myself think instead. *You've got the long, strong arms of love. You can hold on across continents and the oceans in between.*

So this is war-love.

Justine, I think. *Remember Justine.*

Remember her, maybe. Just don't *become* her. I can almost hear Linda's voice, saying this.

I wonder if Linda's right.

I open the stall door. I step out, blinking against the harsher light.

Linda is bracing herself against the sink. Her face is flushed and damp with sweat. Her arms are covered with little red welts from the hot rims of plates.

"I can't even believe you've been in here this long," she says. "We're practically dying out there, and you're sitting in here."

"You told me to," I mutter. But then I glance at my watch. It's been close to twenty minutes that I've been in here.

Linda must be too wiped out to yell. She speaks softly. She sounds discouraged, not mad. Disappointed.

"I want this for us this summer." She plucks a paper towel from the dispenser, turns to the sink, runs cold water over the towel, swabs her face, and dabs at the welts on her arms. "We need this, you and me. And it's not just about money or discipline, Penelope. We need to make something work *together* again." She stuffs the paper towel into the overflowing garbage can, then snags another paper towel and holds it out to me. "Wipe your face, and get back out there."

I'd say something if I knew what to say. But I'd be talking to a swinging door.

Already, Linda's back out there.

Nine

My first official shift ends with a bang, not a whimper, at 10:45 p.m. when I drop an entire tub of dirty dishes on the kitchen floor.

Isaac stares at me like I'm a cockroach lurking in his daily special. Caitlin swears a blue streak under her breath. Linda says, "Go. Home. To. Bed." She has her hands pressed to either side of her face. With her mouth open in horror, she reminds me of that famous painting *The Scream*. But Linda doesn't scream. Not right now at least. She just says, "Rest up for tomorrow."

"Tomorrow?" Caitlin, Isaac, and I groan in unison.

Linda plants her hands on her hips. "Oh, we're not getting off that easy. We'll make a waitress out of Penelope yet."

Then Linda gets to work cleaning up my mess. I offer to help, but she practically shoves me toward the door.

"Take the VW," she says. "Isaac, you'll give me a ride home?"

"You bet," Isaac says grimly. "If it'll get her out of here."

"Now, now. That's my daughter you're talking about," Linda says, but she sounds grim herself.

As I flee, I hear Caitlin and Isaac laying odds on my failure. Caitlin gives me a week, tops. Isaac, three days. I'm nobody's favorite except Linda's, who says with hesitation that I'll be fine. We're cut of the same cloth.

I'm at the back door when I remember my bag. I go back inside to get it, skulking past Linda, Isaac, and Caitlin. I left it under the bar, I remember. I slink through the dining room and duck past Tom, who's still busy eyeballing the TV. I grab my bag, then turn to leave again.

That's when I see her, hanging where only Tom typically looks.

Justine.

In the photograph nailed there above the upside-down wineglasses, she stands at Red Earth's bar beside a guy I think might be a much younger version of Tom. In his white T-shirt, he looks like a sweet greaser, giving my grandma a big, adoring grin. She is looking straight into the camera, forcing a tight, weary smile. Her hair has been whipped into a Jackie O. flip. Only Justine's widow's peak keeps it from being solid Jackie O. There are dark circles under Justine's eyes. Her heart-shaped face is sunken now, and lines etch her mouth. She *is* Justine—I think I'd recognize her at any age, even eighty years old. But she *is not* Justine too. At least she is not the same Justine that sits at the dressing table in my photograph at home. This Justine is miserable.

From the hairdo, the sheath-like style of Justine's dress, and the swelling in her belly, I'd say this picture was taken in 1969, just before Linda was born.

"Tom?"

He turns from the TV. He frowns, seeing me. "I thought you were gone."

"Almost." I point at the photograph.

Tom flicks his eyes where I'm pointing. Then he fixes his gaze on the TV again.

"A real lady," he says gruffly.

I clench my hands and wait for more. But Tom won't look at me. From the set to his shoulders, I know not to push it.

I stumble off to the VW. I back out of the parking lot. I drive toward home, speed through the dark, cooling night. I try to remember how easily David drove his scooter, how it felt to hold on to him so tightly while he did.

Home, I park the VW in the garage.

Inside the house, I realize I haven't eaten since mid-afternoon. I'm bleary and numb. Except for my feet. They're like burning-hot bricks. I drag off my Doc Martens, collapse into a kitchen chair, and prop my feet on the table. Now what? Is it exhaustion or adrenaline or anger that's making me vibrate?

Somehow I'm on my feet again. I stuff my face with dry cereal. Drink a large glass of orange juice, then another. Eat a few tablespoons of peanut butter swiped on a bruised banana. I try drawing a portrait of Tom, but all that comes out are two eagles that look like buzzards on Popeye-like arms.

I stagger to my bedroom and drop down at my desk. Open my laptop.

I catch my breath.

There's an email.

> Hey there, Penna.
>
> I don't have much time. I just want to give you this little look into my life, since you want to know. Get this. My bunk is really uncomfortable, you know? If I weren't so beat from the heat today, I wouldn't be able to sleep. Even beat, it's hard. But at least lying there I can look at your pictures. I've got this wall beside me, and I've covered every square inch with you. You're the last person I see falling asleep, the first person I see waking up. You get more beautiful very day. You're beauty, Penna. Just like I always said. Remember that, no matter what happens. I still believe that.

And there's an attachment. A drawing.

There he is—sketched in black marker, a mix of fine point, medium weight, and broad stroke—my favorite superhero, David's manga look-alike. He's wearing camouflage and (as if he's been talking to Ravi too) a billowing superhero cape. His hair is thick and curly again. He kneels over two little vines, just planted, it looks like, from the way little mounds of dirt are sketched up around them. Manga David is twining the vines around the bottom rungs of an old ladder, which is propped against the side of a tent.

David always helped Bonnie with the little garden she kept in their backyard. Tomatoes, cucumbers, green beans—it's hard to tell from the drawing which vegetable these little vines are. But it looks like David is trying to bring a little bit of his backyard to Iraq.

I rattle off an email. I tell him I love his email and drawing. Draw more, I beg. I tell him about Red Earth. It's not so terrible, I say, which I probably wouldn't have said if I hadn't seen David's drawing. When someone you love plants vegetables in the middle of a war zone, how can you complain about your job? I tell him I can't wait to hear his voice. I miss him. I love him. All that and more.

I press *Send*, and the email whooshes away into the great beyond.

I throw myself on the bed, then. I smell like the daily specials. I cover my nose with Plum Tumble and try to breathe through my mouth. I can't stop thinking about David's drawing. I feel guilty and hopeful and inspired all at the same time. I feel such love for him, a love that's getting stronger because of all this, not weaker, the way I was afraid. There. I've said it. I was afraid of that—being weak—almost as much as I was afraid of David getting hurt, or worse. Almost. But in the middle of the night, at the darkest hour, this is what it's coming down to inside me: love.

● ● ●

I can't sleep.

I get up and sit down at my desk again, open a new document, and start typing.

Dear Mrs. Weaver,

I think we might be related. I think I might be your granddaughter.

I think I live in your old house in Killdeer now and sleep under your quilt and look at your picture. I think we have other things in common too. I would very much like to talk with you. Will you email me or write me back if you have any connection to Killdeer, Oklahoma? I'll write my phone number below, should you prefer to call.

Sincerely,
Penelope Weaver

I copy this over and over, until I've copied enough letters for every Justine on my list. Then I print them all.

Linda is home. She made the right choice and didn't interrupt me. She ate and showered, watched a little TV. I can hear her now, faintly snoring beneath her covers. It's nearly two in the morning, after all, and she wants to be rested for tomorrow.

As should I.

I think of the tender way the figure in David's drawing bowed over those little plants.

I stick all the letters in envelopes and address them.

Only when I'm sealing the last envelope do I remember the envelope beneath the attic floor.

Even David would say, "Enough already," I tell myself. And I fall into bed.

● ● ●

Penelope,

You were sleeping so hard, I didn't want to wake you. I'll come and pick you up at 3:30. Things will go better tonight. I promise.

Mom

I discover her note—and her previously unsung ability to read the future—on the kitchen table when I grab my breakfast or lunch or brunch, I guess it is, of old, cold pizza.

Chomping on the last of the crust, I look out the window and spot the clockwork lady passing by. She's got more energy than I do this morning, that's for sure. The attic seems a long way up—the Mount Everest of Killdeer, Oklahoma. I watch the old lady disappear around the corner. Guess I'll take my inspiration from her. From David.

I go back into my bedroom and check my email. Nothing. Facebook. Nothing new there. Cell phone. Ditto.

Moving on.

Still wearing my pajamas, I tug on a pair of thick socks, go into the hallway, pull the cord to the attic's trapdoor, jump out of the way as the attic ladder descends, and climb up.

Linda must have been up here in the past few days, because she's taped thick plastic over the hole in the broken window. Now there's barely enough dusty light to see by. My socks snag on the wood planks as I hunch around, looking for the loose floorboard.

When I find it, I lift the board aside and, quick as I can, plunge my hand into the hole and draw out the envelope. No scorpions or spiders on the attack, but I sneeze at the dust. Holding the envelope close, I scuttle across the attic, climb back down the ladder, and go back to my room.

If it's nothing more than some old tax document or bill of sale, I don't know what I'm going to do. It has to be more.

Turns out it is.

● ● ●

January 10, 1945

Sweet Justine—

    Thank you for the gloves! They sure help, these winter nights. Remember how we once thought Europe would be like something out of a fairy tale? Well, it's a bitter cold fairy tale. I'll say that for it.

I think about our honeymoon all the time now.

Remember that souvenir shop in the Badlands, and the funny plaster airplane, how I got you to climb into it with me? You climbed right up in that ticky-tacky thing. You slid right down in front of me, closer than life. I can feel you against me now.

All the other tourists stared. Remember? We might as well have had tin cans dangling from our waists and Just Married painted across our backsides. We were that much of a sight to see—a real treat, right up there with Yellow Rock Drug's claim to fame: free ice water, fresh donuts, and bottomless cups of coffee, and all those wooden Indians and totem poles.

I tickled you and I wouldn't stop, not even when you begged.

I think it was in the Badlands when we started saying we were dropping in on George, Tom, Abe, and Teddy.

And then at Mount Rushmore, we left our old Ford parked in the little bit of scrub-pine shade that we could find. (How's the radiator doing, by the way? Remember it gets thirsty. Give it a drink.) It was a long hike into the park, but you never complained. Just like you don't complain now about my being gone now. Brave girl.

First thing I want to do when I get home? First real thing? I want to go back to Yellow Rock. I want to have our honeymoon all over again without knowing we'll have to leave each other so soon after.

Take care of our little house, brave girl. I'll be back as soon as I can.

Always yours, as you are always mine—
Owen

●●●

Always yours, as you are always mine—

Owen.

For you, because of you.

David.

I have to find Justine.

I look again at the envelope. It's addressed to a *Mrs. Justine Delmore*. She lived at this address then too. Owen must have lived here before he went to war.

So this was *their* house first. Hers. Not my grandpa's. The house must have been hers when he married her. Not that it matters really, but still.

I go to my computer and find Justine Delmore. Not Justine Blue or Justine Weaver. Justine Delmore. When she left my grandpa, she left him this house and took back Owen's name.

Justine Delmore lives in Yellow Rock, South Dakota. She has an address and a phone number. A newspaper article pops up too, a feature in the *Yellow Rock Times*.

Turns out she is a librarian in Yellow Rock, a member of the local chapter of the GSW (whatever that is). And an artist. The brief article celebrates Justine's retirement from the library. She has donated a painting for the entryway. The article includes a tiny, fuzzy photograph of the woman who must be Justine standing next to the painting. She looks bird-like. In any strong wind, it looks like, she could just blow away.

My heart starts thudding in my chest. I can feel my pulse in my throat. A white cloud of hair frames her aged face. But the girl in her painting—I recognize that blue dress from the photograph on my desk. The girl balances on the rails of the train tracks that divide the canvas, her arms stretched wide. With her left hand, the girl reaches toward a steep bank of jagged yellow rock. With her right, she reaches toward red clay plains and the little gray house there that is Linda's and mine now.

"What are you doing?"

From behind me I hear Linda's voice, sharp with frustration.

In a flash I put my computer to sleep. I spin around in my chair.

"It's time to go, and you're still in your pajamas." Linda folds her arms, juts a hip. "Snap to it."

When I say that I'll be ready before Linda knows it, she turns on her heel and storms off. I hear her in the kitchen, stuffing things she thinks she doesn't want or need into the recycling and garbage. When she gets in a fury like this, she thinks everything is junk. She throws important stuff away.

I don't try to stop her. I get ready as quickly as I can, almost before she knows it. This seems to satisfy her. At least she doesn't say a word all the way to Red Earth. She doesn't ask me about the painting on my computer screen of a girl balanced on train tracks, reaching between here and there.

Ten

Linda was wrong. It may be my second day working, but I'm still the worst thing to hit this joint since the waiter two years ago who hid vodka in his OJ and served food with the shakes, only to finally pass out cold on top of the elementary-school principal's order of home fries.

This according to Caitlin, who is covering my butt again.

"You need help," Caitlin says, ringing her tray with glass after glass of Long Island iced teas. "I mean, this is so not your calling. I'm either going to strangle you or we are going to let loose after work. I think we'd better let loose, don't you?"

She strides off, delivering the drinks to her table and going to one of my tables to take the order I would be taking if I were a better waitress.

Tom watches me from across the bar. He is *staring* at me. I chew at my lip, waiting for the slow burn of fury to rise in his eyes. But instead he just shakes his head.

"Like that—" Tom clears his throat huskily. "Standing there like that—"

Behind Tom the TV blasts another war clip—this one from Afghanistan. "The real hot spot," the reporter proclaims as the camera pans a barren cliff, then zeros in on the mouth of a cave and the group of bearded men huddled there, machine guns clutched to their chests.

"All worn out like that," Tom finally says. "Well, you look so much like her, young."

"Like who?" Though, of course, I can guess. I just want to hear him say it, that's all. Do I look like Linda or Justine, or both of them finally meeting in me?

I expect Tom to turn back to his sink full of dirty glasses or the footage that's spinning now about Iran.

But he keeps looking at me. He says, "Like a person who might let bad things get the best of her if she's not careful. That's who."

Only then, when he's delivered a sharp blow to my ego, does he turn back to the sink.

●●●

Linda is running herself ragged, trying to do all of her job and most of mine, trying to prove that she's right: we can do this, together, again.

Isaac finally hunts me down and stops me in my tracks. He takes the jumble of menus I'm holding. I'm supposed to be seating the little crowd that is waiting with increasing irritation at the front door. But given the fact that I'm also supposed to be clearing tables, I haven't gotten around to it yet.

"You're sweating," Isaac says, "which is not terribly appealing to our clientele, I'm sure."

"Oh well." I try to sound like I don't give a rip. I don't pull it off.

Isaac deftly taps the menus into a neat stack. "Last night's break helped? That little siesta you took in the ladies' room?"

I try to remember. "Kind of."

"Disappear for a while." Isaac flicks his fingers at me. "Go on. Scoot. Scat."

I scurry back to the bathroom. I find my special stall and lock myself inside. I perch on the toilet. For the heck of it, I pull out my pen and graffiti a tiny killdeer flying over the toilet-paper holder, and then a nest beneath the bird, and me and David sitting inside. The killdeer will watch over us, if only here in a bathroom stall. This makes me feel a little better for a moment. Then I realize that when Linda gets a load of my little doodle, she'll really have my hide.

I bury my head in my arms.

Minutes later my black apron rings brightly. I nearly fall to the stall floor. I scrounge through my apron pocket with my left hand and pull my cell from the rumpled pages of my check pad. It rings again. Clumsily, I flip it open.

"Penna?"

My heart thuds in my throat. There is the little nest I drew and us inside. Here we are.

"David?"

He laughs. He still sounds tense, but he also sounds giddy with relief. It's him again. It's me again.

"You can hear me better this time?"

"Yes!" There's no static. He's coming through loud and clear. I close my eyes so I can focus on the sound of his voice.

"It's noisy here, though. Talk as loud as you can, okay?"

I wait, eyes closed, but now David is silent.

Finally he says, "Where are you?"

"Oh, I'm at this wild party." I laugh. "This guy's parents are out of town and—"

"Which guy?" His tone has turned hard and unfamiliar.

I open my eyes. *Kidding!* There is that little nest I drew. It's still there. "I'm at Red Earth, waiting tables like I wrote you. Didn't you get my emails yet? I thought they'd be waiting for you. I've written letters too. Lots of them. Guess they haven't arrived yet either, huh? Stupid army."

"Hey. I'm in that stupid army."

"I didn't mean it that way." I swallow hard. Why does this feel like a first date—one I've had with other guys, but never with David, because from the beginning David and I were completely comfortable together? "I'll be waitressing for the rest of the summer and for the school year too, I guess. Linda's idea."

"Oh."

I wait for more. The silence gets long. This is the guy who draws hearts in the dust, I remind myself. This is the guy who tends a garden. Maybe he just needs to remember that the world is bigger than where he is. He just needs to remember our plan.

"I'm saving the money for college," I say. "With you."

David clears his throat. "Okay." And then, less warily, "I can't believe I got this connection. I'm standing on a rooftop."

Seems like he's back on track. I laugh, giddy with relief. "Any cool buildings? Mosques or minarets or whatever?" My words come out in a rush.

"Not exactly." There's a moment of garbled noise like David's lowered the phone to look around.

So that's what the wind sounds like in Iraq. Not so different from the wind in Oklahoma when you get right down to it.

I hear a rubbing sound—as if the phone has brushed against David's cheek. Lucky phone.

"Unless you count the interesting patterns from all the mortar holes in the walls," he says.

"Mortar holes? *Recent* mortar holes?"

He doesn't seem to hear my question. "It's supposed to be a hundred and fourteen degrees today. They told me that I'll start patrolling soon. Mostly right now I'm sitting around. We're stationed just outside town." His voice brightens. "Did you get my emails?"

"I loved them! The photograph, the drawing—they were great. What did you plant?" I'm so afraid we're going to be cut off again that my words come out in a rush.

"Tomatoes. Mom and Dad were happy about that. I just got off the phone with them."

"Oh good. About the tomatoes. And about your parents." I'm biting my nails, I realize. I never bite my nails. I stop. "Will that be okay? The patrolling, I mean?"

"It's my assignment."

I can almost see David shrugging, careless, relatively carefree, considering his situation. I don't get it. I don't say so. I say, "Keep sending me drawings, then. Or plant some…I don't know…some zucchini."

"I'll try." His voice sounds fainter, as if he's looking away from the phone, distracted by mortar holes or something else I can't imagine.

"How are your tattoos?" I practically shout this into the phone.

"Great." He's back again, loud and clear.

"Mine too!"

We share this. No matter what Linda thinks, no matter how they look when I'm older, the tattoos were definitely worth it. I glance at mine. More and more, I love the delicate braid, the statement it makes. It makes me feel pretty. Unique. It's a part of me.

"Do you like yours?" I ask.

"They make me think of you."

My heart lifts. I start telling David everything I can. I tell him about Caitlin and Tom and Isaac. I tell him my tips suck right now, but they should improve as I get better at my job. I tell him I'll put everything in the bank and save for the future.

"I miss you," he says. "I miss you so much, Penna."

"Ditto," I say. "Double, triple, quadruple ditto."

I tell him I'd give anything if he'd be able to phone every day.

"I'll try," David says. And then, "Listen, I've got good news."

In the far distance I hear a voice come over a loudspeaker. Maybe it's an imam. But I don't ask if this is so. I want to hear David's good news, and only that.

"They say I can schedule a Skype session with you. I want to set a time to make sure you're home."

"Yes! When?"

"Soon. Nine o'clock tomorrow morning, actually, your time. I won't have very long—maybe ten minutes—because I want to Skype Mom and Dad too while I can. They say sometimes you can Skype, sometimes you can't. That's how it goes here. Like everything else."

Static fills my ear.

"David? I can't hear you."

His voice crackles in and out—dislocated consonants and vowels.

"David!" I practically shout his name.

His voice comes clear as a bell then. "Losing you."

He's gone.

My ear aches with the pressure from my cell. I drop my phone back into my apron pocket. I take a deep breath.

Tomorrow I'll see his face.

I get up off the toilet and go back out to do my job. Anything to make this night go faster.

●●●

I do a little better at my job. Just a little, but enough to win a nod from Isaac, a smile from Caitlin, a pat on the back from Linda. When the last customers finally leave, the tables are cleaned and reset, and I have scrubbed the graffiti from the bathroom stalls (everything but my nest), Caitlin and I sit down at what I now think of as "our table." We have to settle up before we can go home. We match checks to credit-card receipts. We count out tips.

We don't say much, which is nice, since I'm doing another kind of math in my head at the same time. If it's twelve o'clock here, then it's eight o'clock in Baghdad. I hope David's eaten a great bagel by now. I hope he's eaten two.

When Caitlin has smoothed out her last wad of singles, she stuffs them in her wallet, gives me a long look, and says, "I heard you talking in the john."

I've been lost in thoughts of tomorrow, 9:00 a.m. I fumble with my money. "Oh?"

She tucks a lock of pink-streaked hair behind her ear. "Property of the U.S. Army, huh?"

I frown. "Not exactly."

Caitlin shrugs. "My friend wears a T-shirt with that on it. Her boyfriend's over there. In Iraq or Afghanistan or wherever."

"Oh." I sit up a little straighter. "My boyfriend is in Iraq. But I'm nobody's property."

"You sure sounded tight." Caitlin stuffs her wallet in her purse. " Must be hard, huh? Being apart?"

I glance at Tom, who's listening in on Caitlin and me. How much do I really want to get into this?

"I deal with it."

"'It's not a job! It's an adventure!' Isn't that the way it goes?" Caitlin gives me a second look. "Geez, Penna. End of conversation. Except…" Caitlin shrugs. "If I were you, I'd think twice."

"About?"

Caitlin shrugs. "Staying with a guy who could be dead tomorrow. Or worse. That's what I tell my friend with the shirt."

I can't say anything to this. I just stare at Caitlin until she puts her hand on my shoulder. She gives me a sympathetic smile, and now she's asking me to come out with her tonight. She's telling me that she knows some great guys. I'll have a blast.

Everything has gone into sharp focus, like I'm suddenly seeing Caitlin, the room, the world through the right pair of glasses. I ease my way out from under her hand. I haven't finished counting all my tips yet, but now I'm not going to bother.

"You know what? I really owe you for all your help, the way you kind of jump-started me here at Red Earth. So take this. It's yours, all of it." I push the bills and change across the table toward Caitlin. I don't even feel angry. I feel…clear. "Some other night we can hang out. But no guys. I've got a boyfriend. He just happens to be in Iraq."

Caitlin shakes her head. "That's exactly what my friend Jules says—Miss Property of the U.S. Army. At least let me set the two of you up. You and Jules'll have a lot to talk about."

"Fine," I surprise myself by saying. "Whatever," I add, dialing it down a bit.

Caitlin's eyes brighten. "Tomorrow then? You, me, Jules?"

"Maybe."

Right now tomorrow is only about David. I can't think beyond 9:00 a.m. In my new clearheaded way, I realize all I want right now is to get out of here. I grab my bag, say my see-you-laters, and go.

Justine survived this already—the unknown, the waiting. For better or worse, she came through to the other side. I take some comfort in that as I walk out into the night.

●●●

It would be one thing if home were only a few blocks away. But it's over three miles. About one mile in, I wish I'd hung out a little longer, gotten a ride from Linda, or borrowed the car and let her get a ride from whomever. But no. I had to escape. And now as I trudge along the familiar route, each footfall feels heavier than the last.

David, Skype, 9:00 a.m., I repeat with every step.

About twenty long, dusty minutes closer to the house, my phone rings.

Is it possible twice in one night?

I grab for my phone. I don't recognize the number. Maybe his phone went dead. (He always forgets to charge it.) Maybe he's borrowing a phone from some other guy.

It's some other guy, all right. I recognize him as soon as he says hello.

"Hi, Ravi." I start walking again. I hadn't even realized I'd stopped. My feet really ache now. "What's up?"

Ravi clears his throat. "Not much. I was just…I don't know. I'm on my break at work. There's something I've been wanting to ask you."

Now he sounds shy as well as sweet.

"What?"

"It's about school."

"Yeah?"

"How do you like it over there?"

I shrug. "It's okay. I mean, I like the art classes. It is what it is, you know?"

"Oh."

Ahead of me are the park and the playground. A branch stirs in the wind just above the slide, and for a moment I think Ravi is perched there on his skateboard and about to sail toward me. Then I remember he's calling from work.

"Why are you asking about school?"

I hear something tapping through the receiver, like a pen being drummed nervously against a table. "I'm thinking about going back," Ravi says.

"You are? That's great!"

"I'm glad you think so."

I feel my face go hot with sudden, startling guilt. I shake my head, shake away the feeling. I've got nothing to feel bad about. Ravi is about David for me. He's David's friend.

David, Skype, 9:00 a.m., I remind myself.

"I've been talking with the guidance counselor," Ravi says. "She's been great. Because I've taken some classes online, I can come in as a senior. I can even take AP classes if I want."

"I'm in AP Art," I say. "That's about all the AP I can handle, though."

"I'm going to take AP History and English."

"Cool."

"Yeah. If only my dad—"

"Hey. Ravi. Break's over." The man who interrupts Ravi clearly has no patience for slackers.

I hear Ravi apologize. Then he tells me he has to go. Maybe we can talk again soon. He has other things he wants to ask me about school.

"Later," he says.

Not good-bye.

I'm past the park now. I can't keep up this pace when I've got no one to talk to. I slow down. Way down. Way, way down.

Just when I think I might stop walking altogether, a car swings over to the side of the road. Linda's VW. The door pops open.

Linda leans across the front seat. "Going my way?"

I get in. We've only got a mile or so to go, but I slump in the seat and close my eyes.

●●●

"Home again, home again."

That's the next thing I hear. I open my eyes to Linda's smile. David, Skype, 9:00 a.m.! I sit up straight. "What time is it?"

"Like, five minutes past when you climbed in. You fell fast asleep." She brushes my hair from my eyes.

I wipe drool from my cheek. "I was totally out."

Linda nods. "The restaurant biz will do that to you. And walking home. And a phone call from Iraq."

I look at her.

"Tom told me. He told me what Caitlin said too, about ditching David. Guess you're getting it from all sides."

"People can say whatever they want. I don't care."

Inside, Linda fries us some eggs. I make toast and chamomile tea. We sit at the kitchen table, eating in silence.

"You think there's some ice cream crystallizing in here?" Linda goes for the freezer, opens the door.

She shrieks at the sight of the four frozen honey hands.

I laugh. "Incoming. Low-flying art project."

Linda stares. Then she shuts the freezer door. She turns to me. She has to clear her throat before she can speak.

"You know him better than I've known any guy."

I sit very still, taking this in.

Linda and I say good night then. No hugs. No kisses. Just good night like everything is okay, because in that moment, with the Skype call only a few hours away, everything is.

I take a shower, wash off the long day, check for messages that aren't there, set my alarm for 8:30 a.m., and slip under Plum Tumble.

Eleven

Linda shakes me awake, saying, "Penelope! Your alarm has been going off for forever!"

Forever?

Pushing Linda aside, I leap from my bed. I grab my clock and stare at the numbers: 8:55. I let out a yelp. Then I whirl around and face Linda. She's still wearing her pink nightgown. She must have overslept too. She's usually dressed and ready to go by this time.

"Are you okay? Your cheeks are so red." She puts her hand to my head. "Do you have a fever?"

"I need privacy." I say this as calmly as I can, which is to say, not so much. "David," I say. "Now. Please."

Linda gets it. She slips swiftly from my room, closing the door behind her. I lunge for my computer and log on to Skype.

Wait for him. *Wait for him.*

And suddenly there he is, breathtakingly recognizable but different too, flattened across my computer screen. And paler than he's ever been, than he ever could be, like the harsh Iraqi sun has bleached out his skin. I know probably the reverse has happened, of course. It must be my monitor, ghosting him up like this. He's beautiful and spooky, all at the same time.

He leans closer to his computer, as if this will bring him closer to me, and in the little box in the bottom corner that shows me, I glimpse my look of surprise. David's movements aren't fluid, as I know they would be if I were sitting right in front of him, because David is always graceful. His body stutters and freezes and skips. The video transmission is out of synch.

But still, there are his features that I've been trying so hard to draw. His straight eyebrows, his brown eyes, full lips, strong jaw.

"It's so good to *see* you," I say.

There's a beat, two beats, three, and still his expression hasn't changed. Then that crazy, crooked grin breaks across his face as he finally hears what I just said.

"That's a major understatement," he says.

I laugh. "Can you do better?"

Again that weird delay. But now he laughs too. "I don't think so. Not in words. But watch this. Just watch."

He lifts his hand, the one with the ring tattoo, which looks to have healed nicely. He puts his fingers to his computer screen, nearly blocking my view of him. I start to tell him this when I realize what he's doing. He's tracing my face with his fingers—my cheeks, nose, lips, chin, neck. He's touching me the only way he can, slowly, tenderly, until I feel my skin tingling where his hand has just been.

With a weird, stuttering motion, he lowers his hand. "There. Did you see what I said?"

I lick my lips, which have gone dry. I nod. "A picture is worth a thousand words."

When he hears this, he moves his head in a Skypey nod. "Exactly."

So I trace him too, hoping my hands remember every angle and curve of his features when I sit down the next time to draw his portrait.

"So tell me," David says then.

"What?"

"Anything."

I tell him about the frozen honey hands waiting for his return. I fill him in on Red Earth. The letters I sent out to Justine. Late-night eggs and chamomile tea with Linda. The birds outside my window in the honey locust this morning.

I don't tell him about Ravi. There's no time for Ravi.

As I talk, guys pass back and forth behind David. Moving in the background like that, their figures break apart and blur. I catch the flash of a muscled arm, the butt of a rifle. Some of the guys call out to David. "O'Dell. Hurry it up. You see the line back here?"

There is a line. I see it snaking darkly in the farthest corner of the room. Maybe they're standing at such a distance to give David some privacy. To be honest, I can't tell how much privacy David has. He keeps glancing up to his left. He appears to be making eye contact with someone there. An officer, maybe? A censor?

"Where are you?" I ask.

David isn't listening to me. He's listening to whoever is standing up to his left. He nods at that person, whoever it is, then turns back to me. His mouth is set in a hard, firm line, but his eyes look troubled.

"We only have about five more minutes left, Penna. Then I've got to log off. It's someone else's turn."

My heart drops. "Did you get to Skype your mom and dad?" I manage to keep my voice steady.

"Just got off with them. Good talk. When Mom wasn't crying and Dad wasn't making stupid jokes in an effort to keep her from crying. Maybe you could give them a call?"

"I will. I promise." Desperate, I grip the edge of my desk. "It's your turn now, David. Tell me something."

"'Something,'" he says.

I stare at his face on the screen.

He blinks, waits, looks surprised when I still don't respond. "Don't you remember? Our last night, riding on the scooter? I said that exact thing. *Something.* It made you laugh."

"Did it?" I remember kissing his neck, that's all. "I need to go back to the viaduct with you," I say.

"Do it. Don't wait for me."

David swallows hard; I watch the muscles in his throat moving. His beautiful throat.

"Take a picture and send it to me, okay?"

"Okay." *Breathe in. Breathe out.* "Now, could you *please* tell me how you're doing? Have you been drawing much?"

"Not really. Let's see." He furrows his brow. "We managed to get enough guys together to play a decent game of baseball. And oh yeah, the most important thing. We've been doing a lot of target practice. Guess I'm pretty good. Sniper good, the other bums here say. Oh! And one other thing—the *most*, most important thing." He turns his head in that herky-jerky way, and his eyes widen in surprise. "Hey, no way. A-holes!"

Again that little picture of me looks surprised. I've never heard David say that word before. Usually he's less predictable when he's laying into someone. More creative.

That's what I'm thinking when two big guys appear from the edges of the screen and jump on David. One grabs him in a headlock. The other rubs his knuckles hard across David's scalp.

"Hey! Stop! I'm talking to my girlfriend here!" David yells.

From above, in that corner that held his attention before, I hear someone yelling, "Get lost!" And then there's a scuffle of bodies I can't make out— shadows and shapes all gathered around David, who's completely hidden from me now. There's pushing and pulling, shoving and kicking. There's yelling, cursing—David's voice again, swearing a blue streak—and laughter.

As quickly as they appeared, the shadows and shapes dissipate. Someone shouts from the background, "She's got you pussy-whipped, O'Dell." Someone else shouts, "Leave him alone, why don't you?" And someone else shouts on top of this, "*All* of you! Shut up! I can't hear myself think!" And then from the left corner, loud and clear: "You've all lost your Skype privileges for today. All of you. Get ready for inspection. *Now*."

David looks at me, and I can't read his expression at all.

"Gotta go." He touches the screen again, where my lips must be. "Smile."

I try.

"Love you," David says.

"Love you too." I reach for him, touch the screen. "But you didn't get to tell me the *most*, most important thing!"

David shakes his head. "Can't now. Gotta hustle. I'll write you."

He logs off.

I log off too.

I sit there for a moment, feeling all mixed up. Happy. Sad. Scared. I look up at the photo of Justine.

I go into the kitchen then and dial the phone number that I found listed for Justine Delmore in Yellow Rock, South Dakota. The phone rings. And rings. Five rings. Maybe she sleeps late too. Maybe she's moved on yet again.

But then there's the click of a phone being lifted from its cradle.

"Hello?"

The woman's voice is high and reedy. The word hangs in the air between us, suspended on a line that stretches like those train tracks from this little gray house to those jagged yellow cliffs.

"Justine?" I say breathlessly. "Is this Justine Delmore?"

The woman tells me that no, Justine Delmore doesn't live here anymore.

Justine moved back to her hometown a little while ago. Maybe a month. Maybe two. Maybe more. The woman's not sure. "Time isn't the same when you're my age," she says.

I sit down hard on the kitchen chair.

Justine lives in Killdeer now too.

"Who is this?" the woman asks then, suddenly suspicious. "Is this a scam? You aren't one of those identity-theft people, are you?"

I shake my head no. It takes a few moments for me to actually say the word. And then I tell the woman thank you. Thank you so much. I can't tell her how grateful I am.

I go into the kitchen, take out the local phone book, and look up Justine Delmore. She's not listed.

But she's here.

• • •

I'm still sitting at the kitchen table when Linda strides in, freshly showered and toweling her hair. She's wearing her favorite robe. It's white terry cloth. Even feeling so mixed up inside, I realize that it's a relief to see Linda in something other than that black uniform. Something other than boss clothes.

"Lawd have mercy," Linda says, using her poor excuse for a drawl. She steadies herself against the counter, making a show of surprise. "She's emerged from her den." Linda grins. "Doing some schoolwork? Portfolio stuff? Hope so." She looks over my shoulder.

She frowns.

For the last half hour or so, ever since the phone call to Yellow Rock, and my failed effort to locate Justine's address and phone number, I've been drawing David and Justine. One after another, I draw them. I have five Davids now, and I'm working on my fifth Justine. I'm working quickly, spontaneously, drawing David here and in Iraq, Justine here and in Yellow Rock.

Some of the drawings are as realistic as I can make them. (David sprinting toward the viaduct wall and riding on his scooter; Justine brushing her hair and standing on the porch of this very house.) Others are the best I can imagine. (David in camouflage playing baseball with his buddies; Justine and someone I'll call Owen sitting in the cockpit of a plaster airplane.) They're rough sketches, sure, but still these are the best things I've drawn all summer.

"You're obsessed," Linda says.

"I got them right," I say. "You've got to admit that."

The coffeemaker spews out its last drips and fills the pot. Linda flings herself at it and pours a cupful.

"We have just over a year before you go away to college. We have time for just you and me. We could have a better time than we've ever had before." She takes a steamy glug of coffee.

"Now that David's gone. And as long as I keep Justine out of the picture." I flatten the eraser ball against the table. It's a little pancake now.

"I'm not talking about David here, Penelope. I understand about David. Don't give me that look. I *do*." Linda gives me her own version of my look back. "I *am* talking about *her*, though. I don't want to even think about her, let alone see her—pictures of her, just lying around in plain sight." Linda shudders, sloshing coffee onto the floor.

"You're living in her house," I say.

Linda swipes her foot across the spilled coffee, mopping it up with her sock, and then takes another sip. "It doesn't *matter* whose house it was. I will *not* be haunted by your imagination."

"You're haunted by your mother. Who lives right here. In Killdeer."

I didn't expect to tell Linda so soon. But there. I have. It's a rush, the relief I feel. So why not say this too?

"I'm going to see her," I say.

Linda is shaking her head so hard that the coffee is sloshing all over the place now. On her hand. Her favorite robe. The counter and, of course, the floor. But she doesn't seem to notice. Fiercely she says, "That woman would never come back here."

"But she has." And I tell Linda how I tracked Justine down, how I learned of Justine's return. "I'd think you'd be a little happy," I say. "I mean, now we're not the only family we've got."

"With family like her, who needs enemies?" Linda slams her dripping coffee cup on the counter and walks purposefully past me. At the kitchen door, though, she hesitates. She grips the door for support as she looks back at me, wrinkles furrowing her brow.

"I don't want to have anything to do with this, Penelope. Keep me out of it. And you'd better be ready for work this afternoon when I come to pick you up."

Then she walks down the hall past all the pictures of just the two of us. She goes into her bedroom and closes the door. No doubt she's putting on her black uniform now, like every other morning, like nothing will ever change.

Twelve

I want another mother. I want another home—a place as familiar as the life and love lines in my palms and David's. I want David.

I'll settle for his house.

And Bonnie.

I get dressed and get on my bike.

When I bank into David's driveway, I screech on the brakes so fast that I nearly go headfirst over my handlebars. The pink impatiens I helped him plant last spring need weeding. The bird feeder he always kept filled stands empty now. Our names, scratched into the sidewalk last fall when the concrete was just poured, are caked with red clay.

For some reason, all this makes me want to turn right around and bolt. But before I can, Bonnie appears at the front door. I can see her mouth moving behind the glass—"Penna!" Then she opens the door and her arms, and comes toward me, her spiky blond hair shining in the sun.

"We Skyped!" she cries, throwing her arms around me.

"Us too." I hug her back, hard. Maybe I'll absorb some of her happiness through osmosis.

Bonnie steers me into the dim kitchen. She turns on the light, and the room's paintings spring to life—sloppy, colorful paintings David did when he was a kid.

"I've missed being here," I say.

Bonnie takes me by the shoulders and sits me down on a stool at the counter. She backs away then, holding up her hands like she's saying, *Stay. Keep me company on this long, lonely Saturday.*

"Could I have something to drink?" I'm not thirsty. I just know this is exactly what Bonnie wants to hear.

She goes to the refrigerator and opens the door. She stares into it as if it will tell her something. "Iced tea okay?"

"Great."

She pulls out a pitcher and whirls toward a cupboard, takes out two glasses. Pouring, she talks. "Beau's at work all the time these days. I think it helps him keep his mind off David. I'm just so glad it's Saturday. I've been neglecting things with David gone. It's like I just don't care what the house looks like anymore. Not that I ever did, much."

Bonnie sets a glass of tea down on the counter before me. The counter is a mess, covered with dried spilled food and crumbs. But the tea is good when I sip it, laced with lemon and mint. Bonnie takes a sip too.

"I like life comfortable, you know? But with David gone—well, I've really let things go. I've given myself today to regain some semblance of control." She rolls her eyes. We both know what this means. She won't be in control until David's home again. She won't be comfortable either.

Bonnie sits down on the stool beside me. I drain my glass. Then I stand and start scrubbing the counter.

"Don't you go cleaning up my mess," Bonnie says.

"I like to do stuff like this." I rinse the dishrag in steaming hot water. I dry my hands swiftly and snap on some yellow rubber gloves. With yellow rubber gloves I can deal with almost anything.

So I clean and we talk. I tell her about working at Red Earth. Somehow I manage to make it all sound funny. I'm a real crack-up, with all my mistakes. I am even worse at the job than I really am. I love the sound of Bonnie's laugh, deep and booming, like she doesn't care what anyone thinks, she's just going to let it rip. David must have picked up his laugh from her. Before OSUT, when he laughed, everyone laughed.

Bonnie's laughter makes me feel so comfortable, so at home, that I find myself telling her about Ravi and his pictures. "I hope you can see them too," I say.

"Oh, I will! Soon, in fact." Bonnie smiles. "I knew you and Ravi would hit it off. You're both high-quality people, you know?" Bonnie's smile fades. "Poor kid. He's been through so much. I can't even believe, really, how he keeps on keeping on."

This seems a little extreme to me. I mean, 9/11 and all that followed for Ravi was a little while ago. But I don't want to get into it. I don't want to talk about Ravi anymore. With David's mother. In David's house.

Flustered, I turn to another counter, hoping Bonnie didn't glimpse my expression. I spritz on some high-powered cleanser and scrub hard.

Bonnie tells me about her job. She tells me that Beau got a promotion at the public relations firm, which is really good timing since the value of their house and their retirement accounts have taken a beating in this economy.

We've been talking for nearly an hour, mostly talking around the subject of David, when Bonnie suddenly says, "How do you think he seemed this morning? How did he sound to you?"

I look up from the stove top. I'm scouring away at what look to be ancient drippings—eggs, maybe, that have adhered like glue to the black burners. I've poured on the cleanser, but these drippings don't seem to be going anywhere.

"Good. He sounded good." I blink. I sound like I don't mean it. I *don't* mean it. "I mean, it's hard to tell on Skype, right? But he looks healthy. Real healthy, don't you think?"

Bonnie nods. "It *was* hard to tell. But it was better than nothing."

"Anything's better than nothing. Even noise."

Bonnie slaps her hand on the spill-free, crumb-free counter. "Did you get one of those phone calls too? Talk about an exercise in frustration! I nearly lost my mind." She turns sober. "I'm going to have to work really hard at not doing that, Penna."

I look at her. "Are you okay?"

She bows her head and runs her fingers through her hair—that gesture David makes when he's anxious. She looks up at me and forces a smile. "Positive attitude, right? Beau's got that in spades. I just have to work a little harder."

I set down my scouring pad, tug off the yellow gloves, wash my hands, and go over to the counter. I take a deep breath.

"David said he had something big to tell me. But then we had to stop talking. Did he tell you anything important? That you can tell me, I mean."

Bonnie sits very still, watching me.

"What have *you* heard?" My voice rises. "Bonnie?"

"He's doing okay." Her voice is quiet and careful. "No action to speak of in these first days—at least not against the U.S. military. Those Iraqis, though. Already, he's seen some awful stuff when it comes to the citizens. There's a certain marketplace he happened to be passing through. That's what we always hear about on the news, right? 'A marketplace.' Well, I guess some are worse than others when it comes to casualties." Bonnie looks at me, her blue eyes pained.

Suddenly my head is spinning. It must be all that cleanser, too many chemicals inhaled. I go to the fridge, open the freezer door, and look inside as if there's something I want in there. All I really want is frosty air to clear my head. It helps a little. I shut the door and sit back down beside Bonnie, who doesn't even give me a second look. She keeps talking as if a girl sticking her head inside a freezer is an everyday occurrence.

"What's the connection between 'casualty' and 'casual,' I want to know." Bonnie presses her fingertips to her forehead like she's got a bad headache. Maybe the chemicals took a toll on her too. "Anyway, he's starting night patrol duty tomorrow. Actually, it's today for him now." She glances at the clock on the stove. "He'll be on patrol soon, most likely. He didn't say much more about it. He tried to sound happy just to be doing something that makes all that training worth it. Maybe he *is* happy. I don't know. I did more looking around on the Net than I should have. Don't do that, Penna, if you can stop yourself."

"He planted his own little garden over there," I hear myself say. "Already he figured out how to do that. Can you think of anyone else who would pull that off? He's resourceful. And lucky."

"A good combination." Bonnie takes my hands in hers. She taps her finger gently against my tattoo. "I was so upset when I saw that he'd gone and done this. I know I didn't act like it—why waste the precious, little time we had left—but I was. But now I'm glad he did it. Anything that makes him happy, as long as it doesn't hurt him, makes me happy."

"Are you happy about patrol duty then?" My voice is shaky.

She sighs heavily. She starts to speak and then can't seem to find the words to say. She stands and comes around the counter to me. She puts her arms around me. I let her hold me for a while. Finally I pull away.

"Is there anything you need, Penna?" Bonnie gives me a sad smile. "Now that you've cleaned practically my entire kitchen?"

I start to shake my head, but then I change my mind. "Can I use your bathroom?"

She nods. "Upstairs. You know."

Of course I know. I know the way like the back of his hand. I know the worn plaid fabric on the couch cushions and the smell of the cinnamon-scented broom by the fireplace and the array of pictures of David set at strategic angles on the mantelpiece. There is the one of little David in his baseball uniform. There he is with braces and zits—on the verge of hot, probably just realizing that girls exist. And there he is last December, standing in front of Killdeer High after his last day of classes, an official graduate, with his arm around me.

Upstairs I walk right past the bathroom and into David's room. I shut the door behind me. I look around, taking everything in.

If the rest of Bonnie's house is a mess, David's room is pristine. It's like a museum. A shrine. Same soccer-star posters. Same drafting table, with a drawing placed carefully in the center. Same computer. Same Boy Scout vest, hanging from a dowel like some indigenous weaving. (I wonder if Ravi still has his.) Same bookshelves packed with thick fantasy and sci-fi novels, manga and comic books. Same tower of CDs. Same empty fish tank filled with the dinosaur, cowboy and Indian, and army guy diorama that took over in sixth grade when the fish died. Same pictures of me, on the swings at the playground, sitting on the back of his motorcycle, standing under the viaduct by the mural.

Same picture of the two of us together, standing on the front steps of the art museum in Oklahoma City, the day we fell in love with the same paintings and each other and kissed under the statue of Geronimo in the sculpture garden. A museum guard snapped that photo. He was a big old guy with a thick, gray mustache, and he didn't want to be bothered until David got down on one knee and begged. He barely looked through the viewfinder then, but still somehow he managed to catch what was best about that day—our crazy happiness. Standing in front of this abstract painting that "hummed," I said (and David agreed), we have our arms flung around each other. It's one of my favorite pictures of us too.

Relief. That's what I feel. Here, everything is the same. Nothing has changed. When he comes home, he'll be the same too. Nothing will have changed for us.

In this room it's like David never went away.

I lie facedown on his bed and breathe him in.

After a while I get up again. From the window I can see the backyard and also David's dog, Mars, sprawled on his side in the shade. Mars doesn't look so good. He's panting hard. He looks kind of mangy. Little big dog, lost without his master. If I weren't afraid he'd tear my hand off, I'd go outside and pet him.

Instead I go to David's dresser, open the drawers, and touch his carefully folded T-shirts, socks, jeans, shorts. I open the door to his closet, part the hangers, and slip inside. I draw the closet door closed. In the darkness I hide in David's clothes.

If I'm not careful, I'm going to make a mess of things. I open the door and step back into his room, blinking against the light.

I stumble over to David's drafting table and look at the drawing there. It's my superhero Manga David, the drawing he did for his tattoo, complete with the heavy artillery and the circle of barbwire and tumbleweeds. I pick up the drawing. I run my fingers over its back just to feel the indentations David left using his favorite 0.50 millimeter Rapidograph pen.

That's when I see the drawing that was hidden beneath this one. It's my Manga David again. Only he's not packing heavy artillery. He's not jumping around like he's half crazy, his mouth open in rage. He's holding hands with a wavy-haired manga girl that looks like me. The two of them are surrounded by a wreath of hearts and flowers and killdeer, and the letters of our names.

We're smiling at each other. Sparks fly from our bedazzled eyes.

It's a beautiful drawing. It's a beauty.

But David chose the other one.

● ● ●

No one can stay shut away this long.

I have to come out.

I make sure David's drawings are exactly where I found them on the drafting table. I take one last, long look around, one last, long breath of him. Then I cross the room, open the door, step into the hallway, and go back downstairs.

I find Bonnie in the kitchen, staring into her glass of iced tea. She looks at me. *Feel better?* her eyes ask.

I don't answer, not even with my eyes. I put those yellow gloves back on and get to work on the stove top again. Never mind the chemical inhalants. I'm not going to leave a job half finished. Bonnie and I chat about this and that—school starting up again, the weather. I work quickly. Working quickly keeps my mind off that hidden drawing in David's room. I can't think about it now. I will think about it later, when I can find a way to be okay with the fact that he chose the other one instead.

When the stove top is sparkling, I rinse out the rag for the last time. I tell Bonnie that I should go.

"Come back soon," she says. "Come back when Beau's here. Come for dinner. I'll make something decent, I promise."

Closing the front door behind me, I nearly run smack into Ravi.

We draw back from each other.

He is not in worker or skater mode. He is wearing a trim, blue polo shirt, baggy khaki shorts, and yellow flip-flops.

He cleans up real nice.

He's holding a manila folder, which he now lifts like a kind of offering. "Same old, same old."

"She'll love them."

He nods. "I thought I'd deliver them on my way over to the high school. I've decided. I'm definitely going."

"I'm glad." I smile at him, and he smiles back—a wide, square grin. I hear the O'Dells' door open behind me, and Bonnie says, "Well, if this day just doesn't keep getting better and better. You're just in time for lunch, Rav."

Rav? I mouth at him.

He shrugs, then looks at Bonnie in such a warm, familiar way that I see the little boy she once knew so well. "Sandwiches?" he asks.

Bonnie laughs. "You know it."

To me, Ravi says, "Bonnie makes a mean sandwich."

"It even surpasses my lasagna." Bonnie puts her hand on my shoulder, and now we stand in a tight little circle, my boyfriend's mother, my boyfriend's friend, and me. Bonnie gives my shoulder a squeeze. "You want to stay too, Penna? I'm sorry I didn't think to ask before."

I shake my head. "Gotta get ready for work."

"Next time, then. Is turkey on wheat okay, Rav?"

He nods. Bonnie hugs me good-bye all over again, then playfully snatches the manila envelope from Ravi's hands and goes back inside.

Ravi looks at me. "So."

"So." We're standing too close. I edge away. Better. Though the sun is really hot, I suddenly realize. I wipe sweat from my upper lip. "You see Bonnie a lot now?"

"Second time." Ravi smiles. "She *does* make a good sandwich."

"When she's on, she's on."

"And when she's off, she's off."

We laugh.

"Penna," he says. Then he says my name again. "Next year—I'd still like to talk to you about it."

"I'll be working a lot. And going to school." I say this quickly. I sound defensive.

"Me too. My schedule will be crazy." Just as quickly, just as defensively, Ravi says this.

For a moment we stand there.

"Well," I say.

Ravi blinks. "Yeah."

"Wait." I find I'm shaking my head. "Listen."

He waits. Listens.

"Tonight," I say. "I think I'm going out with some friends after work. You could come, if you want."

"*I'll* be working," he says.

"Oh. Yeah."

"I could meet you tomorrow morning, though, at the viaduct."

I shake my head. "I don't really like going there that much anymore. I'm kind of over it, you know?"

What I don't say is that place is feeling more and more like Ravi, less and less like David. Next time I go there, the only company I'm going to have is my camera. I'm going to take a picture of me in front of the mural and send it to David. Just like he asked.

I don't want to do the playground either. Same reason.

"How about breakfast?"

Ravi looks surprised, like I've asked him for a date. Which I haven't.

"Okay."

We agree to meet at 'Round the Clock, the only diner in town.

David and I only went there once. He didn't like the place. Said they couldn't even make a decent piece of toast.

● ● ●

Home again, I sit at the kitchen table and draw David on his motorcycle over and over again until I get him right. Mythical. That's what he looks like. This drawing could go in my portfolio for college. It could help get me where I want to go.

Only when I'm in bedroom, slipping the drawing into one of the plastic sleeves of my portfolio, do I realize that for the first time since I met David, I didn't think something like, *This drawing could help me get where I want to go with him.*

Justine seems to be watching me from the photograph.

I need to find her.

Thirteen

That night, work is a blur that passes bearably.

"You might be getting the hang of this," Caitlin says at one point.

I smile. I like Caitlin, I realize. I *appreciate* her. I mean, she's covered my butt.

"You still want to go out tonight after work?" she asks.

I'd been thinking about biking around Killdeer in the dark, looking for…what? Signs? Clues? Hints of Justine?

A little pointless, I guess.

I nod.

Caitlin cocks her head. "So that's a 'yes'?"

"Yeah."

"Awesome. You'll come over to my house. Jules'll meet us there, and then…we'll see what the night holds."

Caitlin darts away to take another drink order. She's added purple streaks to the pink in her hair. She reminds me of a bright, exotic bird, flitting from table to table, plucking up shiny, round objects and wrinkled, green slips of paper to take back to her nest, wherever that may be.

I look over at the door, which has just swung open. A slew of people stand there, middle-aged folks mostly, with a few little kids thrown in for good measure. Looks to be five big tables at least. I feel my heart racing, the adrenaline kicking in. From behind me, Tom says, "You better get going."

Craziness ensues, but it's not nearly as bad as it used to be.

When the shift ends, Caitlin and I clean up and settle up as quickly as we can, and then we scram.

We climb into Caitlin's car, a white beater parked right beside Linda's VW and drive off into the night. We listen to music on the radio. Loud. Louder. I haven't listened to music since David left. I hardly listened to music all the time he was at OSUT either. The songs that reminded me of him—some girls might want to go there, but I couldn't. It hurt too much. The songs that didn't remind me of him felt empty.

We listen to rap for a while. Tonight, with the windows down and Caitlin rapping along beside me, never missing a word, it feels just right. It hits me right in the heart. Hard. Makes me feel like I'm receiving CPR or something. In a good way.

"Find something else," Caitlin finally says, turning down a tidy little street. "Something quieter. There are folks down this way who throw a fit when they hear a bass beat. And rap's no good soft."

We're in a part of town that I don't know that well. David and I came here a couple of times to play tennis at the YMCA. But neither of us like tennis that much, so we didn't come back. Other than the YMCA, this part of town seems to be made up of streets like this, lined with rows of neat, little brick houses.

I turn down the volume and troll up and down the dial until I light on an oldies-but-goodies station.

"…one of the most popular hits from nineteen forty-five, 'It's Been a Long, Long Time,' by Harry James and his orchestra, featuring Willie Smith on alto sax and the very pretty Kitty Kallen on vocals," the announcer is saying.

I sit back. Caitlin cuts me a look. I tell her I've got to hear this.

Justine and Owen would have heard this.

A trumpet swoons, the notes filling the air around Caitlin and me. The orchestra moves like smoke behind it, the strings rising—Justine and Owen might have slow-danced to this—and then Kitty Kallen starts singing, something about words not sufficing.

The song takes my breath away. When it's over, the announcer starts talking about a favorite little number from 1939, and I turn the radio off. I don't want to hear anything else. I don't want anything to confuse my memory of that song.

"You okay?" Caitlin asks, turning the car into a gravel driveway.

I nod.

"Good." Caitlin puts the car in park and turns off the engine. She drops her keys in her bag. "Come on in."

Caitlin's house is small, cluttered, dark, and quiet. She puts her finger to her lips, and we tiptoe down the narrow hallway, past the single bathroom and four closed doors that I assume must be bedrooms, and into the cramped kitchen. Caitlin shuts the kitchen door behind us. Only then does she turn on the light. When it flares, I blink. I hope she thinks it's my eyes adjusting versus the surprise I'm feeling, seeing plates and glasses and bowls and pots and pans stacked on every possible surface. Some things are reasonably clean, but others are…not. There are open boxes of cereal, crackers, and cookies on the kitchen table, and an open carton of milk sitting on top of the refrigerator. It's worse than Bonnie's house.

Caitlin sighs. She takes down the milk and puts it inside the refrigerator, closing the refrigerator door quickly before I can see inside. She looks at me then.

"I know. It's a mess. There are a lot of people in my family, and I seem to be the only one who got the cleanliness gene."

She tells me then that she's the oldest of seven. Her parents both work long hours to make ends meet. Until the past few months, when most of the other kids could manage without her, she's always spent a lot of time caring for her siblings.

"I love coming home late like this when everyone's asleep," she says. "They sleep like logs, all of them, unless one of the little ones has a nightmare. With the kitchen door shut, I don't have to worry about making a little bit of noise. Sometimes I'll clean like crazy. Other times I'll just sit on the back porch and listen to music. Either way I get to do what I want, alone or with friends. And that, Penna, is the ultimate in my book."

With friends like me, I think. The thought makes me astonishingly happy.

Caitlin grabs two spoons and a carton of chocolate ice cream from the freezer and leads me through the back door to the porch. She asks if I want music, and I say the quiet is fine. She shrugs, okay, whatever. We kick off our shoes and put our tired feet up on the porch railing. We don't say much as we dig into the ice cream.

For the first time since David's been gone, I feel almost relaxed.

After about fifteen minutes, Jules texts Caitlin to say she's finished babysitting. She's on her way.

So much for being relaxed. I dig for more ice cream, but it's gone.

Caitlin gives me a sock on the arm. "Chill. Jules is great."

I look out over Caitlin's tiny backyard. There are toys and bicycles everywhere. "It takes me a while to get comfortable with people, that's all. Maybe it's an only-child thing."

Caitlin snorts. "Or maybe you need to get out more often."

I sigh. "Maybe."

From inside the house comes a faint wail.

"Oh shoot." Caitlin leaps from her chair. "That's Connor. He's five, the baby. If he has a bad dream, forget it. He'll wake the whole house. And if he gets too worked up, he won't be able to go back to sleep. Then guess who'll be spending the rest of the night singing lullabies?"

Connor cries out again. Louder.

"Stay put. I'll be right back." Caitlin goes inside the house.

I set the empty ice cream carton on the porch floor. All of a sudden I'm warm with worry. I strip off my socks and rest my feet on the railing again, but I can't relax now. I don't want to compare army-boyfriend notes with a stranger. Only with Justine.

Something tickles the bottom of my foot and I yelp, nearly falling from my chair.

From below me comes the sound of laughter. I look through the slats in the porch railing to see a tall girl with long blond hair. She's about my age. When she sees me, her eyes widen and she stops laughing.

"Sorry! I just saw your foot! I thought you were Caitlin!"

I shrug in a way that I hope looks casual. "Penna."

"Oh! I've heard a lot about *you*." She flicks back her hair, and it ripples in the moonlight. "Jules."

"I've heard about you too." I clear my thought. "Not a lot, but, you know. Some."

Jules comes up the porch stairs and flings herself into the chair that Caitlin just vacated. She picks up the ice cream carton, frowns into its empty depths, and drops it again.

"Is Caitlin consoling the masses?"

"Connor."

Jules nods. "A drama king in the making. This whole family's got *a lot* of drama. It's not just Caitlin. But you watch. Caitlin is going to burst through that door any minute, saying, 'Get me the heck out of here.' She's so fed up with taking care of those kids. I don't blame her. I have only one brother. He's older than me. I'll tell you what, when I come around here, I'm extra glad about that."

I shrug. "I'd take a brother or a sister. Younger or older."

"Oh, I guess it can be nice to have someone to talk to. Just not six someones who treat you like you're their second mom." Jules cocks her head and looks at me. "Your boyfriend's serving, right?"

Here it comes. Here I go.

"He just left."

"Mine too. For the second time."

Before I can think, I've touched her arm. "*Second* time? I'm sorry."

Jules shifts in her chair. For a minute I think she is drawing her arm away from my hand, and I feel stupid. But then I see she's showing me something on her wrist.

"See, two bracelets. One for each deployment." Jules jingles the two red, blue, and silver-beaded bangles, and I see lettered charms as well: *Zach*.

"Nice," I say.

Jules nods. "Caitlin told me you guys got tattooed. Beats a bracelet any day in my opinion."

I flash my right ring finger, the beautiful braid there. "Whatever works, right?" My mouth twists, suppressing a goofy smile. I never thought I'd feel so proud of a couple of tattoos—like I *won* or something. "We probably would have done it sooner or later anyway."

"But you did it because he was going, right?" Jules leans forward, peering at me. It seems important to her that this is the case.

"Well—" I consider this. "His going made everything so intense, you know?"

"I sure do." Jules turns the bracelets on her wrist. "I was like that the first time. I went through every typical response in the book, actually. I got all reclusive. Not a good choice. Then I turned into a party animal. A very not good choice. Then I got some new hobbies. A better choice. Then Zach came home the first time, and that was a whole other challenge." Jules sinks back in her chair.

I must look like I'm feeling: sick with sudden worry. Jules gives me an encouraging smile.

"Don't worry," she says. "I survived. We survived. Now I'm working, and when I'm not working, I'm over at the community college taking classes, so that helps." She clasps her hands to her chest, suddenly overcome by excitement. "Zach's back in six weeks, and that should be it for him for a while. I can't believe it really. With the National Guard it's been feeling like it's never over. And I guess it never really is. You know."

"It'll be over for us after this deployment," I say firmly. "That's all David's in for."

"Oh yeah?" Jules shakes her head. "Honey, it goes on and on. If I didn't believe in what Zach was doing—"

"I'm just in it because David is in it."

Jules stares at me, open-mouthed, confused now.

"I mean…" I hesitate. What do I mean? It sounds like I don't believe in what David is doing. Is that the case? I pull on my socks again, buying time. I'll explain. Or cover my butt. One of the two.

"I just never thought I'd date a soldier, that's all," I finally say. "And he's not a *soldier*. Not totally. He's *David*." I give a pathetic little laugh. "Honestly, I don't even know that much about what it's all about."

Jules stands. She leans against the porch railing, folds her arms over her chest, and stares down at me. "What what's all about?"

This is what I've been dreading, I realize. Interrogation. Like I'm not good enough, or I'm not doing this right or something. Suddenly I feel angry.

"This war. Any war."

"Well, *I* know what it's about. I've worked hard to know." Jules clenches her jaw until tiny cords of muscle ripple beneath her cheeks.

"Good for you." I glare at her. "I just think there's lots of ways to be, you know. Bottom line, I love David, and that's what matters."

Jules studies me, her eyes narrowed. "I guess."

Caitlin bursts through the back door, closes it behind her, and leans against it. "Get me the heck out of here!"

Jules and I look at each other. We start to laugh.

"What? *What?*" Caitlin says.

Jules and I can't stop laughing. We're wiping tears from our eyes.

"Oh, for heaven's sake," Caitlin huffs. "Connor spilled milk all over my shirt. I'm changing my clothes. And then we're out of here." She turns back to the house, then glances over her shoulder at us. "See? I knew you all would get along."

With Caitlin inside again, we finally stop laughing.

"So, bottom line, the *real* bottom line?" Jules fiddles with her bracelets again. "You hanging in there? I ask because a lot of times that's all I ever want anyone to really ask me. How are you holding on?"

I catch my breath. *Holding on. Holding on across continents and the oceans in between.* I say, "I don't know."

Jules sighs. "It sucks, doesn't it? I'm on this message board that really helps—Girlfriends of Soldiers in Iraq. They've got one of those for practically every country in the world, in case you know someone who's got someone in, like, Panama. And there's Army Girlfriend Support. I like that one too. And I send Zach lots of packages, which he says helps."

"I should do that." My words surprise me—their urgency—and then the sudden rush of guilt I feel. My cheeks burn with it. "I don't know why I haven't done that. I've had other stuff going on, I guess." I pause for a breath. *Breathe in, breathe out.* "How long does it take for a package to get to Iraq? What should I send?"

Jules shakes her head. "It can take forever sometimes. But it'll get there eventually. Listen. Give yourself time, Penna. It's takes a while to figure things out."

"But...what should I send?"

"Oh, anything he likes." Jules smiles reassuringly. "Let's see. Shampoo, soap, razors. That's always good. But send big bottles because they share. And send his favorite magazines. No porn, though, okay? One tool in Zach's troop hid porn behind a ceiling tile, and when the sergeant found out about it, they were seriously disciplined. Send some good books. Oh, and beef jerky—not pork, because they don't allow any pork in Iraq.

"Beef," I murmur, making a mental note.

"And especially cookies! Send cookies—but not like a dozen, because those will be gone in five minutes. I learned what a 'gross' is, sending cookies to Iraq. It's about one hundred and forty-four nice-sized cookies, FYI. Last time I sent a package, I sent one hundred and forty-four peanut butter and chocolate chip. Jack said they actually lasted his unit for almost two whole days."

"Cookies." I sound as dazed as I feel.

But then I look at Jules, and I say it again, and I don't sound dazed at all. My head is as clear as clear can be.

●●●

Outside the all-night grocery store, Jules and Caitlin help me make a list on a wrinkled Red Earth cocktail napkin that Caitlin scrounges from the bottom of her bag. On the other side of the napkin, they both write their phone numbers.

Inside the all-night grocery store, Caitlin and Jules pitch things into my shopping cart as I check them off the list.

I spend that night's tips on:

1. Two big bottles of shampoo.
2. Two big bars of soap.
3. Two packages of David's kind of razors.
4. Ten packages of beef jerky.
5. The current issues of *Sports Illustrated, Rolling Stone,* and, as a joke, *the National Enquirer.*

6.   Five packages of turkey jerky. What the heck?

7.   Chocolate-chip cookie ingredients—enough to make at least a gross.

8.   A small stuffed dinosaur, because he had a thing for dinosaurs when he was just a kid.

They come to my house. We bake chocolate-chip cookies until three in the morning. We play loud music, dance, and laugh a lot. We don't eat too much of the batter. I make popcorn instead.

When they leave, Linda still hasn't come back.

I decide not to worry about this. Linda has her life. And, looking around the kitchen at all the cooling cookies, I realize that even with David gone, I have mine.

Fourteen

Late the next morning, I stumble out of bed, tired but happy. It's hard not to smile when the scent of fresh-baked cookies lingers in the air. Knowing Linda, she probably sampled some when she got home. I hope not too many.

I go to her room, only to find her bed still pristinely made. It appears Linda didn't deplete my cookie stock, because it appears Linda never came home. Fine. I have things to do too.

I go into the kitchen, eat a single cookie for breakfast, and then pack the rest of them, along with the rest of David's care-package items, into one of the boxes we used to move dishes from Chicago to Killdeer. I seal the box with some of our leftover packing tape.

Linda never throws away packing stuff. "You never know," she always says. I should remind her of this, next time she promises that Killdeer will be our permanent home. I should say, "Hey. If you really mean it, then recycle, why don't you?" And I'll point her to the pantry, where the rest of the boxes are stashed.

I'm addressing the box at the kitchen counter when I look out the window, and there she is, the clockwork lady, passing by. Doing her bit as I'm doing mine. The wind whips her pale yellow dress. She leans into the wind, her thin arms lifting from her sides with its force. I wonder if the clockwork lady could use a steadying hand.

I tap on the glass, but she doesn't hear. I start to go outside, but then I realize I'm still in my pajamas, or what constitutes my pajamas: an old T-shirt and my panties. I run to my room and throw on some clothes. But by the time I step outside, the clockwork lady is gone.

I'm sure she'll be fine. So it's a windy day. It's sunny too. She's walked in worse weather than this. Once I saw her pass as heat lightning skewered a yellow sky. They were predicting tornados. She's not the kind of lady who lets a little wind get her down.

I won't go looking for her. I'll mail David's package instead.

● ● ●

By the time I get home from the post office, it's nearly one in the afternoon. If Linda comes home at all, she'll arrive in the next couple of hours, in time to take me to work. If she doesn't come for me, I guess I'll have to call her and remind her that I'm kind of stranded here. I'll lay on the guilt, what the heck. She owes me a little guilt. If she says, "Bike it," well, then I'll be late.

For once, though, I'd like to be on time. I'd like to share a Coke with Caitlin before our shift starts, tell her I got David's care package in the mail.

I realize I haven't checked my phone since last night. I find it lying in a pile of cookie crumbs on the kitchen counter.

There are three new messages.

I will never leave my phone at home again. I will never let it out of my sight.

I play the first message.

"Hey, Penna. It's Jules. Now you have my number *in* your phone, so you have no excuse not to call me! I had so much fun last night. When Caitlin dropped me off, she said something about going out again. There's this new place we love—you've got to come. You'll have a blast. Maybe tonight? Call me! Bye."

I call her back and get her voice mail. Without hesitation I say I'd love to do something tonight.

Feeling almost giddy, I play the next message.

"Hi there. I'm sitting in 'Round the Clock. Where are you? We said nine, right? Did I get the time wrong? Anyway, I'm glad you suggested this place. There's this treasure chest, and when a kid jumps on it, the lid opens and the kid gets to choose a prize. It's kind of magical. I would have loved it when I was little. Someone's got to be pushing a button somewhere, but the kids don't know. I'm thinking maybe we said ten. I'll hang out. They keep bringing me coffee, so I'm good. See you soon."

Ravi.

I completely forgot.

I play the next message, which is not a message, only the sound of someone hanging up, who is Ravi.

I call his cell, but he doesn't answer. I don't leave a message. I call 'Round the Clock instead. I describe Ravi to the husky-voiced woman who answers the phone. She says, yeah, he was there. He drank about a gallon of coffee, ate some toast, paid his bill, and left.

They can't even make a decent piece of toast, David said.

I feel a little sick to my stomach. I'd better eat something besides a cookie.

But first I call Ravi's cell again. This time I leave a message. A long, apologetic one. I was up late baking cookies, I overslept, blah, blah, blah.

I don't tell him I completely forgot that we were going to have breakfast (not a date, no, definitely not a date), I was having too much fun with some friends, I was thinking about this old lady who walks by my house, I was thinking about David.

"Any chance you're off work tonight?" I say. "I'm going out with some friends. It'd be great if you came too. Call me, okay?"

Somehow I doubt he will.

• • •

I'm in my room getting ready for work when I hear Linda come in the front door.

"Yum," she says brightly. "It smells great in here! Have you been baking?"

I don't answer.

I hear her go into the bathroom and start the shower. She must really be grungy if she's been at Red Earth since yesterday. Now she's the one who's going to be rushing to get it together for the evening shift. She's the one who's going to make us late.

I finish getting ready. I glance in the full-length mirror that hangs on the back of my closed bedroom door, slick on some lip gloss. There I am. All black all the time. Red Earth ready.

Linda turns off the shower. The hair dryer goes on.

I sit down at my computer, check email. And there's David.

No message. Just three attachments.

I open them all. Then one by one, I take them in—David's drawings.

The first drawing is silly, a collage of sketches of David, my manga super-hero, doing various menial chores: fixing a shower, plunging a toilet, digging a trench, his cape snapping heroically in the invisible wind.

Funny.

In the next drawing, the wind is stronger. It whips Manga David's cape over his eyes. It doesn't seem like he'd be able to see, but still he's firing a rifle. Chocolate bars, not bullets, explode from it into the air. The bars rain down into the outstretched hands of laughing boys who look a lot like David did when he was little.

A little strange, but not so bad.

I look at the next drawing, which shows David playing cards with three other soldiers, who are also wearing capes. Their capes are draped over their shoulders like blankets. If I didn't know it's so hot over there, I would think it's very, very cold, from the way they're all huddled together around a single candle. Every card in every hand is a joker.

I shiver.

"Penna, let's go! We're late," Linda calls.

Once again this apparently is my fault.

Still, I take the time to write David an email. Short but sweet. That's all I can pull off right now.

> I love your drawings. Thanks for sending them to me. Write me too, okay?
>
> I just sent you something special in the mail. It's going to rock your world. Just wait and see.

As if his world hasn't already been rocked.

● ● ●

By the time Linda and I get to Red Earth, Caitlin is in full Happy Hour mode, waiting on about twenty people at once. It's an hour before we have a chance to talk, and then only in passing. But when she asks if I want to hang out again tonight with Jules, I immediately agree.

Hours after this, the last table finally empties. Caitlin is arranging the table settings for tomorrow. I'm swabbing down the menus. Then we'll be ready to go.

That's what I'm thinking about when Tom comes up to me, points to the fireplace mantel, and says, "You might want to check out that photograph. Linda just put it up today."

"Oh really," I say.

He takes the menus and rag from my hands. "Really."

I go over and look.

Up close I realize it's another photo of Tom as a teenager. He stands at attention in front of Red Earth's sign. This time he's wearing a sharply pressed army uniform. The photo has that Technicolor sheen of the 1960s, so his uniform looks lichen green. He wears his cap cocked on his head; the black bill shines glossily in the sun. He seems to be saluting the person who's taking the picture. Her heavily pregnant shadow falls at his feet.

Justine.

Pregnant with Linda.

I spin around and look at Tom.

He's watching. He jerks his head—*Come on, then*—and I hurry back to him before he can change his mind.

I'm afraid he might already have changed it, from his deep sigh as I approach. But then he says, "Right after that was taken, I went to Vietnam. And then I went MIA. Justine went MIA her own way not long after that." He's still holding the stack of menus. He swipes the rag across the topmost one. Again and again he scrubs at it, though it's clean enough already. "She didn't think I'd ever come home. She called me 'son,' see? I guess I was the last straw." He looks up at me, his eyes wary. "That's what she tells me, at least."

I grip the edge of the bar. "*Tells* you?"

Abruptly, Tom slaps the menus down on a nearby table. The rag he flings at the bar, and it lands with a thwack near the sink. He gives me a hard look then, like once and for all he's taking the measure of my character. "She says I'm taking care of her now, but really she takes care of me just by being there," he says. "It's like old times almost. Justine brought me into her home when my ma died, see. Justine raised me like her son."

"She's my grandmother." My voice cracks.

Tom nods. "You want to see her?"

"Yes!"

"I'll tell her that."

"She's my *grandmother*."

"I know. She wants to see you too. But I have to make sure she's strong enough. She's up and down, you know?" Tom glances at Linda, who is walking toward us, a tray of dirty glasses in her hands. "That one," he says sadly, jerking his head. "I haven't told her Justine's staying with me. I've heard Linda say it often enough—she said it the first day I came in for a job interview. She doesn't want to know anything about Justine, and she doesn't want you bumping up against Justine either. Why Linda's putting all these new pictures up, I'll never understand. I asked her once, and she said they're *authentic*. They're just *decoration*. Seems to me Linda doesn't know what she wants." Tom looks at me again, his gaze softening at whatever expression is on my face. "Seems like you do, though."

I nod.

"Linda might never get over what happened," Tom says. "There are people like that."

I swallow hard. Tom has just said what I haven't been able to say, haven't wanted to hear.

Tom goes back over to his typical place at the bar. He's got more than enough to do now that Linda is standing there too. She's right by his side, passing him sticky coaster after sticky coaster. It's up to him to clean off the rings, left by all those happy people drinking glasses of wine and steins of beer.

"Tell her," I call to Tom.

He looks up at me. Linda looks up too.

"Tell me what?" Linda says.

"Not *her*," I say to Tom, and turn away.

• • •

I find Caitlin then.

"Let's go," I say.

She flicks her pink and purple hair. "One last setting," she says. She takes care of it, rolling the paper napkin tightly around the knife, fork, and spoon, and setting them to the left of the clean, white plate. And then she says, "Done."

Next minute we're in Caitlin's car. She drives us to Jules's house, which is a little brick box much like Caitlin's own, only with fewer people inside, I guess.

"Where are we going?" I ask.

"Just wait!" Jules says, climbing into the backseat.

And then we take off.

A few minutes later I'm saying, "No. No, really. We don't need to go here."

Because I know where we're going. We're going to the viaduct.

"It's not the *ultimate* destination," Jules says. "But we've got to see it. Right, Caitlin?"

Caitlin nods. "Your mother, *Linda*, has only been talking about it for months."

"And then we'll go to the *ultimate* destination," Jules adds.

I remember then what David asked for, last time we talked on the phone. "Do either of you have a camera?"

"On my cell," Caitlin says.

"Oh, all right then," I say.

We pull to a stop about a block away from the viaduct.

"That's the *ultimate* destination." Jules points across the street and the empty lot beyond to what was the abandoned factory but now radiates neon and noise.

With David, I didn't want to go there. With Caitlin and Jules, I'm interested.

"What is it?" I ask.

"This new laser tag and paintball place." Jules grins. "You're going to love it. When Zach was home on leave, we went there together. He loved it too."

I think of David and me shooting paintballs at the guy on the Internet site. "I don't know."

"You won't know until you try. Now show us your mural," Caitlin says.

We get out of the car and walk toward the viaduct.

And that's when I see Ravi, whipping around the viaduct on his skateboard. He banks high up the curved wall, down again, and flies across the ground and up the other wall, then does it all again. His wheels skim across the killdeer and their nest, and across David and me, big and blue.

"Hey!" Caitlin yells. "Stop!" She gives me a fierce look. "He's going to wreck it, Penna."

Ravi keeps doing his trick. I can hear the whir of his skateboard's wheels.

"It's okay," I say, but Caitlin and Jules don't listen. They run toward Ravi. I run after them. Ravi skates fast, smooth and steady, back and forth, back and forth, repeating that same move.

We're at the entrance to the viaduct when Ravi spots us. Still, he doesn't break his pattern. He keeps on skating back and forth, up and down the walls. He glances over at us as we approach, and his look surprises me. His black eyes are stone cold and distant. It's like Ravi and I have never talked, like we've never seen each other before. He's dressed in that hooded sweatshirt again.

"Tough guy," Jules murmurs.

"He's not so tough," I say.

"Well, he better not ram into me with that board, or I'll show him what's what," Caitlin says, and she marches beneath the viaduct and right into Ravi's path.

He jumps off his board and kicks it up into his hands before it hits her.

"How do you do?" Playing polite, Caitlin sticks out her hand to Ravi. When he doesn't take it, she pumps it up and down, miming a handshake. "Nice to meet you too."

"Ravi," I say. "This is Caitlin. And this is Jules. Caitlin and Jules, Ravi."

Ravi drops his board on the ground and braces it with his foot. "What are you doing here? I thought you don't like coming here anymore."

I laugh, trying to keep it light. "How about you? I thought you had to work."

"I traded nights." He glares at me. "I was too tired to go to work. I got up early this morning for no reason at all. Now I can't sleep, so I'm here."

Caitlin and Jules glance at me.

I clear my throat. "That sucks."

Ravi nods.

"I hate it when I don't get enough sleep."

Ravi studies the ground. "Me too."

"I'm sorry that happened to you. I mean it."

Now Caitlin and Jules are really looking at me.

To my relief, Ravi looks up at me too, and his expression has softened. "I'll be all right. Just give me a day or two," he says. And he smiles.

I show Caitlin and Jules the mural then. They ooh and ahh over it. All the while, Ravi skates around us. Then I have them all stand back, and Caitlin takes a picture of me before the mural on her cell.

"I'll email it to you," Caitlin says, tucking her phone away. Then she tugs a hair band from her pocket and whips her hair up into a ponytail. She points at the skateboard. "You want to show us how to use that thing?"

"What about paintball?" Jules asks.

Caitlin rolls her eyes. "There'll be other nights for paintball. We can play paintball when it's raining. It's nice outside tonight. Let's enjoy the weather."

"Spoken like the mom of six," Jules mutters.

But then Ravi starts to show us how to skateboard, and even she gets a lesson.

We fall some. We laugh a lot.

When I ride the skateboard, I get lost in the feel of it, skimming over the ground, with Ravi, Jules, and Caitlin running by my side. I feel confident, daring. I feel like I can do anything.

I can ask Linda where Tom lives. I don't have to wait around if I don't want to. This one thing, this one thing I really, really want, I can make happen.

●●●

It's one thirty in the morning when I get home. Linda's not back yet. I go right to my room. I check my computer.

There it is. An email from David. No drawing attached. Just words.

I've never been so happy for words.

> Hey, Penna.
>
> I got an email from Mom that said you stopped by to visit. Thank you.
>
> I guess you know that I started night patrol. I'm okay. I don't exactly know what's dangerous for us here anymore, so late in the game. So don't worry. I'll tell you more soon. I just don't feel like thinking about it right now. That's all.
>
> Here's something good. Or as good as it gets here, I guess. We've started to go to the local orphanage to help the kids here. It's practically bare except for beds and toilets and sinks. But it's clean. There are kids of all ages. The youngest are tiny. The oldest look to be about sixteen. There are so many kids roaming the streets here. They keep trying to sell me stuff—stuff you can't believe. Broken combs. Half-empty matchbooks. Stuff like that. Or they'll try and shine my shoes. And the begging—you wouldn't believe it. Or the number of kids sniffing and huffing. Totally stoned on old cans of spray paint and other stuff I don't know. They'd be better off in the orphanage, but I guess there's no room.
>
> The orphanage woman told us that since our occupation, nearly four million of her people have been displaced from their homes. Nearly half are children.

We just stood there.

There's one little girl with big dark eyes and a red dress. I've heard she's ten, but she looks about six. I haven't been able to make her smile yet. I keep trying. If I had a little sister, she'd probably look a lot like this girl—at least, what I can see of her through the bandages.

Ravi said you guys talk too. It was good to hear from him. Kind of surprising. Leave it to Mom.

Ravi didn't say what you talk about, though.

What do you talk about?

I mean, he's there. I'm here.

What do you talk about?

Gotta sign off. I'll write again, soon as I can.

Love,

David

For the second time in one day, I write David back immediately. I ask him to tell me more about what he's doing, more about where he is. What is the food like? Has he seen any good TV? Do they show movies at base? Does he take pictures? If he does, could he send me a picture of himself with the little girl in the red dress?

I tell David I'm okay. Work is better. I tell him I think I'm about to meet my grandmother, and I'll tell him all about it once I have. I miss you, I tell him. I tell him that Ravi showed me the cutest pictures. *You'll be receiving them in the mail soon*, I write. *That's what we talk about, Ravi and me. We talk about you. Oh, and the girl I work with, Caitlin, she took a picture of me tonight down at the viaduct. I'll get it to you as soon as she gets it to me.*

I tell him I love him. I press *Send*.

Linda comes home then. I go to her, chat her up. Then very casually I ask where Tom lives. Linda tells me. She knows the exact street and address. She knows the few blocks between our house and his. She knows nothing else.

Linda thinks it's nice that I'm interested in knowing more about Tom. "He's an *old* friend," she reminds me. "And he was in Vietnam, you know. He had a terrible time there, I think. Isaac has told me things I didn't even know." She gives a funny, little sigh. "Isaac and Tom talk," she says.

That night I dream of a little girl in a red dress and a young woman in a blue dress and me in the green sundress that David loves. We are all balancing on train tracks, trying to walk without falling.

Fifteen

Next morning I'm up earlier than I've been all summer. I take a quick shower and slip into the green sundress of my dreams. I scarf a bagel. I leave a note for Linda, who's still sleeping: *Went out. Pick me up for work? I'll be ready. I promise.* By nine I'm walking the few blocks to Tom's.

Tom lives on a dead-end street in a little yellow brick ranch. I start up the weed-ridden driveway and then panic, turn around, and scuttle back to the sidewalk.

I pace up and down Tom's street. Five times I walk it.

I'm working up the nerve to start up Tom's driveway again when Tom's front door opens.

A frail figure steps out—not much more than a shadow in the shadows.

The figure crosses the porch and comes into the sunlight, shading her eyes with a thin hand. She's wearing a white dress.

The clockwork lady.

I walk up the driveway toward her. I see more clearly her heart-shaped face.

Justine?

I must have said the word aloud, because she nods.

"I knew you'd come." Her voice is thin and reedy.

"How?" I say. "How could you possibly know?"

She doubles over then. Drops right down on the top porch step.

I run to her. To my relief, she is sitting up by the time I reach her side. She is resting her forehead on her knees. I kneel beside her. I haven't been around old people much. I don't know what to do now. I ask her, foolishly, if she's all right.

"I couldn't come to you." Justine says as if this is the answer I'm looking for. "I could only pass by. Linda."

"I'm Penna," I say. "I'm Linda's daughter, your granddaughter."

Justine shakes her head. "I know that. I *know* that. Penelope, isn't it? I love your name."

I reach out my hand to her. She's shaking. Her skin looks clammy. My hand wavers by her bony, bowed shoulder. I'm afraid of her, I realize. How can I be afraid of a little old lady?

I remember.

She practically ruined me.

It's like Linda is hovering again, repeating the words, restraining my hand.

I should be able to touch Justine. I should be able to touch anyone who's this sad, no matter their past.

Instead the words burst from me—my voice as harsh as Linda's when she speaks of Justine. "Why couldn't you come? Tell me. All these years, why couldn't you come?"

I remember her photograph on my shelf. She is so changed now, a lifetime older. This Justine's dark eyes have faded to a murkier golden brown. Her skin is a maze of wrinkles. Her lips are thinner. In her sadness, she is disintegrating before my eyes. She crumples like Linda does when Linda is upset. Only worse.

"Easy." Tom's deep voice descends from above. "Easy now."

He's hulking over us, bearishly big. His broad face is softer than I've ever seen it. He narrows his eyes, swiftly evaluates Justine, then bends low and swoops her up. Her thin, bare legs swing beneath the fluttering hem of her dress. Her sandaled feet dangle. She rests her head on his shoulder.

"It's all right. It'll be all right," Tom says. The tattooed eagles ripple on his sinewy arms, though Justine weighs next to nothing, I can tell, from the way Tom spins around and heads back into the house.

I leap to my feet. "Wait."

Tom casts a furious look back at me. This wasn't what he wanted, me barging in like this.

"Come on, then." He kicks the door open with one foot. "If you're going to play nice."

• • •

Tom lays Justine on the couch in his front room. The couch is big and red. Justine, so pale in her white dress, looks ghostly lying there. Her closed eyelids are nearly as thin as tracing paper. Her fine, white hair spreads like a cloud across the couch cushion.

Tom looks from her to me. He jerks his head to one side. "Water."

I run in the direction of his gesture to the tiny kitchen. I turn on the tap and fill a plastic cup, then hurry back.

Justine is sitting up now, pushing Tom's protective arms away. She looks at me and manages the shadow of a smile. "Not dead yet," she says. She holds out a shaky hand and takes the cup from me. She spills a little, drinks a little, and rests the cup daintily on her knees.

Tom forces a smile. "You might as well be at a tea party."

"I was raised right." Justine lifts her chin at this attempt at humor. "I am *all right*, Tom, just as you said I'd be." Justine looks at me. "Are you all right?"

My throat tightens with emotion. My arms wrap tightly around my ribs. *I've been searching for you*, I want to say. And, suddenly, *I'm furious at you.* "I'm all right," I say.

Tom stands. "Call if you need me," he tells Justine. He doesn't look at me. He goes to the kitchen. He bangs around some pots and pans, just to remind us he's there. Then there's the sound of running water and sloshing in the sink.

Justine shakes her head. "Doing dishes is a comfort to him. But you must know that from work."

I don't want to talk about Tom.

"Ever since his war, he's liked things tidy." Justine raises her plastic cup to the room, and I see how sparely furnished and neatly kept it is. "He can't cook for his life, though. At least I can still sometimes help out with that." She closes her eyes wearily. "Though yesterday I couldn't think of the word for soup, and I couldn't, for the life of me, remember how to work a can opener. It's like there's a click in my brain and such things are blocked out or blacked out. Something."

"Why couldn't you come?" The words explode again from me.

With a resolute breath, Justine opens her eyes. She bends and sets her plastic cup on the floor, then slowly sits up again. Everything she does is done cautiously, like she might break if she's not careful.

"Please," she says. "A moment."

I drop down on a hardback chair and give Justine her moment. She smooths the skirt of her dress, accordion-pleats the fabric, then smooths the fabric flat again.

"I tried," she finally says. "For years and years, I tried. But he didn't want me here. He said he would make it worse for everyone if I came."

"He who?"

"Your granddad. Ernest. Truth be told, he wasn't the only one who stopped me from coming. Someone drinks like that, eventually you can't let them stop you. But your mother—once she got to be a certain age, she didn't want anything to do with me either."

What can I say to this? I know it's true.

Justine covers her eyes with her hand. "He was sick. She was hurt. Years had passed. Still, there's no real excuse for my actions, I know. I should have tried harder." She lowers her hand. Tears stand in her eyes. "I was afraid."

I hear footsteps from behind me, and now Tom stands over Justine again, watching her carefully. Justine swipes the tears from her eyes and waves him away. He glowers but goes.

"Penelope." Justine stands then. Carefully, slowly, she walks over to me. Her hand settles lightly on my shoulder. "Forgive me. Please."

● ● ●

Justine and I sit together on the red couch, and she tells me what happened. She was sick at heart and in her head, she says. She made a new life in the place where she was briefly the happiest.

"Yellow Rock," I say.

When Justine draws back in surprise, I tell her about her photograph and Owen's letter too.

"I had to hide things like that from Ernest." She shakes her head wonder-ingly. "I'd hide them in the strangest places, places he'd never think to go. I guess I forgot about the photo and the letter."

"I'll give them back to you."

"They're yours now." She sounds relieved at this. "I'd like to see them, that's all."

"Sure." I tell Justine how I found her then. I tell her I saw the newspaper article and the painting she made. I tell her I like to draw and paint too. I'll show her my drawings and paintings someday, if she wants. There's a viaduct I want to show her—

I think of Ravi banking up the mural wall, and Caitlin and Jules running beside me, laughing there, and then I think of David and me, painting each other big and blue, and I can't say anymore.

"I want to see everything," Justine says. "I want to live my life now, the way I wasn't able to then."

I put my hand on her arm. "How did you finally decide to come back?"

Justine pats my hand. Her fingers are startlingly cold. "Tom found me years ago. When Ernest died and left everything to Linda and you, Tom let me know. A few months ago I sold my little place in Yellow Rock to a friend. I moved here. Hoping."

Hearing his name, Tom descends again. He tells Justine that she's getting tired. He tells me I'd better get ready for work. I glance at my watch. He's right. Tom holds out a hand and hoists me up. He walks me to the door.

I hesitate there. I look back at Justine, who, leaning deep into the red couch cushions, looks nearly lost again.

"It's one thing with me," I say. "It'll be another thing with Linda."

"At least I'll have tried," Justine says.

"But how—?" I can't even finish the question.

Justine glances at Tom. "Could we come to the house? I'd like to see it again on the inside." She smiles at me now. "It's my old house, you know, from my first marriage. Ernest moved in when he married me."

I nod. "I've been wondering if you slept in my bedroom or Linda's," I say, realizing that, yes, I want to know that. Like Justine, I want to see and know everything I can.

Justine's smiles, and in her smile I see her eighteen-year-old self—the girl before so much sadness and so many mistakes. I see me.

"Why don't you all come to Red Earth some time?" This idea hits me out of the blue, and my words tumble over each other. "Linda will be more likely to behave there. I mean, she *is* the manager."

Tom shrugs. "It's possible."

"Sometime soon," Justine agrees. "From Yellow Rock to Red Earth. How do you like that?"

Tom follows me out of the house. We stand on his driveway, eyeing each other.

"I know you think I should have waited," I say. "But what if I waited one day too long?"

Tom nods. "And there's something else." His voice is rough with emotion.

"What?"

"The doctor, he says she's in the early stages of Alzheimer's. It comes and goes now. She can be real bad, or she can be clear as a bell. But you're right. We shouldn't wait too long for anything or anyone that we really care about."

●●●

I don't walk home. I run, the hem of my green sundress fluttering at my knees.

I hurry to my bedroom. There is my window. I go to it, breathe in fresh air, morning sunshine, life now. There is the honey locust tree, the tree that I love. I love the smooth, silvery brown bark and its long, lean, lithe shape, and the delicate little leaves that extend so neatly from their stems. I love the way the tree shades my room and cools it. I love the shadows it casts on my walls by day and night. I love the way David used to stand beneath it, waiting for me. I love knowing that Justine and Owen must have stood there too.

I will never forget any of this. I will remember for her.

I grab a piece of paper and start sketching shapes that grow into the honey locust.

I check my computer then. No news from David. No message on my cell from him either, though Caitlin has left a text telling me to check my email.

She's sent the picture of me at the viaduct. I look good in it. I look happy. I might even look too happy. But I promised. So I write David an email, telling him I've found Justine. I can't wait for the two of them to meet. Then I attach my picture at the viaduct and send it off.

If he asks who I was with, I won't lie. I've got no reason to lie. "Caitlin, Jules, and Ravi," I'll tell him. "I can't wait for the five of us to hang out when you get home."

Don't wait too long for anything or anyone that you care about.

But I'll have to.

I guess I'm figuring out how.

●●●

"Justine won't come tonight." Tom has joined me at the coffeemaker, where I'm filling two cups for the couple arguing at the table in the corner. "She says she's not ready yet. She's old, Penna. I'm old, and I think I've got it rough. But she's *old* old. I can just imagine. She's got to take it easy. When she doesn't take it easy, that's when her mind seems to go. Even she knows that now."

It's nearly ten. Except for an arguing couple, Red Earth's tables are empty. No one is even drinking at the bar. It's been so dead tonight that Linda is talking about shutting down early. She and Isaac have things they need to take care of in the kitchen—measurements for some new appliances. They'd just as soon do it now as after midnight.

Tom heads back to the bar, and I turn toward the couple, steeling myself to interrupt what seems to be an increasingly heated disagreement.

Caitlin elbows me.

I am getting better at balancing things. Barely a ripple breaks across the coffee.

Caitlin laughs. "Good job. You passed the test."

I stick out my tongue.

"I'm so into getting out of here early." Caitlin sounds giddy with the possibility of a few extra hours of freedom. "I texted Jules, and she said she's already on her way over to Total Rush. The paintball place, you know. She's picking up some other kids too. She asked them about you. Some of them are going to be seniors this year. They remember you from school."

"Really?" I hesitate. Then I think of Justine. I think Justine would want me to go. *Live your life*, I think Justine would say. *It'll help you hold on.*

"Oh, come on, Penna! Don't do this. Don't make some dumb excuse."

"I'm not." I grin, realizing this is true. "Let's see how quickly we can get out of here."

Caitlin beams.

I head for the arguing couple, balancing the brimming cups like a pro. The couple—an older man and a younger woman—barely look up as I set the cups down. They are in the thick of it, that's for sure. I sweep crumbs, straws, and cracker wrappers from the floor until the man throws a bill on the table, and the two of them push back their chairs and storm out.

I go over and pocket the cash. I don't want it ever to get that angry between David and me.

From the kitchen door, Linda calls, "Closing time!"

Together, Caitlin and I have prepped everything for tomorrow. All I have to do is clean up this table.

I'm wiping it down when Caitlin walks over, dangling her key chain from her hand. She swings it like a pendulum before my eyes. "You are getting sleepy, very sleepy," she intones hypnotically. "You are going to have a very good time."

I pull this zombie look, slack jawed, empty eyed. I stick my arms straight out in front of me, turn, and lumber mechanically toward the kitchen to get my bag from the closet there.

That's when I see Linda and Isaac through the kitchen door's round window.

Linda and Isaac, kissing like crazy.

I stop lumbering. I lower my arms.

"Ooh-la-la," Caitlin mutters from behind me.

Like she senses something, Linda comes up for air. She sees me seeing her. She pulls away from Isaac. She bangs open the kitchen door and comes at me. *Wait, don't run away. I can explain everything—just let me hold you*, her expression says.

I hold up my hand, and she comes to a stop just in front of me.

"It's fine," I say coolly, keeping my voice under control. It's not hard, actually. I'm that stunned. "Call me crazy, but I've always believed in true love. You know that."

Though who knows what kind of love this is for Linda? She's never been exactly the "true love" type.

I push past her, go into the kitchen, stride past Isaac (catching a scent of the musky cologne he wears, which I realize only now I've smelled on Linda too), grab my bag from the closet, and go out the back door, where I meet Caitlin by her car.

"Did you know?" I ask.

Caitlin shrugs. "I had a hunch."

I sink down in the seat, grimly grateful for the pebbles Caitlin accidentally spews onto Linda's VW peeling out. I brace my feet on the dashboard.

Caitlin glances over at me, but she doesn't complain.

"Good thing you've got on those kick-ass Docs," she says. "You're going to need them where we're going."

Sixteen

Caitlin doesn't seem to need to talk or listen to music, and I'm glad for some quiet. So we drive in silence toward the viaduct and Total Rush.

It burns me, I realize, staring out the car window. It burns me that I've waited for Linda, wondering where she is. All my curfews, the ones I tried so hard to keep. All that stuff she said about independence, all that stuff about letting go of David—that really burns me. And yet there she was, holding on to just who she wants.

So that's what she's been doing all those long hours at work. Getting all dependent on someone besides herself.

I think of our house, the little hallway there, lined with photographs of me, of her, of me and her. Am I jealous of my mother? Is that it? Or am I just mad that for once she's caring more about herself than me? More about what she wants than what I want—which happens to be David, safe and sound at home again. And Justine, who lives right around the corner but might as well live a world away. Would it hurt Linda to be a little more accepting of what I want? Then maybe I'd be a little accepting of her.

"Almost there," Caitlin says, interrupting my thoughts.

Just as well. I'm sick of thinking about Linda.

"Good. Except I've never played before," I say.

"No worries," Caitlin says. "It's not hard. Soon you'll be addicted like the rest of us."

And then we're there.

●●●

Except for the cars parked in the dirt parking lot out front, the spotlights illuminating the metal steps leading up to the entrance, and the neon sign reading "Total Rush" above, the big old factory looks just the same on the outside as it did when David and I used to drive by: crumbling brick, boarded-up windows, lots of graffiti.

Or it seems just the same from inside Caitlin's car. Once she and I get out—well, then it's another story. Music thuds from inside the warehouse—metal so loud it makes the air jump. I press my hands to my ears, and the throbbing baseline gets muffled, but like that it reminds me of the raves David and I used to go to, just over there at the viaduct, and then I'm thinking of David and how he loved those raves—and how he loved.

I wish he were here.

I lower my hands, and the warehouse music hits me hard.

"Come on!" Caitlin yells. She grabs my hand and drags me across the parking lot and up the metal steps to the warehouse's doorway.

"Don't be scared." I think that's what Caitlin says as she leads me inside. The entryway door swings shut behind us, and the music settles on my head like a heavy helmet. For a moment I can't see straight—sound dementia. And the black lights have turned everything ghoulish—most notably Caitlin's glowing teeth as she smiles. The flashing strobes pepper blasts of brilliance into the darkness. When Caitlin turns, a strobe fractures her body. She jerks her way over to a counter, and there's a cash register there—I see that now—and behind loom what look to be lockers for gear. Then I register the bulky guy in blaze orange standing behind the cash register. He's taking a credit card from Caitlin. I tug at her arm, protesting, but she waves me off.

"You'll get me next time," she yells at me.

"Thanks," I yell back, but she waves this off too, shouting, "We're in this together."

Somehow Caitlin lets Blaze Orange know that I've never been here or played before. He glowers like I've done something wrong, and then he hollers, "Got to brief her, I guess." He turns, flings open the lockers, and grabs kneepads, face masks, and padded vests for Caitlin and me. He shoves these things across the counter at us. As we scramble to hold on to everything, he grabs a couple paintball guns too.

He gestures with the guns for us to follow him, and then he hustles Caitlin and me down a narrow hallway and into a room that reminds of the walk-in freezer at work—not because it's so cold, but because I feel claustrophobic the minute I step inside. In the dim light, I make out a couple of benches. I follow Caitlin's lead and sit down on one of them. The guy slams the door shut, and the music is instantly muffled. It's at mall decibel now; this must have been some kind of vault or meat locker or padded cell, once upon a time. I can hear myself think. I can hear Blaze Orange's words too, when he starts giving the lowdown about this place.

"You're starting the newbie with paintball, right?" he says.

"Yes, sir." Caitlin nods like a good soldier.

Blaze Orange nods back. "My personal preference. I mean they're both about the territory and the goal, the *killing*, but you can't beat the realism of paintball. The fog of war, man." He pumps his fists in the air. "It's all about the fog of war. Know what I'm saying? I'm talking Capture the Flag gone gonzo. Battlefield action. Everything and everyone, fair game. I mean, the sound of those paint pellets flying overhead, the smoke and the mess, the slippery floor—it really pulls you in like nothing else. Know what I'm saying?"

"In laser tag nothing really matters except having accurate equipment."

Caitlin is clarifying this for my sake, talking fast as she slips on the protective vest. She can't wait to get out there. That's clear from the way she's grinning. "In laser tag there are a lot of beeps and lights, but it just isn't the same as blasting and getting blasted. You know those old-lady bath beads? Well, any thoughts you ever had about those are about to change."

Jules barges into the room then. She's all geared up and looks like she's been playing for a while, because she's sweaty too. She has two rectangles of black smeared beneath her eyes. They remind me of tribal markings, war paint.

"'Scuse me," Jules says to Blaze Orange, and she plants herself in front of Caitlin, pulls a little jar from her jeans' pocket, opens it, dips her finger inside, and then smears two rectangles beneath Caitlin's eyes. Then Jules does me.

We all bash knuckles and whoop.

"Now that that's done…" Blaze Orange hoists his pants up over his gut. He's built like an ex-linebacker, his muscle only just starting to turn to fat. "Here's the deal. You two may know how to play." He jerks his head at Caitlin and Jules. "But you, I got to fill in." He jerks his head at me. "It's a legal thing."

I nod, twisting my face mask around and around in my hands.

Blaze Orange talks about teams, rules, referees. "No physical contact whatsoever allowed," he says loudly. He clears his throat and lowers his voice, but just a little. "Just point and shoot. Does it hurt? Sometimes, like when you get snapped with a wet towel. Little welts, maybe you'll get some of those. Big injuries, probably not. But remember, no shoving, no hitting. No *touching*. Got it?"

"Got it," I say.

"Watch the uneven surface," Blaze Orange continues. "There are these steel supports—watch for those. When you get splashed, you're *out*. You go to the safe area in the sidelines with the other girls." Here he pauses to catch his breath, glowering at me like I'm a born rule-breaker. "You stay in the safe area until the next game. Got it?"

I'm frowning at his assumption about girls being the only occupants of the safe area. But I'm antsy. The mask feels clammy with the sweat that's suddenly slicking my palms. I want to get on with it, end the suspense, solve the mystery. So I don't comment other than to say, "Got it."

"When all the players on one team are out or one team captures the other team's flag and gets it to the opponent's home base before the time runs out—that's when you win." Blaze Orange pumps his fists in the air again. He loves his job. "Now get your gear on!"

Jules and Caitlin help me suit up. The goggles on my mask make everything that was already strange go a stranger green.

"Number one golden rule," Caitlin says, adjusting the straps on my vest. "If some dude starts talking smack about you because you are a girl, kick his butt."

So that "girls' safe area" crack bugged her too.

Before I can respond, Jules turns me toward the door and gives me a shove. I stumble toward it.

"To the Wild West Room!" Jules cries. "Everybody's waiting there. Yee-haw!"

Blaze Orange flings open the door then, and we fall out into our version of some war.

●●●

David would die laughing, seeing this place. That's what I think when I walk into the Wild West Room. David liked to play paintball outdoors; he did it all the time before he met me. But he wouldn't have been able to take this indoor version of the West seriously. Nobody should—not with the paintings of cowboys and bucking broncos covering the walls, the small, rickety oil derricks, and the gigantic hay bales, water barrels, and tumbleweeds.

Everything's off scale, even the child-sized skeleton dressed in Indian garb hanging from a fake tree and the mummified mini-rustler dangling nearby.

The sign above the big fenced-in area right in front of Jules and me reads "Corral," and inside hulk lumpy, mangy-looking cows, bulls, and horses—all fake, of course. There's a covered wagon that's definitely seen better days. And then there are the two other hallways that lead out of the Corral, down which I glimpse other signs set on posts outside other rooms—Bank, Depot, Saloon—all waiting to be explored and seized as territory.

At least the music is lower, and it's not metal. It's country—rough-riding hillbilly rock, the kind David could dance to but I never could.

Two teams are at war in here, one in greenish-yellow vests like Jules, Caitlin, and me, the other in yellowish-green. I think I might recognize a few kids from school, but it's hard to tell. Everyone is yelling and firing guns; dodging, sliding, and somersaulting for safety; hiding behind the derricks, hay bales, water barrels, tumbleweeds, cows, bulls, and horses; and firing some more from there.

"Get down!" Jules and Caitlin scream. They pull me to the floor, and we crawl on our bellies to the covered wagon. Somehow we scramble through the tautly cinched opening of the wagon's paint-spattered cloth cover and inside the wagon, tumbling over each other and knocking down the guy in the yellowish-green vest who's hiding there.

An enemy, I'm thinking as the wagon rocks beneath us.

"Hands up!" the guy gasps, though he's flat on his back, Jules squatting with one knee on his chest and me straddling his legs.

Jules points her gun right at his chest. "My, what close range. This could hurt." She glances over at me. "Think of our guys. Think of what they're going through. This is just a taste."

My heart starts pounding so hard that I'm sure it's going to burst through my vest.

The guy tries to curl into a ball, but with us on him he can't do much but twitch.

So much for no touching, I think.

Boom, boom, boom, goes my heart.

"We can do this the easy way or the hard way," I find myself saying.

Caitlin laughs. "Did you hear that in a movie or what?"

The guy flings aside his gun and we give him a little room. "On your knees," Jules barks, and he goes there. With our guns trained on him, he scrambles from the wagon. We hear him holler, pummeled by paintballs as he hits the ground.

"He is so out!" I shout. I grab Jules's arm in my excitement, and she jumps, reflexively jerking her gun away like I'm trying to steal it or something.

"Whoa." I can barely get the words out; I'm that breathless. "We're on the same side, remember?"

"There are three girls in there!" someone shouts from outside, and then the covered wagon heaves like someone is shaking it.

I scream.

"Don't wimp out on us now," Jules says. And Caitlin cocks her gun.

I don't wimp out. I get lost in the fog of war. There's the literal fog from the haze of paint, splattering all around outside the wagon, turning a sulfuric color when it mixes. And there's the fog of colored lights that even the sheen of paint across my goggles can't hide when I peek out at the Corral. There's the fog of sound too—music, yelling, guns firing, pellets splatting, and more often then I would have thought, the sound of bodies banging up against things. The wagon keeps shuddering with that impact.

My shoulder aches from the gun's kick. I never fired a gun before today. Once David tried to take me hunting—just gophers, he said. It's the only time he asked me out that I refused to go.

But now here I am, squinting as I aim my gun at the Corral and the yellowish-green vests there, pulling the trigger, relishing the kick and the pain. When I think of David, I shoot even better. *Blam.* Someone else is out of the game. I think of Linda and Isaac—*blam, blam*—and that works too.

●●●

We're the last women standing.

We climb out of the wagon, triumphant, and swagger across the paint-spattered floor and out of the Wild West.

"Didn't you love it?" Caitlin asked.

"I did!" I'm sweaty and breathless. My heart is still racing, though it doesn't feel like it's going to burst through my vest anymore.

"I could play every night. It makes me feel closer to Zach," Jules says.

I nod. I did feel connected to David in there. Though this is nothing compared to what he's going through.

And, come to think of it, I hope he's going through nothing like this.

I feel suddenly sick. I look around at the smeared floor, and images from Tom's special reports flash through my mind. The guy in the kaffiyeh on that Internet site. And then I remember David's drawings: the gun spewing candy bars, not bullets. The soldiers playing only with jokers. And the kids in the orphanage that he told me about. The little girl in the red dress.

I think of Justine. I wonder how she would feel about all this.

I start walking.

"Where are you going?" Caitlin asks.

"We're going to play again," Jules says.

I look back at them and shake my head, smiling. "I want to write David. I need to go home."

"How will you get there?" Caitlin asks.

I shrug. "I'll walk. I need some air. It's not so far."

"Maybe you'll play again tomorrow night?" Jules asks.

I nod. "Maybe."

• • •

Blaze Orange is nowhere to be seen, so I drop my gear on the counter and walk out of the warehouse. I hesitate on the metal stairs outside, my eyes adjusting in the bright spotlight. A moth darts past my cheek toward the light above. I start down the stairs then. I don't want to listen to the moth, banging its dusty body to a pulp against the hot light it thinks might be the sun. A deathtrap it thinks might be an open door.

I go to the viaduct.

I hear Ravi before I see him—the wheels of his skateboard skimming across the concrete.

And then there he is in his hooded sweatshirt, skating over the mural, sailing up and down it, up and down.

"Trade nights again?" I call.

Ravi stops skating, but awkwardly, stumbling from his board, falling to the ground. Slowly, he stands, dusts himself off. Then, not looking at me, he nods.

"You're going to have to watch out or you just might lose your job," I say. And then I notice that Ravi's cheeks are wet. That isn't sweat, I realize. I'm the sweaty one. Ravi's been crying.

I take a step toward him, then another. "What's wrong?"

He rolls his skateboard back and forth beneath one foot. He looks at the ground.

"Are you okay?"

He looks at me then, and his black eyes are as striking as the first time I really saw him, the night David and I went on our last roundabout ride. His black eyes look haunted I realize now.

"Ravi?"

"I traded because a month ago tonight, my father died. Heart attack." Ravi's voice is low and quiet, almost formal. "He died thinking that my only goal was to work the night shift at the Walmart for the rest of my life." Ravi dries his cheeks with the sleeve of his sweatshirt. Then he straightens his shoulders. "This is why I'm going back to school, Penna. For me, yes. But also for my father."

"You're doing the right thing." I blink at the tears that are building in my eyes now. I laugh, and it comes out all broken. "Going back to school, I mean. And taking tonight off work too, if that's what seems right."

"I'm scared." The statement is so simple and so weird coming from a guy that I blink in surprise. I don't want to cry anymore. I want to give him advice, snap him into shape, shield him in a suit of armor, smear some war paint beneath his eyes. If I only could.

"Keep a low profile," I say. "That's the advice all the army dudes give in the chat rooms and stuff. They say the best way to make it through the army is to keep a very low profile. I read up on stuff like that while David was at OSUT. I wanted to understand, you know? I wanted to really be there for him—almost with him, if I could. If only I could. So I read all this stuff, and I'm thinking sometimes just everyday life, high school and college and all that, is like a war and you just have to get through, do the best you can, try not get hurt, try not to hurt anybody. If we can remember that, then maybe David can too."

Ravi nods.

Carrying his skateboard, he comes over to me and puts his arm lightly around my shoulder. He guides me out from beneath the viaduct. We talk a bit. Ravi tells me he's got an older sister. She's come home from college to help him get through this year. I tell him about Justine. I tell him more than I've told David, because I tell him about Owen too.

Then we fall silent, and Ravi walks beside me the whole long way home. Then he skates off to wherever he lives, wherever he's starting his life over again.

• • •

Linda's not home yet.

But David's there waiting.

Hey, Penna.

Thanks for the photograph. How long has it been since we were there together? I'm losing track of things like time over here. About three weeks, right? Seems like another lifetime.

You look great. Better than ever.

I'll send you a pic of the little girl as soon as I have one.

I'm going to try and think about now. About everything that's been going on.

You'll get this, I bet. When I first got here, I thought the graffiti—Arabic, I guess—was cool. I still think this, mostly. Only at night on patrol it looks kind of scary. It makes me think of snakes or vipers, if there's even a difference between the two.

But then everything looks different in the dusk and the dark. Garbage, especially. And cardboard boxes. And packed-down dirt (though all the ground is pretty much dirt here, it's so dry). And burned-out cars and buses and donkey carts. Burkas. Ali Babas.

Remember that guy we shot paintballs at over the Net? I keep thinking I see him. I feel like he's stalking me, even though I know he's a U.S. citizen, just like me. He lives in Colorado, for Pete's sake.

All these things sometimes make it hard for me to keep my mind on the game. Guess I haven't told you what the game is exactly.

I'm working nights, sleeping days. Patrol is a little different than it used to be, because we're also helping train the Iraqis who are going to take over when we're gone. I ride around for six hours straight, trying to find and detonate roadside bombs. Route clearance, it's called.

They say pretty soon all the training is going to happen inside the wire. We won't even have to leave camp. The Iraqis will come to us. We'll show them how to sweep and purge an area there, I guess.

Until then, don't worry. I wear full battle rattle. And I'm in a truck that's got armor at least an inch thick all around. A real Frankenstein. That's what some of the guys call our monster trucks. We scrounge around for the extra armor we need for protection, and then we spot-weld the seams. There are two other trucks like mine in our unit. And then there's the Buffalo.

The Buffalo is this mega-war machine. It's got this claw—or more like a giant scoop with a nasty spike on the end. We call it the "spork," like that plastic fork-spoon thingie you get in the cafeteria when you're eating mac 'n' cheese. If we think something's trouble, like a plastic bag that wasn't in the road the day before, then the Buffalo rolls up and sporks it. Usually the plastic bag is just a plastic bag. But sometimes the thing blows.

Last night the streets were looking really lonely. Nobody and nothing around. We were rolling along, talking sports, girls, politics, family. Drinking Gatorade. One of the Iraqi guys was teaching me his words for *hello* and *good-bye* and *please* and *thank you* and *Where is the bathroom?* We were laughing our heads off at my pronunciation.

Suddenly the earth heaved up and fell in chunks, and our

truck pitched like crazy to one side and then came down on all four wheels. We were safe. But, man.

Now the loneliest road looks crowded with danger.

Another guy is chomping at the bit here. He needs to write *right now*, and I have to whip something off to Mom and Dad. Gotta sign off.

David

I try to write him a real email back. Substantially positive. But I can't. Nothing I say seems like enough.

So I just write: *I miss you. I love you.*

And hope that's enough.

Seventeen

Next morning Linda still isn't home. So I call Tom.

"Come on over," he says. "She's already had her morning walk—no sign of life at your house, she said. She's probably going to need a nap soon."

I get ready fast. I slip the old letter from Owen into my bag, and the photograph of Justine too, and head out.

Tom leads me onto his back porch, where Justine is sitting, bowed over something in her hands. He gives me a quick pat on the back, and then he leaves the two of us alone.

"Hi," I say. And then I try it out. "Grandma."

Justine looks up and gives me a radiant smile. Now I can see what she's holding: a square of fabric. She sets the fabric on the porch railing. Gripping the rocker's rickety arms, she tries to stand.

"You sit here," she says, wavering a bit.

I hold out my hands to catch her if she falls. "The steps are fine."

Still hunched, she looks up at me. "There's a chair in my bedroom. Or we can get one from the kitchen."

For an answer, I plop down on the steps. Shaking her head, Justine sinks back into the rocking chair.

"I'm not being a good host." Her laughter is soft and sad. "But then I never really was."

"You were pretty good to Tom when he needed you."

Justine wearily waves this off. "It was as simple as setting another place at the table. We're family."

Is Tom more like family than I am? I wonder. I remind myself it's not a competition. I pull her photograph and Owen's letter from my bag. "These are for you."

Justine eyes them.

"They won't bite," I say.

Justine takes them from me. She gasps at the picture and quickly puts it facedown on her lap. She puts the letter there too. "I think I'll just save these for later." She draws a pressed handkerchief from her sleeve's cuff and pats her eyes. "I don't deserve any of this. But I'm so grateful."

Justine tucks the handkerchief back in her cuff. She gives me a steady look then. "I'm losing my mind, you see. Bit by bit, it's slipping away—my brain is like a piece of ice, slowly melting." She gives her head a shake, like she's jarring something into place. "It's humbling, sometimes horrible, remembering who I was, things I did. But it's also a gift."

Hearing this from her is somehow worse than hearing it from Tom. My heart sinks. Here is this woman, the person I've been searching for, who was supposed to help me understand so many things. Now she's saying she's nearly gone? I want to cry. I look away from her until I can pull it together. When I look back again, she's watching me closely with the intent, alert eyes of a healthy woman.

"This is my last chance." Her voice is quiet. "My last chance to do something right." She smiles. "Just hope I can remember what I'm trying to do. There's something I must do, something I must find. But now, bless me, I can't remember what it is." She laughs, shaking her head so hard that wisps of her hair fall into her eyes. She blinks and her pale eyelashes tangle in her hair. Still she doesn't push her hair away.

So I do. I push Justine's hair back behind her ear as if she's the child and I'm the mom. She smiles so gratefully that I have to smile back, never mind how sad I'm feeling inside.

"You sound like Linda," I say. "She's always looking for a last chance to do something right."

"Is she? Poor girl. Poor dear girl." A shadow passes over Justine's face. "The things I've *done*. The things I *haven't* done. Someday you'll understand, Penelope."

Justine holds out her hand and I take it. Bone thin and fragile, it weighs less than the killdeer did that night in the attic. But Justine's hand trembles as the bird did. And I can feel a faint pulse at her wrist that seems nearly as rapid as the bird's frantic heartbeat. Not quite, but nearly.

"I pray you don't have to, though," Justine says.

I look away from her hand—that translucent, papery skin—and into her eyes. "Don't have to what?"

"Understand like this—what I'm understanding now. These regrets."

Justine seems to tire quickly then, and she has me call for Tom. He comes immediately and helps her to her bedroom for nap. When he comes back out on the porch, he tells me that he's doing a double shift today. He's got about twenty minutes before he has to leave.

"You're looking peaked," he says. "Want something to eat?"

"Tell me more about what's going on with her."

"While we eat."

I follow him into his small, neat kitchen, where he makes me a peanut butter and jelly sandwich, pours me a glass of milk, and tells me to sit down. "Eat."

I take a small bite and make myself chew.

"So this is how it is." He sits down too and spreads his big hands wide across the table. "The doctor says she's hit a plateau—his word—when it comes to the Alzheimer's. But when she worsens, she'll probably worsen quickly, and there will come a time when I won't be able to *do* for her anymore. She'll be harder to manage. There will be falls, infections. Not just her brain, but her body will shut down. She won't be safe unless she's living in a facility."

I put my sandwich on the plate. "A nursing home, you mean?"

"An assisted-living facility. There's a difference. She can have more independence if she's not in a nursing home—or at least not yet. We'll postpone that as long as we can. We've talked it all through, Justine, me, and the doctor. She went with me and we chose the place together. It's right outside Killdeer. She never wants to be a burden, she says." Tom flexes his fingers, puts a hand over his mouth. But not before I see that his lips are trembling. "This is the first time I've talked about this with anyone but her," he says.

"She's good here for now, though?"

Tom takes his hand from his mouth. He's in control again. "She's good here until I think—or *we* think—she's in danger. Believe me, I keep an eye on her when she insists on taking her little walks. Every day I weigh the odds. What if she stumbles? What if she wanders away? She hasn't done either yet, and she's let me know loud and clear that if I coop her up like a caged bird, she'll stop singing. So to speak." Tom runs his hands over his bald scalp. "She'll die. That's actually what she says."

I stare at my barely touched sandwich.

Tom says, "You gonna eat that?"

I shake my head. "Not now."

Tom gets up, goes to a cabinet, pulls out a plastic bag, and puts the sandwich in it. He hands it to me. "In case you get hungry later."

I look at him, grateful not for the sandwich but for who he is.

"I wish—" I hesitate for a moment, but then I say it. "It should be Linda and me doing this."

"You can do other things. Things I can't do as well."

"Like what?"

"Oh." Tom sighs. "Like listening to her. I don't have the patience, Penna. I'm a doer, know what I mean? But Justine needs someone to listen. And then there's all the *stuff*. I hate stuff."

I sit up a little straighter at this. "What stuff?"

"She left this trunk in storage with my things when she ran away to Yellow Rock. I just pulled it out for her the other day. She took one look and burst into tears. And then she was calling me Owen and asking me to help her. She was in bad shape that day." Tom shakes his head.

"I'll go through the trunk with her," I say. "I'll do it as soon as she's able. I want to know about Owen. I want—" I can't put the words together anymore. I've never seen Justine struggle half as hard as I am right now.

Tom folds his arms across his chest. He nods slowly, evaluating me with something like pride.

Before I leave, I peek in on Justine. She is still sleeping deeply beneath her intricate quilt. The seams are separating on this one too. Maybe I can help her sew them up.

I'm thinking this as I shut the door and remember the little rectangle of cloth she was working on when I arrived.

Curious, I go back out onto the porch. I pick up the little rectangle and drape it open across my hands.

It's a banner, not any longer or wider than a shoebox, bordered in red with frayed gold fringe at the bottom. At the center of the banner is a gold star.

"That's the one thing she pulled out of that trunk."

I start at the sound of Tom's voice just behind me. I turn, lifting up the banner. "What is it?"

"A flag to hang in your window when your soldier got killed." Tom clears his throat, suddenly uncomfortable. "You haven't heard of the Gold Star Wives?"

I shake my head. Carefully, Tom sets the banner back on the porch railing, right where Justine left it. "It's the organization she joined after Owen was killed. It's for folks whose spouses get killed while they're serving. She was one of the first members, back in forty-five."

I remember the newspaper article then—how it said Justine was the leader of the local chapter of the GSW. Gold Star Wives, I guess.

"She's still on their mailing list. We got a letter just the other day. She's fixing to get to a meeting in the city soon as she's able. I'd drive her, of course."

"Can I come?"

Tom looks at me. "You'd want to?" Something in my expression answers his question, and he says, "You better talk to Linda then."

I roll my eyes. "I think Linda's got other things to think about right now."

Tom laughs. "You finally caught on, huh?"

● ● ●

I'm doing my hair for work when I have my first opportunity to talk to Linda.

I'd pass, to be perfectly honest. But she knocks on my bedroom door and then comes in before I can invite her.

"Well, look who's here," I say, regarding her in my mirror.

Linda frowns. "I came back. Isn't that what family is about? Family always comes back."

"FYI, *Justine* just came back." I finish off my second braid and secure it with a black band, then whirl away from my mirror and face Linda. "Justine is waiting for you, and she might not have much time." I let out a snort. "A lot of people seem to be waiting for you these days, wondering what you're up to."

With a weary huff, Linda drops down on my bed. She plants her elbows on her knees. Still in her work uniform from yesterday, having worked the lunch shift already today, she looks more than a little grimy. "I won't let that happen again." She shakes her head. "I got carried away. I know it sounds stupid, but we didn't do anything except talk. We sat at the bar all night." She rubs that sore spot in her neck. "My aching back."

I roll my eyes, though Linda is staring at the floor now and won't see. "You could have called."

"I should have. I don't know when I've felt like this, Penelope. It's the first time, I think. It took Isaac and me completely by surprise. I'm all confused. He's all confused. I'm—"

"'*Confused.*' Uh-uh." I shake my finger at her. "I've tried that excuse. Didn't work so well."

"If you're talking about David," Linda says quietly, "it was just so soon after that thing in Chicago. I was making sure you were safe. That's all."

"'That thing in Chicago?'" I have to laugh. "I got hurt in Chicago. I made a lot of bad choices, and ultimately I got really hurt. How well do you know Isaac? I mean, really?" I stalk around the room, suddenly enraged. "You might be making a bad choice too."

Linda glares. "I haven't done a thing with Isaac."

"I'm not talking about Isaac now. I'm talking about Justine."

Linda claps her hands to her forehead. "Oh, for heaven's sake, Penelope!"

"You're making a mistake, and—" I point at the clock on my desk. "Now we're late for work."

Linda glances at the clock. She stares at the photo of Justine there and then opens her mouth to speak.

But I cut her off. "Don't say another word."

For once, Linda doesn't. Instead, she gets to her feet and stumbles from my room, exhausted.

• • •

At work all the tables are full, even though it's still only five o'clock, and hordes of people are lined up at the bar and at the door. Caitlin is in her element, taking names, raking in tips. Pretty soon I've kicked into gear too.

As I pocket a particularly juicy tip, it hits me. This isn't just about getting through the summer anymore. I really am making money for college. And I kind of like the work.

By the end of the night, though, I'm wiped out.

Caitlin has already cleaned up and prepped her stations for tomorrow. Her family has plans tonight—some sibling's birthday party—so she's heading home. It sounds like Jules is busy too. Linda is in the kitchen with Isaac. I go over to Tom, who's wiping down the bar.

"How was she when you left?" I ask.

Tom frowns. "She was still sleeping. I just hope she remembered to eat when she woke up."

I think of Justine, her thin frame. Tom scrubs vigorously at a sticky spot. He scrubs and scrubs until I reach out and grab the rag, stopping its swift revolutions. Now he looks up.

"Go check on her." I'm suddenly breathless with fear. "I can finish here. Remember, I'm good at cleaning too." He starts to shake his head, and I blurt out, "And you're good at taking care of her. So please go. For me."

●●●

I go slowly, finishing up for Tom. I do it right.

I'm taking off my apron when I see inside the pocket—my cell phone, flashing.

The call was from David. How could I have missed him? I sit down at the bar and listen to his message. It's garbled and shaky. Sometimes his voice is so distorted that it doesn't sound like him at all. He sounds like a machine. He sounds like an animal. He sounds really, really afraid.

I play the message again, making sure I heard right.

"Penna, pick up. Please pick—I gotta talk to someone. I gotta—Oh, I'm just gonna tell you. I was on the truck and saw—a wire. It was going through this lump by the road. I was thinking IED. The Buffalo moved in—stopped.

That lump? Dead body. A person murdered—bound, gagged, blindfolded, wired to blow, dumped, facedown. A kid. A little kid. Where are you, Penna? Where *are*—"

Even the second time through, the loud static and whistling at the end of his call takes me so by surprise that I have to yank the phone from my ear.

"Penelope?"

I turn at the sound of Linda's voice. She's come up behind me. She's watching me, worried. Isaac is just behind her, and he looks worried too.

"Mom?" I say. It's the first time I've called her that in months. Now that I've started, I can't seem to stop. "Mom?"

"Penelope? What's wrong?" She puts her hand to her mouth. "Oh God."

I shake my head. "He's okay." I can't seem to stop shaking my head. "But could you take me home now? Please? I want to go home so bad."

"Let's go." Without another word, Linda wraps her arms around me. It's like she's been waiting for this—waiting to be my mom again. In the VW, I babble something about David. I babble something about Justine. It's not clear what I'm saying, even I know that. But Linda doesn't ask for clarification. It's like for once she knows that the last thing I need now is a question. I've got too many questions already.

Home again, she leads me from the car into the house. While she makes some chamomile tea, I text Ravi.

Heard from David? Anything at all? I'm scared.

If Ravi can admit he's scared, I can too. I know he's working. I probably won't hear from him until tomorrow. That's okay. No matter what David says, any news, any time is better than no news at all.

But Ravi does text me back. Right away.

— 178 —

On break. Haven't heard from D. He wrote 1 email from
Kuwait. That's all. You ok?

A little scared. But ok.

I text this back. I *am* as okay as I can be, because now Linda is beside me,
a steaming cup of tea in her hand. She slowly steers me toward my bedroom.
She situates me under Plum Tumble. She hands me the cup of tea. I drink
a few sips, then set the cup on my nightstand. I sink down into bed. Linda
lies beside me. *She's still here*, I think, finally drifting toward sleep. She came
back with me. This is what families do. They come back.

Come back, I think as I close my eyes.

Eighteen

Next morning I wake to my cell ringing. I can't reach for it through my dream of tanks plowing toward children and David standing in the way.

Somehow the receiver gets thrust against my ear. I hear Tom's voice.

"She's asking to go for a ride. She wants to see some of the old places. You want to come?"

I blink.

There's a murmur from beside me in the bed. I start, realizing Linda's still lying there. She's the one who put the receiver to my ear. Her eyes are closed. She's fallen back asleep. Quickly, I slip my hand under my pillow and slide my list of reasons—Why I Fell in Love with David and Why It's a Good Thing I Did—away from Linda. Funny, I haven't thought about that list in days. Still, I don't exactly want her finding it. I extricate the phone from between Linda's fingers and turn away from her toward the window. "I'll come."

"Pick you up in half an hour," Tom says and hangs up.

I study the familiar curve of Linda's hip, the dip at her waist, the slope of her shoulder. I could be little again, seeking my mother after a restless night, pressing against her spine or spooning into her belly. Whenever Linda woke, she was always glad I was there. She'd hold me closer, tell me stories, listen to mine. It wasn't so long ago that we did this. I'd forgotten. I'm glad I remembered.

I pull myself out of bed, check my cell. There's another message from Ravi.

You want to talk?

I text Ravi back:

Soon.

● ● ●

I sit between Tom and Justine. In comparison to Tom, Justine barely takes up any space. I'm trying not to think about David's message last night. The panic in his voice, the things he said. I can hardly breathe, thinking about it. I'm so afraid.

Justine is staring out the window. "So much has changed. But then there are other things—oh my goodness, like that weather vane—that are exactly the same."

I watch her watching Killdeer roll by and try to feel reassured. *She's here now. I wanted this. I wanted her to come home. She did. David will too.* I tell myself this over and over again.

Tom ends up taking us out on the road that David and I always used to drive, looping through the outskirts of Killdeer and into the country. We're approaching the bankrupt shopping mall when Justine rolls her window down all the way. She rests her arms on the frame like a little girl. Her gossamer-fine hair whips back in the wind, revealing her scalp. "I'm looking for something," she says. "I'll know it when I see it." She grasps at the window frame until the pink beds of her fingernails turn white.

"Look!" Just past the mall's parking lot, she points out at a big tree, shading the vacant JCPenney. "I climbed that." She reaches across me and grabs Tom's arm. "Oh, Owen. Do you remember?"

I look at Tom, who looks at Justine, who looks at Tom.

"What did I just say?" Justine asks.

"Never mind." Tom tries to smile. "Tell us about the tree."

Justine nods, relieved. "Pull over," she says. "Please."

So Tom turns into the empty parking lot and drives right up to the big old tree—the kind of blackjack oak I'd never seen before I moved here and David showed me.

Justine clasps her hands tightly to her chest. "I'm almost positive this is it."

I lean forward to get a better view of the tree. The bark is rough and very dark, nearly black, cracked and broken into small pieces. It looks almost charred, like it's been struck by lightning, but somehow it has managed to thrive.

"This was the tree between our farms. I'm almost sure of it. It's where Owen and I first met, the day his family moved to Killdeer. We were just kids. We were playing right here, not even knowing each other was close by. It's like yesterday. It's clearer than yesterday!" She laughs.

"What happened then?" I want to hear everything. I want her yesterdays.

"That mean old bull from the ranch down the road got loose and charged us! We ran smack-dab into each other, stumbling for this very oak. We scrambled up it and tucked ourselves out of reach. The bull gored the trunk, but the oak held strong. Finally the bull wandered off to another part of the field, but it was most of the afternoon before someone came and herded him home, so we had plenty of time to get acquainted."

Justine looks out at the oak as if it's a long-lost relative. "When we finally climbed down, I showed Owen the little violets I loved best, nestled over there in the shady spot near the creek." She smiles, remembering. "We picked violets from that very bed so that I could carry them on our wedding day. On our honeymoon we hung them from the Ford's rearview mirror. By the time we came home from South Dakota, they were dried into a tight little fist of flowers." Justine frowns. "I put that bouquet somewhere. I just know it."

"Maybe in the cedar chest?" Tom asks.

And Justine says, "Oh, maybe that's where it is. Let's go look. Right now!"

But then she heaves open the truck's door and steps carefully out into the parking lot. She goes over to the oak and touches the trunk. She shows Tom and me the ancient marks there, deep gouges in the cracked, black bark that very well could have been made by the horns of an angry bull.

●●●

We drive back to Tom's house, Justine remembering all the way. "Every fellow in the town was serving back then," she recalls. "Felt it was his duty."

Tom turns down the street to his house. He says, "I knew I had to serve too. No matter the consequences."

David, I think. David.

I was on the truck, looking through my binoculars when I saw it. A wire. It was going through this lump by the road.

A kid. A little kid.

What are the consequences of seeing something like that?

●●●

Tom leads Justine and me out onto the back porch. The Gold Star banner is still draped over the porch railing. I study Justine's thin, lined face. She's looking weary now too.

Tom gestures to an old cedar chest, shoved off in a corner. "There she blows."

"You can stay," Justine says, as Tom turns to go.

He shakes his head and claps his hand to his gut. "We need to eat. At least, I do. How do BLTs sound?"

Without waiting for an answer, he heads off toward the kitchen.

For a moment Justine looks confused. She grasps the porch railing for support. "I have to sit down," she says. I take her arm and lower her into the rocker. She relaxes there, resting her head on the wooden back. She closes her eyes then, and as soon as they're closed, her mouth opens. She's asleep.

I wait for a few moments. I shift my weight, but Justine doesn't awaken. So finally I squat down beside the cedar chest. I lift the lid.

The smell of cedar wafts up. Then there's another odor I don't like nearly so much: mildew and mold. I sneeze once, twice, and open my eyes to Justine, who's bending over, nearly tipping in the rocker, so that she can look inside too.

"Careful!" I catch hold of the rocking chair's arm.

"Bring it all out," she says. "Everything."

Here's what's inside:

1. A yellowed obituary, circa 1945, with a small photograph of a hand-some, dark-haired young man.

2. A bundle of church programs tied together with a faded blue ribbon.

3. Two halves of a broken globe.

4. A dark blue silk dress—the same one with the pearly buttons, neat collar, and capped sleeves that she wears in the photograph beside my clock.

5. A cardboard tube filled with what look to be sketches.

6. A shoebox full of black-and-white photographs.

7. A U.S. flag, folded neatly into a tight, thick triangle.

8. A tarnished bugle.

9. A bunch of dried flowers, mostly disintegrated now—but still it's clear they once were violets.

10. Another letter, this one tucked into an unaddressed envelope.

I start with the yellowed newspaper article. I read it out loud to Justine, who stares out into Tom's backyard, listening.

"'To our great sadness, yet another of our brave Killdeer boys made the ultimate sacrifice. Our beloved Owen Delmore was killed while deactivating a mine in the vicinity of Oppenheim, Germany. His young wife, Justine (née Blue), survives him.'"

Then I show Justine the stack of programs from Owen's service at the First Baptist Church. They played "At the Cross" and "When the Saints Go Marching In." Justine dedicated a memorial to Owen.

"For the life of me," she says quietly, "I can't remember that day or any memorial."

We study the two halves of the broken globe, and there, near the banks of the Rhine River, she points out the black X where Owen died.

"His hands were always so cold in the minefields, so I knitted him gloves," she says.

She turns Owen's bugle over and over in her hands. Slowly, slowly, so they don't rip, I tug the sketches from the cardboard tube. The old paper smells like dust and lead.

"That was life," Justine says wonderingly, riffling through the drawings.

She drew the Killdeer she knew—those old buildings and the landscape that David first showed me. Honey locust leaves. The gnarled oak, gored in the trunk. Oil rigs. Water towers. The viaduct, minus my killdeer. Our little house. But mostly Justine drew Owen—sitting in the cockpit of a plaster airplane, holding a bugle to his lips, climbing a tree, standing with his fists on his hips.

Her Owen is very like the Owen in old photographs. I know this because I take the photographs from the shoebox, and we study those too. Owen is Clark Gable handsome, with shining black hair and a thin black mustache accenting a wide grin. He looks comfortable with himself, leaning casually against things, hip cocked, one foot crossed over the other. In some of the photographs he wraps his arms around Justine's shoulders or waist. He looks smitten.

Justine nods at the blue silk dress. "It would look lovely on you. Would you like to try it on?"

I dash to her yellow bedroom, close the door, and put on the blue silk dress. There are only a few small moth holes. It fits nearly perfectly. I go back to Justine and she laughs, shaking her head in amazement. But it's Tom who, seeing me, cries out in surprise and nearly drops the plates of BLTs.

"You're a ghost," Tom says.

We eat out on the porch then, but Tom can't seem to get comfortable, eyeing me warily, like I just might say boo.

After Tom has cleared away our plates, Justine points to the blank envelope.

"Open that," she says. So I do. When I start to skim it, she gives my shoulder a rap. "No more secrets."

So I read the letter out loud, so we both can hear.

> *Dear Owen,*
>
> *Today is the anniversary of your death. Twenty years gone. I am a middle-aged woman, almost forty. You would not recognize me. I sometimes think this, but mostly I believe you would know me anywhere.*
>
> *I allowed myself to write this only today. I wanted to tell you that a week ago I received your ring. They found it near a riverbed in Germany.*
>
> *I want you to know that the inscription is still there, the words we chose, engraved in gold. I want you to know that just when I had given up hoping for you, a little piece of you came back to me.*
>
> *I cannot wear your ring on my finger or on a chain around my neck. I am married—I have been for ten years. I have the recent surprise of a little daughter. I've been raising a boy for some years too. He came into this house needy only a few years after you left it.*
>
> *I never thought I would be a wife again, Owen, or a mother either. Somehow this has happened. I am still in Killdeer, where we vowed we would never stay.*

I have hidden your ring in a place no one will find it. There it will remain, buried again.

I cannot lie: I've tried to write you before. I've failed, either because of my lack of fortitude or because Ernest came upon me or the baby cried. Linda, that's what he named her. I never had much of a say, but I like her name well enough. Ernest and Linda are better off without me, Owen. That's what I think.

Oh, what am I to do?

Someday I will dig up your ring and give it to someone who will remember you, even after I'm gone.

Always yours, as you are always mine—

Justine

I fold the letter and put it back into the blank envelope. I hold this out to Justine, but she doesn't notice. She's gazing out into the backyard at something I can't see.

"That's what I was looking for."

Pink has risen in her deeply lined cheeks. She looks at me. She tells me exactly where the ring is.

Nineteen

"It's okay," I tell Tom when he looks wary. "Linda's already at work. I'm ninety-nine percent sure."

"Call and check." Tom sounds really nervous.

I was right. Linda's helping Isaac shuck corn for today's lunch special.

So Tom drives Justine and me to my house. "Watch, I'll lose my job over this," he says on the way, only half joking.

"I *hope* I lose my job over this."

But Tom doesn't laugh. And I realize it's not funny. I want to keep my job too. And I want to keep peace with Linda.

Tom parks in the driveway. As he helps Justine from his truck, I find a spade in the garage. Then I go to the honey locust tree that grows just outside my bedroom window. With Tom and Justine watching, I start to dig. The clay is hard and dry. It takes some effort, breaking it into hunks and heaving it aside. In the summer heat, I'm soon sweating hard.

But then there, about two feet down, is a little black leather box, coated in red dust.

Justine gasps. "That's it."

I drop the spade, grab the box, and hold it out to Justine. But she shakes her head.

"You open it."

"You sure?"

She nods.

The box's lid, caked with clay, resists at first. Then suddenly the spring gives. The lid snaps up. Inside, tucked into a fold of black velvet, is a thick gold band.

Justine cries out. Tom puts his arm around her.

Carefully I draw the band from the box. There's the inscription engraved inside: *Always yours as you are always mine.* I hold the band out to Justine, but again she shakes her head. She's weeping now. She steps away from both of us. She makes it to the honey locust tree. She leans against its trunk.

"I remember now," she says, "the hurt when this came to me. All those years, I never had a dog tag or a tooth or a chip of bone. Nothing. And then there was his ring, out of the blue like that. Once I'd buried it, I knew there was no use waiting anymore. He really was gone. I lived his death all over again, only worse because I wasn't numb. I felt it."

"It was a bad time then," Tom says quietly. "But you're here *now*, with us."

Justine shakes her head. "Not Linda."

Tom frowns. "Maybe not. But look." He gestures at me. He slaps his hand against his broad chest. "*Look.*"

Justine looks. "Yes," she says.

"Good girl," Tom says.

My cell phone shrills like some kind of bad joke. I nearly drop the little black box and the ring too, snatching my cell from the pocket of my shorts. I flip it open to silence it, but then I see David's number.

"I have to get this." I give the box and ring to Tom. I say something into the phone to David. "Wait. Hold on," I say. And then I say, "Hi."

"Penna," David says. "You're there."

"I'm here. Where else would I be? I'm not going anywhere. I promise."

David is quiet for a moment. Then he says, "This isn't a test."

I suck in a breath. "Good. I mean, I know that."

"I was just talking to my mom, and she gave me this idea, and I had to call you. That's all."

There's a movement from Justine, and I glance up. She's leaning against Tom now.

"Can you make it?" Tom asks. Justine nods, and Tom helps her across the front yard to the porch. He lowers her onto a step, and when she's safely sitting, he hunkers down beside her there.

"Penna? Did you hear me?"

"Yes." I nod hard like David can see. "Go ahead. Tell me."

"You sure you have time?"

This feels like a test. "Of course!"

"Well, okay. Here's the thing." He laughs again, a nervous sound, low in his throat. "Remember that last night when I was home, and Linda said I should let you all know if I need anything?"

I nod again like he can see. "I just sent you a care—"

But he interrupts me. "Well, here's what I'm thinking I need. Toys. Send lots of toys. They don't have to be brand-new or anything. My mom says she knows of some great thrift stores, and she's going to talk to people at church, and she thinks they'll donate. Maybe you can find some too? And kids' books and clothes. Get the basics too—baby soap, toothpaste, diapers. Kids' medicine would be good too, I bet. Like baby aspirin, cough syrup. I hear a lot of bad coughing." He laughs again, and from the air that rushes through the phone, I get the feeling he's pacing. "I haven't even told you what it's all for, have I?"

I start pacing too. "Go ahead."

"We're at that orphanage nearly every day—we're all obsessed now. It's like another *family* here almost. And I figure there's so much stuff just rotting in closets back home. If we could get some of it over here, that little girl—the one in the red dress—she'd feel like she'd won the lottery. Not to mention all the other kids."

My heart is beating so hard that I'm sure David can hear it. I'm glad that he's doing this. I feel the gladness welling up in me, but tears are welling up in me too.

I may be holding on to him, but is he holding on to me?

David clears his throat. "So you'll help?"

I stop pacing. I draw a line in the red clay with the toe of my shoe, and then I step over it. "I can put up a sign at work. When school starts, I bet I can have a clothes drive or something there." I'm thinking Jules will be all over this. Caitlin and Ravi will probably help too.

"Great! My mom has all the information about how and where to send stuff. You guys talk. You can work it out, right? And check your email in a little bit. You'll see what I'm talking about."

Before I can respond, he's hung up.

I slip my phone back into my pocket. I stare at the hole I just dug in the ground. From where I'm standing, I can't see the bottom.

"You okay?" Tom asks.

I look at Tom and Justine, still sitting together on the step. I walk over to them and sit down on the other side of Justine. Now I'm the one leaning into her.

"Here," she says after a moment, shifting a bit so that I have to sit up again. "I want you to have this," she says.

She takes the slender gold chain from her neck and threads it through Owen's ring. Then she tries to clasp the chain around my neck. Her fingers can't do this, so mine do.

Owen's ring is a warm weight against the hollow at the base of my throat. Justine touches the ring gently, and I feel its impression on my skin.

"Remember everything, will you?" Justine asks.

"Always," I say.

●●●

A few minutes later Tom decides it's time to leave. He helps Justine into his pickup. By the time he's pulled out into the street, she's asleep in the front seat. I clasp the ring around my neck, watching them drive away. I've always wanted a gift from a grandma. I go into the house, the ring shifting against my skin with every step. I suppose I'll get used to that. I *hope* I'll get used to that, though maybe I should hope the opposite. Maybe every move I make should feel like an act of remembering.

Or would that be too much weight?

I call David's house and leave a message for Bonnie. "Just checking in. David told me about his idea. Let's talk soon, okay?"

I start to pull up my email, but then I can't take my eyes off my screen saver. There's David, lying in the middle of the big old heart he scratched out of the dust. *This* David I can hold on to.

I check my inbox.

David has sent me another photograph of himself, this time with the little girl in the red dress. She's covered with bandages. She looks like she could be David's little sister. She's beautiful.

David is crouched beside her in the photograph, holding her close. He's lost weight. I don't need a great memory to figure this out. I just need to click back to my screen saver. Now, in comparison to then, his uniform hangs loose on his limbs. If it weren't a tattoo, that ring would slip right off his finger. He's not looking at the camera. He's smiling at the little girl. But even in profile like that, I can tell his face is gaunt.

What happened to bagels? What happened to pizza? What happened to MRE—those Meals, Ready-to-Eat, prepared with care by the U.S. Army? Growing up with Bonnie for a mom, David's learned not to be a snob about food. David loves food. He eats like a horse. He only loses his appetite when he's anxious or sad or…what? Or worse, maybe, where he is now. Before big tests he never wanted to eat. Before soccer games. Before he left for OSUT. Even before he left for Iraq. Those chocolate-chip bagels that last morning—that was the most I saw him eat during his whole ten-day pass.

He drops weight fast when he doesn't eat.

David's attached another drawing to today's email as well.

In this drawing, superhero Manga David is straddling a tiny mosque, his arms outstretched. He's trying to catch the pieces of a veiled woman, blown sky-high.

His email is short and to the point.

> Dear Penna,
>
> A picture's worth a thousand words. Right?
>
> I thought I'd come here and learn something about life? How to be a better person? How to be a hero? How to *something*? There are no how-to manuals here.
>
> You all think the war is over back home, don't you? Well, for some of us, it's just begun.
>
> If it weren't for the little girl in the red dress, I'd go crazy. She reminds me there's good in the world, good I can do.
>
> David

I feel like the room is pressing in, tight and close. I feel panicky. I have to do something.

I email Caitlin, Jules, and Ravi. I tell them about the children in Iraq, the orphanages there. I ask them if they'll help collect donations.

Without hesitation, they all agree.

●●●

When Linda picks me up for work, she grimaces at the ring around my neck. Then she looks pointedly the other way.

I think she knows who gave it to me.

I think she's picking her battles.

As soon as I walk in the door of Red Earth, Tom beckons me over to a booth.

"I'm worried," he says.

I'm worried too. I feel edgy with worry. *If it weren't for the little girl, he'd go crazy...* These are the words running through my head now. If it weren't for Caitlin, Jules, and Ravi, promising to help me, I don't know what I'd do. And now here's Tom, worried, which means something's up with Justine, which means I'd better sit down. Right here. Right now.

I sink down in the booth. "Worried about what?"

Tom sits down across from me. "She was really out of it when I left. It was like she was living in the past. I mean, really in the past. Seeing it. Hearing it. Feeling it. I've seen hallucinations like that before, but that was back in Nam, when guys were dropping some crazy stuff." With a jerk of his head, he indicates Linda, who's busy packing the salad bar with ice. "I think we should give them a chance before it's too late."

"Now?" The word squeaks out of me.

"Soon."

"Tonight?" Another squeak.

"No way Justine could do it tonight. I'm hoping tomorrow night."

What can I do but nod? It's what I want too, right?

I throw myself into my job, trying to think of nothing else. I talk to Caitlin every chance I get too, or rather I listen as she talks about a guy she's been wanting to ask her out, who just did. She's going on a date with him tonight, or else she'd love to do something with me. Jules is free, though. Maybe Jules and I can get together and make flyers for a clothes and toy drive. Caitlin thinks this is a great idea. If we do it, she'll help us distribute them tomorrow.

I think this is a great idea too, but when I text Jules, she says she's feeling wiped out. Sick. "Let's talk on the phone, though," she says.

In a way I'm relieved. Maybe I'll just go home and get some sleep. I have a feeling I'm going to need it.

Linda tells me that I can take the VW. Isaac will drive her home. Her face is pale with worry, saying this. Like I might just let loose on her for all kinds of reasons—old and new.

I feel the weight of the ring around my neck, and I remember what's important.

I manage to smile at Linda. I tell her it's okay.

If she asks about Justine, I'll find a way to tell her that will be okay too.

• • •

That night I talk to Jules on the phone for a long time. She tells me more about Zach, filling me in on his looks, his hopes, his strengths and weaknesses. I think she might be feeling run-down because she's missing him so much. I know the feeling. I let her talk and talk. I know that someday she'll probably do the same for me.

We talk a bit about what we'll do for the orphanage too. Jules goes to a big church. She knows she'll get a lot of help from them. "There's money there," she says. "And even the people who don't have money like to pitch in for things like this. Especially if we're talking hand-me-downs."

"Which we are," I say. "Except for medicine and stuff like that. Let's hit the wealthy folks up for formula and diapers."

We agree this is a good plan.

When we hang up, I try Ravi, but of course he's working, so he doesn't answer.

And Caitlin's on her big date.

So I pull out all of David's old letters from last year, and I read them all, from beginning to end.

He sounds so young, I realize. He sounds like a different guy.

And the person on the other end, receiving them? She was young too. She was a different girl.

Twenty

Linda shakes me awake the next morning. She's upset, an anxious furrow between her eyes.

"Tom called. He's busy for some mysterious reason. Can't work the lunch shift like he said he would. There's a special party, some kid's baptism or something. Isaac really needs our help."

We throw ourselves together and fly out the door into the VW.

Red Earth is crowded with people in church clothes. They gravitate toward the center of their universe, at least for today. A glowing baby in a long, white silky gown, cradled in the arms of her equally glowing mother.

The lunch-shift server, a twenty-something, sandy-haired hunk named Josh, who's in the business track at Killdeer Community College, welcomes us with relief. "Isaac is up to his elbows in parsley," Josh says. "He keeps asking me to help him garnish. I don't have time to garnish."

So while Linda manages the bar and oversees the floor, I help Isaac garnish. And dice, splice, chop, grate. And wash knives, whisks, spatulas, and tongs. And load the dishwasher. And fetch tall glasses of ice water for both of us.

We work efficiently. We treat each other respectfully. We are a team.

I have to admit that I can see why Linda would fall for a guy like this.

He's pretty much a champ in the kitchen, and he's not arrogant about that fact at all.

Plus, he's got those dreads.

The baptism party is happy. The diners are happy. Isaac's happy, and so are Linda and Josh.

And me. I have to admit it.

"Satisfaction at a job well done." That's what Linda says we're feeling.

If so, I want David to feel this way, over there. I want to help him feel this way.

I'll put up that sign at work tonight. I'll make one for Jules's church too.

YOU CAN HELP!

One of our own Killdeer soldiers is calling for donations:
Gently used kids' clothes, shoes, toys, and baby supplies
needed for the Iraqi orphanage near where he now serves.
Pediatric medicine, baby formula, and cloth or
disposable diapers deeply appreciated.

● ● ●

Linda and I take a break. We go home. She cleans up for the dinner shift. I grab poster board and markers and make not two signs, but seven. In addition to the one I'll put up at Red Earth, I'll put a sign in the library. One in the community center. One in the other big church in town. I'll give one to Jules and one to Caitlin and one to Ravi.

Just as we're about to leave, Caitlin texts Linda and me both. She's freaking out because Tom still hasn't showed.

Justine, I think. Tom's getting her ready. He'll bring her tonight.

I roll up the sign for Red Earth and secure it with a rubber band. And once again Linda and I fly out the door and into the VW.

"He's never late," Linda says, turning a corner so fast that the tires squeal. "This is just not like him. He'd better have shown up by the time we get there, or I don't know what I'm going to do. Oh, Penna." Now her real concern shows. "I hope nothing's wrong with him. He's just so reliable. You know?"

I nod.

When we arrive, Caitlin is placating Happy Hour folks with free Cokes. Linda gets to work behind the bar. I slap my poster up on the wall by the old, broken jukebox, and then I get to work taking appetizer orders. All the while, my heart thuds. *Maybe* Tom's getting Justine ready. Or maybe, just maybe, something bad has happened to her. I've got to find a way to get in touch with Tom. But Red Earth just keeps getting more crowded, and Caitlin is looking at me in sheer desperation, and I need to keep taking those orders.

I'm at the coffeemaker, filling two cups with coffee, when I hear Linda swear. I turn and look at her. She's holding two overflowing steins of beer, very much the St. Pauli Girl gone all wrong, what with the spilled suds foaming on her hands and the bar. She looks up and sees me seeing.

"Look at this place." Linda's voice is too loud. Now a few customers are noticing. She slams the sudsy steins down on the bar and sweeps her arms wide, gesturing at the crowd, the growing line at the door. "And I don't know a Manhattan from a margarita."

I go over to her, speak quietly, trying to calm her down. "You called his house again, right? If Tom's not there, he's probably on his way." *With her,* I think. *Please, with her, because if he's not with her, then something is really wrong.* I swallow the knot in my throat.

Linda doesn't seem to hear me. She is frantically fumbling among the liquor bottles. So I go over to take an order from a couple in the corner. They've been waiting for a while, it looks like, from the way they've set their closed menus close to the edge of the table. Looks like Caitlin hasn't watered them yet either.

It's only when I've set their glasses of water down that I realize the couple is Bonnie and Beau.

"Surprise!" Bonnie smiles up at me.

"I heard I missed you the other day." Beau stands and gives me a quick hug.

I'm so glad to see them. There's so much I want to ask them. I glance around Red Earth—the growing chaos. Obviously now is not the time for the things I want to say. Things like *Is he really okay? His drawings are scaring me. I think he's lost weight. What do you think is really going on?*

"David said he talked to you about his idea for the orphanage. Don't you think it's a great idea?" Bonnie's round face is flushed to the roots of her blond hair. Breathless, she waves the conversation on to Beau.

"We needed a project. It's a real stress reliever, I've got to admit," he says.

I point at the sign by the jukebox, and they both exclaim their approval.

They rattle on then about their house and how it's already turned into a maze of boxes and bags, all filled with everything an orphanage could need. They'd love my help in organizing it all.

"You think our place was a mess before?" Bonnie says.

"You should see it now," Beau says.

"I could come over tomorrow," I say. "Maybe around—"

There's a crash and then Linda screams.

I tear across the room, dodging tables, crunching through glass to where Linda lies on her side on the floor in front of the bar, a cocktail tray spinning like a gyroscope above her head.

I crouch down, Owen's ring dangling at my throat. But Linda won't care about it now. She won't even notice it. Her eyes are closed. Her face is white. Her breathing is fast and shallow.

Caitlin drops down beside me, then yelps and leaps up again, plucking a piece of glass from her knee.

"Call nine-one-one," I say hoarsely.

"It's my fault."

I know this frail voice. It's Justine's. I look up and see her wavering above me in her white dress.

"No," Tom says quickly, moving close to Justine. "*I* never should have brought you here." He looks at me. "We were at urgent care most of today. Some new issues. But she wanted so much to come here tonight, and the doctor said she could try." He shakes his head. "It's my fault—not calling, not explaining. I just wasn't thinking right."

But I know it was my idea to begin with. I'm the one who made things even worse than they were before.

Linda moans. I feel like I might freak out, which will make things worse yet. *Breathe in. Breathe out.* I turn back to Linda. I put my hand to her forehead. Her skin is clammy. From the corner of my eye, I see the vague blur of Caitlin's arm. She's gesturing so frantically that I have to look. There's an ice tub, tipped upside down on the floor. Some of what I thought was glass is ice.

"I thought I'd set it right on the bar." Caitlin twists a purple lock of her hair around and around her finger. "Misjudged that one by a mile. It spilled all over the place. Linda happened to walk by just at that moment, and wham. All that ice—she slipped."

Customers crowd around us now. There's a hand on my shoulder—Bonnie, peering down anxiously. And there's Beau, standing behind her.

"Nine-one-one," I tell them.

Beau pulls out his cell phone.

Linda's eyelids flutter open. She winces as Isaac crouches beside me. He takes Linda's left hand in his. He presses his fingertips to her wrist and starts counting beats. Tears are streaming into Linda's hair now.

"Don't move. Your ankle is broken," Isaac says.

That's when I see the odd angle Linda's right ankle makes, just below the hem of her black pants.

Linda groans, her voice lower than I ever knew it could go.

"It'll be all right," I hear myself say.

Isaac shakes his head. "Forget the ambulance. I'll take her."

I look at him. "How?"

"That tray. Get it," Isaac orders.

The round cocktail tray has stopped spinning. It lies flat on the floor. I grab it and hold it out to Isaac. He tells me to slide the tray under Linda's ankle. "Gently," he says. "It's important to keep the bone stable while we get her to my truck."

"I don't know," I say.

"Do it," Justine says.

I nod. Isaac braces Linda's ankle, lifting it slightly so that I can slip the tray beneath. Linda howls, an unearthly sound. Gritting my teeth, I slide the tray under the broken bone, and Linda lets out another cry.

"Hold on tight to that tray," Isaac tells me. "I'm going to lift her. When I stand, you stand too. Whatever you do, keep her steady."

The next moment, we stand. Isaac cradles Linda in his arms. I bear her on the tray.

"Linda." Justine's voice is full of longing.

Linda casts a wild look in Justine's direction. "*You*." There's venom in the word.

"Hush, now," Isaac says.

Linda moans. Justine leans against Tom.

"Coming through," Isaac says. He's not even breathing hard, carrying all one hundred and thirty-plus pounds of Linda.

She's out cold suddenly, her head lolling against his shoulder. She's never been that good with pain. Once, back in Ohio, she was working way too late after her shift at the bank, using a weed whacker on the ugly mass of yews that bordered our apartment building.

"Someone has to take a little pride in this place," she told me through the dusk. And then she dropped the weed whacker and cut the tip off her thumb. She howled like a she-wolf then too and passed out on the cold ground. I called the ambulance.

"Lucky you didn't lose your foot, working late like that when you're so tired," the ER doctor scolded her (and me too, I felt like). "But I'm always tired," Linda told him. "So what am I supposed to do?"

Somehow Isaac and I carry Linda out to Isaac's pickup. Somehow we lay her out across the backseat without that bone popping through her skin.

"She's going to be all right?" I ask.

Isaac looks at me. I'm crying. I didn't know it, but I am. His stern, handsome face softens.

"I'll take her right to the hospital. She'll be fine," he says. Then he says, "You, Caitlin, Tom? You all can close up shop?"

I press my hand to the sudden pang at the back of my neck. "Oh God."

"Do your mother proud," Isaac says.

● ● ●

I do it. We do it. Me, Caitlin, and Tom too, once he's taken Justine home again and returned. We do Linda proud.

Or if not proud, exactly, we serve everybody who still wants to have dinner in the restaurant. We feed them the best we can with the food we're able to lay our hands on—stuff that's already been prepared, mostly. Salads, soups, and cold sandwiches. Isaac always preps in advance, so we're able to dig into tomorrow's Irish stew too. Then we get the few people who stayed to pay up, and we get them out the door. We clean the place but good.

Once the restaurant is empty, Tom hunkers down on a stool in front of the TV, a tumbler of scotch in his hand. He's pretty much a basket case, he's so guilt ridden.

"I screwed up," he keeps saying.

I remind him for about the tenth time that it was my bad idea.

Caitlin shushes us both. "Lighten up, already. It'll be okay."

"Sure, thanks, right," we tell her, not bothering to explain about Justine.

"You kicked butt tonight," Caitlin tells me then.

"Nervous energy," I say, undoing the top button of my polo shirt and fiddling with the ring around my neck. When I slip my thumb through it, then it fits. Only then.

Only because of the honey hands in the freezer am I able to remember: David's hands are just about the size of Owen's.

●●●

I'm driving home in the VW when my cell rings. I fumble the phone out of my bag.

Isaac.

"Your mom made the mistake of eating a bowl of soup right before she fell. They have to wait to get all the food out of her system before they set the bone. It's going to be another two hours at least. They've got her on morphine, so she's pretty loopy, but she wants to talk to you."

I pull the VW over to the side of the road and turn off the engine. I can't hear her otherwise. Her voice is that wispy. She sounds far, far away.

"Hello, sweetie sweet."

I have to smile. She hasn't called me that since I was a little girl. "You okay?"

"Fine and dandy."

She tells me how the room looks where she is, the color of the curtains in the ER—golden chrysanthemum, she keeps saying, like that's terribly important—and the nurse's plastic sandals—bubblegum pink, and also important. There's a horrible taste in her mouth and her breath must stink, but Isaac is still by her side. She can't get over that.

"No one's ever stayed by my side but you, Penelope," she says. "Aren't you kind of relieved that for once it's him standing here? Not you?"

I stare out the bug-speckled windshield. Beyond the smear and guts, the dark sky arcs like a spangled bowl—immense beauty I can't yet clearly see. "As long as you're okay."

"It's no trouble, me being here, Linda," Isaac says from the background. "I told you that."

Linda tells me that what she wants is for me to get home safely and rest up. She already has it all figured out. I'm going to be her right-hand man. No, girl. No, woman. I'm going to be her right-hand young woman, because her right ankle is broken, and she's right-handed and footed too, so she's going to need assistance. She's going to need me every day by her side to keep the restaurant going, at least until school starts.

"Can you do that, and the night shift too?" Linda asks. "It's only a few weeks."

"Sure." I rest my head on the steering wheel, suddenly exhausted. How will I spend any time with Justine—the little time she may have left, according to Tom?

"Night, sweetie sweet," Linda says. "I love you."

"Me too," I say, but it's Isaac who answers, "I'll tell her that."

Twenty-One

Next day Isaac calls, bright and early. He and Linda didn't get out of the hospital until close to dawn. He just brought her back to his house. She's out cold now. Mid-afternoon he'll take a break from work, check on her. If she's up for it, he'll buzz her back home.

"I'll see you soon at Red Earth, right? The lunch shift?" he says.

I hear the worry and exhaustion in his voice. "I promised," I say.

I can sleep for about another hour. I lie back in bed. And there's a knock at the front door.

I close my eyes. Next thing I know, rocks hit my window.

That gets me out of bed. I go to the window, open it, and peer down through the honey locust branches.

Caitlin and Ravi stand at the base of the tree, looking up at me. She's holding a drink carrier, which holds three big cups of coffee. He's holding a paper bag.

Caitlin grins. "Meals on Wheels," she says.

They've brought breakfast burritos. We sit at the kitchen table, and immediately I wolf mine down. When I look up, they're both staring at me, open mouthed, their burritos barely touched.

"Guess you were hungry," Caitlin says.

I wipe my mouth with a napkin. "I've been eating a lot of weird stuff. On the fly. This is like the best thing I've eaten all summer."

Caitlin smirks. "I won't tell Isaac you said that."

"I need to have you over for dinner," Ravi says. "My sister is an amazing cook. She's teaching me. The three of us could cook together."

"And me!" Caitlin says.

Ravi smiles at her. "Sounds good."

I sit back and drink my coffee then and watch them eat. We talk a little bit about Linda's accident, but mostly we talk about nothing—movies we've seen, the fall season on television, which can't start soon enough. I give them their posters, and they promise they'll put them up right away. Ravi will find a way to post his at the Walmart—even if it's only in the break room. Caitlin has an idea about the factory where her father works.

"Speaking of which." I glance at the clock. I have to get ready right away, or I'll be late for the lunch shift.

It crosses my mind as they leave that Caitlin's special date might have been with Ravi. I feel something twist in my gut—not a nice feeling. But then I think, *You don't know that for sure.* And more importantly, *Friends, that's what you need, Penna. Just friends.*

• • •

I get to work by ten to prep for the first shift. Lunch turns out to be quieter, easier, and with Isaac's help not so bad. Really the restaurant seems like it can kind of run itself for a day or two. Isaac covers most of the nitty-gritty details, checking stock, opening the till. To his visible relief—the glaze lifting from his eyes, his shoulders straightening a bit—I do a good job, following his orders.

Josh is on top of his game today. He moves efficiently around the floor, slapping down drinks and food faster than Caitlin and me put together.

"Inspiring," I say as Josh whizzes past, balancing three entrees on his left arm and carrying two others in his right hand.

"Now don't get all motivational on me," he calls back over his shoulder.

At two thirty we close the place up. Josh heads off for a class; Isaac goes back to his house for Linda; and I drive the VW over to Tom's. He's sitting on the front porch, waiting for me. He stands as I approach the house, and when I see the set of his expression—stricken—I start to run. I take the porch steps two at a time, and at the top he catches my arm to keep me from falling with my momentum.

"What?"

He shakes his head. "I don't know. After yesterday I'm not messing around with urgent care. That was just intestinal distress yesterday. This is...I've put a call in to the doctor. The nurse said we might need to look into some kind of medication—the first of the real drugs, I guess. She's so depressed— hallucinating real bad. She thinks what she sees is real, no question about it. Seeing Linda like that pushed her into a bad place." Clumsily, Tom pats my shoulder. "You sure you want to come in?"

I nod.

"Sure?"

"Don't leave, okay?"

"Not a chance."

Tom leads me inside and down the narrow hallway to her bedroom.

Justine is curled into a ball on her bed, her back to the door. I hesitate only for a moment, and then I go to stand by her. Her eyes are open, she must know I'm there. But she doesn't look up at me. She doesn't even blink.

"Take it down," she says, swatting at the wall behind me.

I turn. There's nothing to see but yellow paint. When I turn back to Justine, she hides her face in the pillow. From its depths, she tells me again to take it down.

"What?" I glance at Tom.

"A picture." Tom shrugs helplessly. "That's what she told me earlier, at least. I think she means a poster, from the way she describes it."

"Down," Justine says.

I kneel beside the bed, trying to meet her eyes. But she won't lift her face from the pillow.

"What picture?" I keep my voice as quiet as I can.

She clenches the edge of the pillow until her knuckles whiten. "You can't see?"

"No."

"She's everywhere!"

"She who?"

Justine's bitter laugh is muffled. "A real beauty, that's who. A first-class calendar girl, with her auburn hair and hourglass figure. She gets the letters. She gets them, not me."

"What letters?"

Now Justine peers at me from beneath a white lock of hair. "Letters from her boy. I haven't gotten any from mine." Justine shifts her voice to a higher, biting register, apparently mimicking the calendar girl: "'Longing won't bring him home sooner. Get a war job!' Damn it, I got a war job! Isn't that enough? Why don't I have any letters?"

"Hush, now." I try to tuck Justine's hair behind her ear, but she jerks her head away and hides again in the pillow. Desperate, I look at Tom.

He leans heavily into the doorway. "She worked at a factory while Owen was overseas. She sewed American flags."

This is *not* my grandmother. I leap to my feet and run my hands over the wall. The paint is cool and smooth to my touch.

"There!" I give the wall a whack for good measure. "I took her down."

"Finally!" Justine sits up in bed, startling me. "Thank you."

"You're welcome." I glance at Tom, who nods. But when I look back at Justine, she's frowning.

She points at my throat, at Owen's ring dangling there. "Where'd you get that?"

I touch the ring. "From you."

"Oh." Justine pats at her cloud of hair, trying to smooth it, and her focus again seems to shift. "Could you?" she asks, still patting at her hair. Then she gestures vaguely at the nightstand, and I see the silver-backed brush there—the same one from the old photograph. Tentatively I settle down on the bed beside her and start to run the brush through her hair. I brush gently, so as not to hurt her scalp. When there are snarls, strands pull free and settle on the yellow bedspread and me.

"Where is he, exactly? That's what I want to know." Justine speaks softly now, calmed by the brush's gentle touch. "It's been nearly two months. I write him every night."

Justine's hair is perfectly smooth, except for the soft curls at the back of her neck. I make one last careful pass with the brush, and then I set it back on the nightstand.

"There," I say. "You look beautiful."

Justine glances at me, suddenly wary. "You sure? We can't be messy here. There's lots of girls far prettier than me looking for work. And that Mr. Schweitzer—well, he ain't no Albert Schweitzer, as we like to say. He likes the pretty girls."

I smile at her. "You'll keep your job."

"Cold comfort." But she smiles too. Then, just when I think she might be content, her glance shifts back to the wall. "For God's sake! Take her down."

So again I stand, reach up, and pull down nothing. Grudgingly, Justine thanks me. Then she shudders so violently that I catch hold of her arm, afraid she'll lose her balance on the bed. Justine pushes off my hold.

She claps her hands over her face. "When they told me—those two men in uniform standing at attention right outside my apartment on that cold and steely day—they brought me a flag. *I* sewed that flag. I *know* this. I sewed up my husband's death. And now I've lost it and every little bit of him. I've lost my flag."

I can feel her panic, fluttering like a bird at my throat, trapped just beneath Owen's ring. I try to pat her arm, but she bats me away and claps her hand back over her face.

"The cedar chest," Tom says from behind me.

I remember then what's inside the chest. I tell Justine to hold on. Pushing past Tom, I run from the bedroom down the hallway to the front room and the cedar chest. I open the lid. I scrounge through the things there—the newspaper clippings, memorial service programs, drawings, and photos—until my hands grip the thick, rough cotton of the tightly folded flag. I lift the flag from the chest. Holding it close, I run back to the bedroom and Justine. I lay the flag in her lap.

"Oh!" Startled, she lowers her hands. She takes in the flag, her eyes widening. Her hands hover above it for a long moment. Then she slips her hand into the flag's fold. She searches for something there, loosening the flag's triangular shape. Finally her fingers ball beneath the fabric as she clenches something in her fist. She draws her hand out. What she holds makes a metallic clinking. She looks up at me, her eyes suddenly clear. "Take these please. I'll feel better knowing they're gone."

I hold out my hand. She opens hers, and the casings of bullets fall into my palm.

"They saluted him at his memorial service, an honor, I know. But, Lord, I hate the sound of guns. I hate the look of any part of them," Justine says.

Then Justine lays the flag on top of her pillow. She lies down, tucking the flag beneath her head. In a moment she's asleep.

The telephone rings then—a shrill jangling that makes Tom and me jump. Tom goes to answer it. His low voice rises and falls in a conversation that goes on and on.

I am suddenly so cold on this hot summer day. So I lie down beside Justine. I nestle close to her. She smells like dry skin and powder and faintly, faintly like Linda and me.

Some time later Tom jostles my shoulder. I sit up with a start. Justine sleeps on. Tom tells me I've been out for less than twenty minutes.

"I have to get back to work," I whisper, clutching Tom's arm for balance and standing as quickly as I can without waking Justine.

Tom nods. He leads me out of the room and to the front door. There, he tells me that the doctor is stopping by soon. "A nice, old-fashioned house call." Tom says, rubbing his tired eyes. "The doc thinks maybe he can help her better here. It'll be less disruptive, and if we can get her on some kind of meds, it might really make a difference. He thinks we should wait a day or two before we take her anywhere."

"No Linda."

"No way," Tom says.

• • •

We get through a night, a day, another night. Working two shifts like this, and helping so much with opening up and closing down, I don't have time to think about much.

Not even David.

I haven't heard from him since he asked me to help with the orphanage.

I've managed to put some big boxes beneath my poster at Red Earth, and they're filling up quickly with toys, clothes, baby supplies. Bonnie and Beau are stopping by soon to pick up the stuff, and I've promised I'll get together with them to help organize as soon as I'm able. Maybe they'll have news of David.

Ravi has texted and called, and Jules too. It's helped, touching base with them. They're collecting a lot of donations as well, they say, and so is Caitlin.

And now, foraging for breakfast, I open the freezer and see the four honey hands. They are cracked at the wrists and broken at some of the fingers—his right thumb and left pinkie, and my right ring finger, where the tattoo of nettles used to be. There are little dried bits of what used to be baby's breath and nettles, scattered across the ice cube trays and the bags of frozen peas. I take out the frigid baking sheet. *That was then*, I think. *That was like something from another century, another millennium.* I swallow the knot in my throat and scrub the stinging from my eyes. Then I dump the hands into the garbage.

We're changing. It doesn't have to be a bad thing. It will make us stronger.

I study my tattoo, which is still beautiful, which hasn't changed at all, and I try to believe this.

Twenty-Two

My voice mail is clogged. In the little window of time between the afternoon and evening shifts, I sink down into a booth at Red Earth and listen.

I make a quick list on a napkin.

To call:

1. Linda: *"I know it's been three days now, Penelope, but I'm going to hibernate a little longer here at Isaac's. Sounds like you're doing great work...I'm doing great too."*

2. Isaac: *"Your mom wants me to clarify. She'll be home real soon. She's just needed a break for such a long time. This is a mini-vacation for her."* (*Laughter in the background.*)

3. Caitlin: *"It's not too late. Okay, so it's one in the morning, but we can still hook up, right? We want to see you! Yeah, so Jules says she'll come and get you. Are you at home or at work? Don't tell me you're still at work? Whatever. Jules'll pick you up wherever..."*

4. Linda again, cheerily: *"It's garbage day!"*

5. Tom: *"I know it's late, but Justine really wants to talk to you."* (*Muffled rustling.*) *"Here you go, Justine. Hold on there—"* (*The phone goes dead.*)

6. Justine: *"Here? Oh. Hello?" (The phone goes dead.)*

7. Caitlin: *"It's not too late…"*

8. Jules: *"Been thinking about you. How you doing? It's been a sucky week for me. Nothing big. Just lonely. Call when you can."*

9. Bonnie: *"We need you, Penna! We can't even make it through the living room anymore with all these boxes! It's a good problem to have, I know, but…when can you come over and help us organize all this? We really want to send it off to David."*

10. Ravi: *"I picked up some of my prep stuff yesterday. The AP materials are massive. How are you doing?"*

11. David: *"Hey, Penna. I hope you're okay. I'm doing…okay. I'll call back when I can."*

I try to call David back. Several times. He never answers.

I notch the ringer on my cell up to the highest volume. I put it on vibrate too. But over the din at Red Earth, I never hear when anyone calls.

● ● ●

Two more days pass this way. And then a morning comes when I drag myself out of bed, stagger to the kitchen, and, *voilà!* Linda is there, tottering around on crutches, brewing coffee, pouring a cup, doctoring it just the way I like it, and handing it to me.

She owes me, I think, taking a sip. I've been working so hard. She owes me this perfect cup and so much more. Just like I owe her. We owe each other something better.

I touch Owen's ring and say, "I want you to see Justine. I want you to try."

Linda freezes, the coffeepot still in her hand, suspended in midair.

I wait. I wait some more. My hands are a little shaky, so I set my cup of coffee on the table. Carefully, like it might crack, Linda sets the coffeepot on the counter. The kitchen is silent, except for the hiss of the last few drops of coffee dripping onto the pot's burner and sizzling there.

Linda hobbles over to a chair and sits down. She rests her face in her hands for a moment. When she looks up at me again, her face seems to sag with resignation. "Maybe. Just give me a little more time, Penelope. Please."

"Maybe isn't good enough. Soon."

"Maybe soon. *Soon*."

"Really?" My voice goes high and hopeful.

"Really." Linda smiles wearily. "Isaac and I have done a lot of talking. Maybe he's talked some sense into me. Though bear in mind, Penelope, I'm doing this for you. If it were just me, well, it wouldn't be happening."

I take a deep breath, trying to loosen the knot of emotion in my chest.

"Promise," I say.

Linda shakes her head. "If you weren't so into drawing, I'd say you should be a lawyer."

"I don't know what I'm into anymore. Maybe I should be a lawyer."

And then it happens. I start to cry.

"Oh, honey." Linda puts a wary hand on my shoulder. "Honey."

"I'm so tired," I say.

"You've done good," Linda says, "working so hard like that. With David gone, and Justine—thank you. Have I said thank you? Thank you. And Penelope?" Now Linda's arms are around me, warm and familiar. "How about this? I'm sorry."

That knot? I feel it slowly unsnarling into a thin, dark thread that I'll just have to absorb, I guess. I lean into Linda.

"Here," she finally says, nudging what's left of my coffee toward me. "Drink up. It'll do you good."

When I'm finished, she pushes herself up, hobbles over to the sugar and milk, and pours me another cup.

"I *did* miss you all that time I was at Isaac's," she says, stirring it all together.

I bite my lip. Then say it anyway, never mind how pathetic I sound. "You seemed pretty happy without me."

Linda gives me a look. "You always seemed pretty happy without me too."

I shrug. "Only with David." My face warms, realizing how this sounds. "I mean, it's not that I was *without* you, exactly. It was that I was *with* him."

"Exactly."

"Oh," I say, getting it.

"And you seem to be making other friends. That's good too."

I nod. It is good. I can't imagine life without Caitlin, Jules, and Ravi. Not now.

Linda clears her throat. "It's been forever for me, Penelope. Forever since I've felt this way about a man. Actually, it's been never. I'm way old for never."

Linda gives me that second cup of coffee then. She sits down beside me. She tells me a little bit about Isaac. Not too much. Just enough.

Enough for me to be really glad.

● ● ●

I continue to work hard at Red Earth. Tom and Isaac work hard. Josh works hard. Even Caitlin puts in extra effort. Together, we get through two weeks with Linda supervising and getting more involved with every passing day. I see Justine three or four times a week for afternoon tea between shifts. I mostly listen to her stories. A lot of the time she repeats herself. Other times we just sit quietly together. She seems to like that best. Sometimes I do quick sketches of her while we sit, and she likes that too.

I hardly hear from David. He's left a few messages on my cell. It's almost like he prefers leaving messages rather than talking to me.

"Hi. Missing you. Got your care package. It was great. Especially the cookies," he calls to say.

And then, "Penna, I know you're busy with Linda being laid up and everything. I'm just checking in to see how the donations are going."

And a few days after that, he leaves a message saying, "Hey. Only a few more weeks until school starts, huh? Bet you're excited. Bonnie says she's expecting you to come over real soon to help with the orphanage stuff. That's cool."

No matter how busy I am, I always call him back as soon as I get his message.

He never answers.

I remind myself of Justine, repeating the same old stories, because basically my days are about work and that's it.

Bonnie leaves a whole bunch of messages. I finally get a moment to call her, only to tell her that I won't be able to get over to her house for a few more days at least.

When Linda's really back at Red Earth—only a few more days now—and I can get a little sleep, I'll go back to Total Rush if that's what Caitlin and Jules want. I'll complain with Ravi about all the prep work for next year. I'll organize a whole semitruck worth of orphanage donations. I'll personally drive everything to the UPS store or the post office, whichever Bonnie and Beau want. I'll make and send off another care package for David too. I'll write a gross of long overdue mail and email—all of it positive and encouraging. I'll spend twice as much time with Justine.

• • •

And then one day, Linda's really back at work.

"Take the night off," she tells me as the lunch shift winds down. "Get some rest."

Problem is, I'm still so wound up with adrenaline that even now, when I have hours and hours to loll around in bed, I can't sleep. I toss and turn. I nod off and wake up again. At about six in the morning, when the birds start singing really loudly in the honey locust tree, I'm up for good. In a sleepy haze, I get out David's old letters from last year. I make a cup of coffee, sit down at the kitchen table, and read them.

I read one particular postcard over and over again, sent from Florida when David was visiting his grandparents. There's a gator wearing sunglasses on the front, and it really does look like it's smiling.

> *Penna—*
>
> *It's New Year's Eve. I know. We're not together. Do you know how much I wish we were? This much. Just now I held out my arms as wide as they can stretch. If I could break myself in two to be with you, I would.*
>
> *Tonight, walking on the beach, I picked up a whole bunch of shells for you.*
>
> *Love,*
> *David*

He took those shells and strung them into a necklace for me. The string broke when we went out last Valentine's Day. It was the first day it was warm enough to take out the motorcycle, and so we went on our roundabout ride. We were passing the farm fields when the shells went flying. When I got as broken up as the shells, David held me tight. "They were only for wishing on, really," he said. "There were ten shells, right?" I nodded. "So make ten wishes," he said.

I wished, ten times over, that we'd always be together.

I close my eyes as questions wash over me. *What do I wish for here and now? What is he wishing for over there? Is he still writing in the soft, black journals that he thinks are so cool? Why haven't I asked this? Why hasn't he told me?* He bought a bunch of them at the Oklahoma City art museum's gift shop that day of our first kiss. The journals weren't cheap. He spent a good chunk of change, way more than he usually spends on himself, but, "It's worth it," he said. "Made in France, hand stitched, used by dudes like Van Gogh and Picasso. How can I go wrong?"

He didn't go wrong. All last year he didn't go wrong. He filled the journals with words and pictures and little scraps of things—matchbook covers, ticket stubs, seed pods, bird feathers, Japanese candy wrappers, and old postage stamps—stuff anyone else might overlook but that caught his eye on any given day. "I like shiny, little things. Just call me Magpie," he said, which somehow I doubt he's saying to anyone in Iraq. Maybe I'm wrong. David would date every page, and all the pages worked together, each one completing what came before and after.

Once David asked me to kiss an inside cover, just so he could remember the exact shade of the lipstick I was wearing—a red that he especially liked. Another time, I cut off a lock of my hair, and he braided the strands and glued them to a page. And then there was the day when he licked his finger and gently dabbed an eyelash from my cheek, then glued that to a page too.

I open my eyes. I set the postcard aside. I take a deep breath, reminding myself of who I was, who I am. Who we were, who we are. I write David an email, because, assuming everything is okay with the lines, the connections, it's faster than a letter. *Connections*, I think. I remind him about the shell necklace and the Valentine's Day roundabout ride, and I tell him what I wished for ten times over. I want to make sure he remembers. I ask him if he's still keeping a journal. Then I tell him the nitty-gritty details of my life: *Officially survived the intense work schedule after Linda's accident. And guess what. Now Linda says she'll see Justine. I wish you were here for this.*

I send the email. Then I draw awhile to remember that I like to do that, I've always liked to do that, and I will like to do that still, when David comes home. I make it to just after noon. Then I do what I've been waiting to do: I walk to Tom's house.

●●●

Tom doesn't answer when I knock, so I go right in.

I find Justine sitting in the front room in the chair by the cedar chest. She's wearing her white dress. Newspaper clippings, photographs, and drawings litter the floor at her feet. Justine is smoothing the Gold Star banner across her lap.

"Penna," Justine says, smiling at me. "My star."

Her eyes are clear. She's her eighty-year-old self today. I'm so relieved that my knees go a little weak. I lean down and give her a hug.

Tom comes into the room then, apologizing for being in the bathroom (I tell him that's fine, *really*), and with his help Justine gets to her feet.

"Do you want to see Linda this afternoon?" Tom asks. He takes my breath away, asking this. Clearly, Tom's a "rip the Band-Aid off what hurts" kind of a guy. Or else he's just so nervous he doesn't know how to deal. From the way he's chewing at his lip, I think this might be the case.

I know how he feels.

For a moment, Justine's expression darkens with confusion, sadness, and fear. But then she nods.

I have no idea what Linda will do, how she will act, whether she will ruin or rebuild what I've worked so hard to make happen.

Tom leads Justine out the front door, and I follow. We help her into the front seat of Tom's truck. Tom sits down behind the steering wheel, and I sit on the other side of Justine. As we pull into the street and head off, Justine leans against me, weighing no more than a shadow, it seems. The few blocks slip past, and then, as we pull up in front of our house, she says softly, "Home."

Twenty-Three

Linda is back from the lunch shift. She's in the kitchen, rinsing out the coffeepot. When we come in, she practically drops the coffeepot into the sink, and then she just stares at Justine. Her look isn't angry or rude; it's stunned. Her face is as pale as when she broke her ankle. She runs her hand roughly across her mouth to stop its trembling. This doesn't work. She glances at me.

Justine points down the hallway, wordlessly asking Linda's permission to look around. Linda nods. We follow Justine—Tom, Linda, and me. With each slow step, Justine's raised hands hover before the photographs that line the walls. Suddenly she veers into my room. She is saying that she used to draw and paint here, and then it became Linda's room when Linda was born.

"I remember it like yesterday," she says.

We follow her through the doorway to her past.

"I drew so many pictures here." Justine gazes out the window, her fingers on the glass.

She leans closer to the window and her breath clouds the glass. "I drew that very honey locust tree. It was so much smaller then, just a slip of a thing. I drew this street when there was nothing else here. Now look at it all. So much, so many strangers." She turns to us, panic constricting her expression.

"I draw that honey locust tree too." I start at the surprising urgency in my voice. "This is my room now."

"I know." Justine's face softens, studying mine. "I'm glad." She sees the quilt then, Plum Tumble, spread across the end of my bed. She goes and gathers the quilt into her arms. She hides her face in the soft folds. "Still here." There is wonder in her voice.

"You can have it back," I say. I feel Linda watching me. "We found it when we first moved in. You should have it."

Linda has been so quiet since we came inside. Now she clears her throat and says, "I thought you made it. Was I right?"

Justine lifts her face from the quilt and nods at Linda. "I made it for Owen. He couldn't take it with him when he went overseas. He said I'd need it more than he did. Maybe he was right. But Ernest keeping it all those years…I can't believe it."

"I remember Dad wrapping up in it on chilly days," Linda says. "When Penna and I first found it, I thought it still smelled like him. Boozy. You know."

"Oh." Justine buries her face in the quilt again and breathes deep. "He's gone." She looks up at Linda, her brow furrowed with lurking confusion. "Isn't he? He's really gone."

Linda swallows hard. "Who?"

"Why, Ernest."

"Most of the time." Linda's voice is quiet.

"We washed the quilt right away," I say firmly. "So it just smells like us now."

"It smells good," Justine says.

I smile. But I'm still wary, watching Justine's every move and expression for some sign that it's not the twenty-first century anymore, but decades ago, before any of us but Justine was born, before Linda and I were even imagined.

Justine lays Plum Tumble back across the foot of my bed, and then she leads us to Linda's bedroom—the room Justine says she shared with Owen, and later Ernest. Justine doesn't seem to care about the dark purple walls—though I bet they weren't purple when she slept here. Standing before Linda's dresser, she presses her hands to her temple. She rubs at some other pain there—nothing to do with color.

"Maybe I should have moved houses altogether," she says. "Maybe that would have helped Ernest and me. But he wanted *this* house. He wanted it so much. More than me, I think."

Tom mumbles something like reassurance. "But if you'd done that, moved, maybe we wouldn't all be standing here together now."

Justine doesn't seem to hear. She looks at the things Linda has displayed on the dresser's top—my framed school pictures, some stones from Lake Michigan, dried flowers in a vase, two earrings missing their mates that Linda likes so much she can't bear to throw away.

Justine picks up my third-grade school photograph, studies it, and then sets it back exactly where it was. "You grew up good."

I don't know whether Justine is talking about Linda or me. It doesn't much matter. But Linda crosses her arms over her chest and watches her mother, and I see tears in her eyes.

Justine leads us into the kitchen now. "Why, it's hardly changed!" Justine claps her hands, joyful and relieved. "I'd know that linoleum anywhere."

"We'd like to do something about that." Linda strides over to the sink and pours herself a glass of water. She doesn't offer one to Justine. "Some updating. You know."

Justine says, "Of course."

"She understands," I say quietly.

But then Justine turns to Linda and says, "I don't know how to begin."

Linda's mouth twists. "Me either."

I've never heard Linda sound like this, so hopeless. The pain in her voice sucks all the air out of me. *Breathe in, breathe out.* I think of the guy going kill-crazy in that video. I'd strike out in panic at the wall I can almost see rising up between my mother and my grandmother. I'd strike out just like that guy did. I'd go kill-crazy if I could. But I can't move. My arms and legs seem to have turned to solid blocks of stone.

I force out the words because someone has to say something, someone has to push us through this wall.

"We don't have to begin. We're right in the middle."

But Justine is right at the end, I think then. I don't say that—I don't have to, because Justine and Linda turn to me in a movement so similar that it seems planned, choreographed, a kind of dance. They look at me. A minute passes, maybe, a long minute where nobody moves. I can hear Tom breathing hard, the sound of a heavy-set man whose heart just might be breaking.

"Oh, Penelope," Linda says. "Is this what you really want?"

I nod.

Linda hugs herself. This is what she's always done. She's held herself. Since she was a very little girl. She's held it together. For herself, for me, for us. Now she's doing it all over again.

Justine holds out her arms to Linda. "Please," Justine says.

Slowly, one step at a time, Linda walks toward Justine. Linda's still holding herself tight. But she lets Justine hold her too.

Thank you. I think I say this aloud. But I can't be sure.

Only a moment passes before Linda quickly pulls away. Linda's face is flushed now. Her gaze darts nervously, lighting on anything but Justine.

"Why don't you all just sit down for a little bit?" I sound like some kind of hoity-toity hostess who barely knows her guests. When I gesture toward the living room, I might as well be made of rusted metal—my arm moves that clumsily. "Take a seat," I actually say.

Justine and Linda seem grateful for any direction. In an awkward manner that rivals my own—like daughter, like mother, like grandmother—they turn, Tom's steadying hand at Justine's elbow. Like that, they walk into the living room. Tom settles Justine on the couch. Linda sits a safe distance away.

• • •

Tom and I bumble around the kitchen, making lemonade, putting cookies on a plate. Tom wonders if maybe somebody needs something more substantial to eat. We decide to make sandwiches and soup too.

"You really need to do some shopping." Tom is scrounging through the refrigerator.

"I haven't exactly had a lot of leisure time these last few days."

"No need to get snappish." Tom shuts the refrigerator and turns to me with what's left of the ham-and-cheese deli packets in his hands. "You holding up otherwise? I mean, except for provisions?"

I dump some ice cubes into the pitcher of lemonade. "Guess so."

"You heard from him?"

I keep my gaze on the ice spiraling in the powdery, yellow drink. "Some." Tom drapes slices of ham and cheese across a plate. The deli packets empty now, he tosses them into the garbage and then pulls what's left of a loaf of bread from the pantry. "Want some advice?" Tom doesn't wait for my answer. "Don't take it personally."

"How should I take it?"

Tom starts to answer, but I don't hear him. I hear only my cell ringing from the living room.

I run toward the sound. I find my cell in my bag beside the couch where Linda and Justine sit at a safe distance from one another. They are talking in herky-jerky phrases, brief questions and halting answers.

At least they are talking.

This thought flashes through my mind, and only this, before I grab my cell from my bag and head toward my room, saying all in a rush, "Hello, hello, hello. Are you there?"

"I'm here," David says.

"And I'm here," I say.

I wish one of us would laugh. But we don't.

I drop down on my bed and wrap Plum Tumble around my shoulders.

"There's something I have to tell you," David says.

"Like, *everything*. Tell me everything. It's been so crazy here. I know it's been crazy there too." I loop my thumb through Owen's ring. I pull down until the necklace digs into the back of my neck. "But now we can talk. Finally. Tell me. And then I'll tell you."

Positive. Encouraging. Loyal. I am these things.

David draws in a sharp breath.

I feel suddenly ill.

I think it. *Oh no*, I think. *Here it comes.*

David says, "All these guys have been getting these Dear John letters. Some of the girls here are getting them too. Dear Janes."

"Weird. I don't know that many Johns. Or Janes." My laughter sounds like crying. "They all must be in the army."

David doesn't laugh. "Guess you don't know what a Dear John letter is."

I shake my head. "Guess I don't."

"It's crap like, 'Sorry. I can't handle this. Maybe we'll hook up again when you get back. But right now it's over between you and me.' Crap like that."

David waits for me to respond. I can't.

"It's a break-up letter," he says.

Something burns at the back of my neck, and then my necklace snaps and puddles in my hand. I was pulling on it that hard. The thin, gold chain slips to the floor, but Owen's ring stays hooked on my thumb.

"What does that have to do with us?" I hear myself say this. I sound distant, as if I'm in a different room or calling from another continent. "I only write Dear David letters."

"But what if you change your mind?"

I clench Owen's ring tighter. "I won't."

"There are people dying over here, Penna. And it's not always from IEDs. Lately it's mostly been from Dear John letters."

He's almost crying now. He's trying to hide it, holding the phone at a distance, muffling it with his hand. But his voice is thick with tears.

"I can't do this," he says.

He says other stuff too. He says he's still glad he enlisted. That's not it. He still believes in what he's doing. That hasn't changed. He still loves me too. As much as ever. But with fear attached. He can't go any deeper right now. That's it. That's all. That's all there is to it. He can't go on any longer. He's too scared—not of fighting a war, but of being in love.

"When I come home again, then maybe if you want, Penna, we can try again. I'll try again then if you'll let me. But for now, no," he says.

"David."

"You don't have to forgive me. But I am sorry, Penna. I'm really sorry. I just can't anymore. I just can't."

He says he loves me. He says he'll write me. He says good-bye. He hangs up.

I set down my phone. I slip Owen's ring off my thumb and put it on my right ring finger.

Owen's ring is too loose to hide the tattoo.

• • •

"Penna?" It's Justine, standing in the doorway, flanked by Linda and Tom.

I stare at them, trying to remember why we're all here. I shiver under Plum Tumble. I draw the quilt closer around my shoulders, but this doesn't seem to help.

"David says we're done."

I've said it.

I cast off the quilt and push past my family. My *family*. I worked so hard to bring them together. How am I all broken apart? I run to the bathroom and hunch over the toilet, sure I'm going to be sick.

Nothing happens. Nothing but the drip of water into the sink.

I go back to my bedroom. Linda and Tom are at the window, looking down through the leaves of the honey locust tree to the place where David and I once kissed. They are talking quietly. They don't hear me come into the room.

But Justine does. She is standing at my dresser, holding her photograph. There is the girl she used to be, the girl so close to my age, running a silver brush through her hair, looking at a boy she loved and lost.

Justine looks at me. She is really here, looking at me. She is not just a photograph. I go to her. She sets the photograph back in its place. She draws me close.

She is so frail. Her mind is changing. The way she remembers—that is changing too. But I know that when she's able, Justine will listen to whatever I have to say about love and loss. She will listen with the same care and concern that I have felt listening to her.

Only problem, I can't imagine I'll ever have anything to say again.

● ● ●

The first word I say is, "No."

Linda has given me the night off, and Justine is at Red Earth too, eating one of Isaac's daily specials. Justine wanted to spend the evening with me, but when she told me so, I said no. She asked if I wanted her company, and I said no. And when Justine, Tom, and Linda finally left, I kept right on saying no to the empty house. For a while I walked from room to room, whispering, saying, shouting *no*, again and again.

I sit down at my computer and write it to David: *No.*

He doesn't write back. It's unreasonable to expect him to respond. So what? That's how I'm feeling. Unreasonable. And angry.

I turn away from my computer. *I still love you. I just can't.* What kind of logic is that? What does it mean? I look down at my hands, curled like dead birds in my lap. I see my tattoo. I think, *Nothing. This means nothing now.* Then I see Owen's ring, slipping away from the braid of my tattoo.

A dead man's ring means more to me than my tattoo.

I turn back to my computer. I whip off another email to David.

How can you? This is ME. I held on for you.

I send this off too. Never mind the voice in my head. I ignore it. I turn on some music, turn it on loud.

You knew this was coming.

I turn the music louder.

Two or three songs later, I don't hear my phone ringing. I see it flashing on my desk.

David, I think. *He's calling me back. He's calling to apologize.*

What will I say? I'll have to figure it out as I go. Hasn't that been what I've been doing this whole time he's been away—first at OSUT, then now? Figuring it out? Winging it? There's no map for this, what we're doing, what I'm feeling. I'll figure it out.

I pick up the phone.

It's Caitlin. And Ravi. He's there too. And Jules. They're in Jules's car. Jules is driving toward me.

Ravi grabs the phone from Caitlin. "Tom told Caitlin, and then he called Josh, who said he'd be glad to put in a few extra hours over the dinner shift. And Bonnie told me. Bonnie's really worried about both you and David, Penna. And I texted Jules, though of course Caitlin already had."

"No," I say, because I'm in the habit.

Ravi acts like he doesn't hear. "We'll stay in. We'll go out. Whatever you want to do, Penna. But we've decided. All of us. You're not going to be alone tonight."

"No. Stop. I don't want you here. I want to be alone," I say. "But thanks."

After we say good-bye, I take off Owen's ring and put it beside Justine's photograph. If I could take off my tattoo, I'd do that too.

Twenty-Four

Of course they don't listen to no.

They knock on the front door and fling pebbles against my bedroom window until the sound drives me right out of the house.

I find them under the honey locust tree. Looks like they found the old ladder that was in the garage when we moved here. They've propped it beneath my window. Caitlin is halfway up.

"Excuse me," I say.

Ravi and Jules, who are bracing the ladder, jump at the sound of my voice. Caitlin nearly falls from the ladder. She just manages to regain her balance.

"'O Romeo, Romeo, wherefore art thou, Romeo?'" she says, her voice dripping with dramatic longing. Then she claps a hand to her mouth and looks at me, her face flushing. "Sorry!" Her apology is muffled by her hand.

"Nice one, Cait," Ravi mutters.

I don't wait for further apologies. I start back inside.

But Jules has me by the arm before I can take more than a few steps, and then Ravi has me by the other arm, and the next thing I know, Caitlin has zipped past us. She's leading us up the front porch steps and through the open door.

They sit me down at my own kitchen table.

Jules makes herself at home first. She scrounges around and figures out the coffee situation. She puts on a fresh pot. The room is quiet, other than the sounds of the coffee brewing. Fine. They insisted on coming here. They can live with the quiet. Because I have nothing to say. I am empty.

Jules pours us coffee. Caitlin knows how I like mine, so she doctors it the way Linda does. Then we sit there, the four of us, and drink coffee in silence.

I glance up at the clock and see that fifteen minutes have passed.

"Please go," I say.

And as soon as I say it, I realize how much I want them to stay. I've wanted them all along.

David and I were big. Are big. But the broken, beat-up, warring, loving, beautiful, truthful world is bigger than us by far.

I remember the little girl in her bandages and red dress. The way David looked at her, his gaunt face.

That's when I finally start to cry.

They hold on.

I hold on.

After a while, I can finally hold it together.

●●●

They offer to take me out to dinner—somewhere different from Red Earth. Ravi says he texted his sister, the incredible amateur chef. She is up for cooking for me tonight. Or we could get carry-out. They also suggest Total Rush. A movie. A drive out into the country. A drive into Oklahoma City.

"You could come to my house, and we could sit on the back porch," Caitlin says.

"The mall over in Edmond is still open. We could go there. A new pair of shoes might do you some good. Been known to help me," Jules says.

I tell them there's only one place I want to go.

We drive to the viaduct.

I lean against David's painting of me, big and blue. I still fit inside. This surprises me. I feel so different from that girl.

Ravi, Jules, and Caitlin lean against Jules's car, watching me, pretending that they're not.

Ravi doesn't have his skateboard. I miss the sound of it, skimming so freely over the concrete, up and down the mural.

This surprises me too.

I take a deep breath. How long has it been since I breathed? Has it been since David's last phone call?

His last phone call. I close my eyes at the thought.

But I can't stand here forever with my eyes closed, leaning against what used to be.

I open my eyes again. "Let's go get something to eat. Something good. Something at Red Earth," I say.

They smile at me, the three of them, and their smiles are full of welcome.

Hey. Good. You're still here, their smiles seem to say.

● ● ●

A week later I'm eating lunch at the kitchen table with Justine and Linda. I'm beat. In spite of the summer heat and the lunch—soup that Justine whipped together out of a few cans and some forlorn vegetables scavenged from the back of the fridge—I can't get warm. I can't wake up. All I can think of is bed.

In just a minute I'll tuck myself back under Plum Tumble. I'm going to stay there until I have to roll out again and get ready for Red Earth. I've been back working just one shift for five days, but I'm still wiped out from the last few weeks. I'm still grabbing naps whenever I can. Linda's worried it's because I'm depressed, I can tell. And maybe there's something to that. But I'm not going to stop sleeping when I need it.

I might see a counselor, though. If Linda has her way.

"Now's the time to get lost in your job. It's the best way to get over someone. That's been my experience," Linda says, blowing on a steaming spoonful of soup. Linda must have registered Justine's sharp glance then, because she quickly adds, "But that's just my experience. You'll tell us what you need, won't you, Penelope?"

I nod. I finish my lunch. I go to my room, intent only on bed.

But for the first time in a week, I really take notice of Owen's ring, glinting in the sun on my desk. I pick the ring up. I hook my thumb through it. Then I go back into the kitchen, where Linda and Justine are still sitting, quietly talking. They're not nearly as herky-jerky anymore. They're almost comfortable with each other. That's a relief. I hold the ring out to Justine. I ask her if she would mind keeping it just a little while longer.

"Why?" she asks.

I hesitate only for a moment. "I don't know exactly. Just a hunch you might want it."

Which is true, as is what I don't say: *for a little while I think I need a break from the extra weight.*

Justine knits her brow, even as she takes the ring and slips it onto her own thumb. "You won't forget?"

"Never," I say.

Then I go back to my room and write an email to David. It's just a few lines. It's only been a week since he broke up with me, after all. He hasn't called or written like he said he would. But I'm not going to wait around anymore. I write:

> Hold on.
>> I think you probably did us both a favor for now.
>> I'll still be here when you get back.
>> And we'll do what's right then too.

●●●

About halfway through my shift at Red Earth that night, I see Bonnie hovering by the door in the blue jukebox light. She gives me a little wave. I go deer-in-the-headlights still. I don't know why. I trust Bonnie. I do. But if you're someone's mother, whose side are you inevitably on? I don't want anyone telling me I did something wrong, this is my fault, if I'd only X or Y or Z. I don't want to hear about David's troubles from anyone but David. I just want to do my job.

Bonnie is standing before me now. She holds out her hand.

Not knowing what to do, I shake her hand, which feels all wrong. We should be hugging. We always hugged. Bonnie's expression crumples as we let go of each other's hands. She's almost in tears.

"David told me," she says.

I've always liked Bonnie. She's always liked me. I'm not going to forget that now. I manage something like a smile, though it probably looks like a grimace.

"I'm sorry," Bonnie says. "I don't understand my son right now. But if there's anything I can do…"

"Let me help get the stuff together for that place." The words rush from me, taking me by surprise.

Bonnie looks equally surprised. "What did you say?"

I clear my throat, try again. "You've still got those boxes in the house for the orphanage?"

"And at the churches, library, community center." Bonnie nods. "It's a crazy mess."

"Let me help," I say. "You wanted my help before."

Bonnie nods hard, her spiky hair stirring with the effort.

"I can get more stuff too, especially after school starts. Ravi's already emailed the guidance counselor about it." Possibilities flood my mind. "I'm thinking I might try to get art supplies. I could get some books on drawing and painting and send those too."

Then Linda comes over to us and Bonnie just about goes ballistic, telling her what a great person I am. "A real angel," she says.

When I can't take it anymore, I slip away to the bathroom. I hide in the same stall. A few days ago I scrubbed off the grafitti of David and me in the nest. There's some new graffiti now, the typical stuff, written by people I don't know. Otherwise everything would be completely familiar if I had even the slightest hope that David would call.

●●●

Closing time. Almost ready to go home.

"Look at this, will you?" Tom yells from the bar. He's pointing at the television, a war story.

I don't turn away. I make myself watch the footage: Mortar fire in a marketplace. Another IED doing its dirty work. Another jeep blown to bits somewhere. And shrouded bodies.

"'Death blossom,'" the reporter says.

Death blossom, I think. *I have to find out what that is. Death blossom.*

Tom flings a damp towel at the TV. The towel hits the screen with a thwack, only briefly obliterating the image before it falls to the floor.

"Enough already," Tom says.

"Where is it this time?" I ask.

When Tom tells me, I really listen. We stay way past closing, him talking, me trying, really trying, to understand.

Twenty-Five

The weekend before school starts, Tom drives Justine and me over to the viaduct. Justine wants to see what I painted there. She's seen my drawings and sketches. Linda was the one who suggested I show her the mural. We were over at Tom's, sitting on the back porch. Justine had had a few bad days, but this was a good one.

"Penna's mural is incredible, Mom," Linda said.

That was the first Linda ever called Justine that. We all went very quiet. *Mom.* The word seemed to echo in the warm air.

Now, holding Justine's arm, guiding her around the cracks in the dry streambed to stand before the tall killdeer in their single nest and the sloppy, gorgeous paintings of David and me, big and blue, I realize what I have to do.

Justine squeezes my hand. "So there you are," she murmurs. "There he is." She sounds sad saying this, almost like I've painted Owen.

I feel sad too. But I don't turn away. I can look at it. I can see him, me, us for what we were and are. We may not be exactly the same, but we're still alive. We're doing the best we can.

I turn to Justine. "Will you help me?"

For a moment she looks puzzled. But then she smiles and nods. "If I can."

●●●

"It's even better than before," Linda says.

Morning light strikes the viaduct mural just so, warming the feathers on the painted birds, igniting the golden swatches of the Icon Killdeer's halo like fire. Linda and Isaac are sitting on the fender of Isaac's pickup, drinking coffee from a thermos and waiting while Justine, with Tom's help, and I finish up a much bigger picture of the world.

Ravi, Caitlin, and Jules finished their work on the mural a while ago. Now they're practicing tricks on Ravi's skateboard. Back and forth the wheels skim. The steady sound soothes me. When someone falls—and Caitlin and Jules both take their falls—I appreciate the repetitive rhythm all the more. When I get tired I've been able to match my brush strokes to it, and that's kept me going.

Justine is tired. She wearily balances her paintbrush on the open can of gold paint that she used to add the finishing touches to her picture of Owen, a bugle raised to his lips, and to her picture of Ernest, sitting in a chair under Plum Tumble. They look young again, whole bodied and good spirited, there on the front of porch of the little gray house that we've all shared.

I touch Justine's arm. "It's good."

Justine smiles. Leaning on Tom, she walks over to the truck. Isaac stands and steps aside, making room. Justine sits down beside Linda.

"Want some coffee?" Linda asks.

Justine nods. And there it is, flashing across her face, her surprise and joy that she is sitting here with us all on a fine late summer morning, sharing coffee.

They're all right. All of them, sitting there, they're all right. They'll wait for me. As will Jules, who painted a blond guy wearing a bracelet with her name on it, who must be Zach. And Caitlin, who painted herself boarding a train bound for the bright lights and big city. (She's still got that urge to escape this place and make it on Broadway or in LA. She and Justine have been talking.) And Ravi, who painted his father wearing a T-shirt printed with an American flag. They hang out here, waiting for me, holding on.

I look back at the mural. Late last night I made a list of what I wanted to paint this morning, almost too many images to number. A motorcycle. A dirt road. All that and more, simply done, but good enough for me.

Last thing, which is now, because, like Justine, my hand can't hold a brush anymore, I swiftly outline David in his cape, finally a hero. I'll fill in the colors and details gradually over the weeks to come. But for now the bold curves and angles of his form are enough for me. Here, he plucks ripe tomatoes from a hardy vine and shares them with the little girl in a red dress. Her bandages are gone. They both look healthy. Soon he'll be coming home, and God help her, she will be going somewhere that feels like home too.

That's my wish.

Tips for an Army Girlfriend

While he (or she) is away, it's most important to hold on to yourself. Of course there are as many ways to do this as there are people, but we thought we'd offer a few suggestions to help you survive, maybe even thrive, during this challenging time. If, as you read through our tips and resources, you realize you have others to share, please visit whilehewasaway.com. Karen will make sure to post your ideas and experiences there.

- Write constantly. Even when you don't hear back for a while. Be open and honest with your communication, so it's easier to trust each other.
- Learn to be independent, and be supportive. Try to lift his spirits.
- To help your own spirits, spend time with friends and family and others who have endured separations from those they love. Find those people who know how to listen and who will work to understand.
- Make sure you always have your phone on you...and the volume turned up! You don't want to miss any opportunity to make a connection.

- Send care packages as often as you can—and enough cookies to feed all his friends! Try spraying your perfume in the box to remind him of home.
- Stay healthy. Continue to eat right and exercise. Exercise is a great way to release endorphins!
- Learn the military acronyms, lingo, and jargon so it's easier to communicate.
- Keep yourself busy. Volunteer or take up a hobby—just make sure you have something to do with your time besides waiting. You might spend the time you're apart making something for him. You may discover gifts you never knew you had.
- Above all, be positive. Always.

other resources

- **www.dailystrength.org/c/Military-Families** An online support group for friends, families, and significant others of military members.
- **www.experienceproject.com/groups/Am-A-United-States-Army-Girlfriend/41268** Stories, advice, support, and chat from fellow army girlfriends.
- **www.lovingfromadistance.com** Advice and support for couples in long distance relationships.
- **www.marriedtothearmy.com** Information and resources for army families including online support groups for family members.
- **www.militaryfamiliesunited.org** A group that supports soldiers, veterans, and their families through charities and volunteer work.

- **www.militarysos.com** Support and resources for military significant others. Includes support groups, answers to frequently asked questions, and advice on topics such as what to send in a care package.

- **www.militarytimes.com/forum/forumdisplay.php?180-Military-Girlfriends** A community forum within the military news site, Military Times. Includes discussions, advice, and support from other army girlfriends.

Author's Note

As I wrote *While He Was Away*, I worked to better understand the experiences and choices of people most immediately affected by the Iraq War. I turned to the art of wounded warriors, books, movies, blogs, websites, and chat rooms. I am particularly grateful for a series of stories featured on NPR's news show *All Things Considered*. Reported by Corey Flintoff—who was part of the NPR team covering the Iraq War, embedded within U.S. military units fighting insurgents and hunting roadside bombs—these pieces had titles like "Deadly Concentration: Finding IEDs at Night." If you have the opportunity to listen to them online, do so. In his reporting Flintoff achieves what radio does best: he makes an experience live through sound. He took me into the lives of people patrolling the streets in Iraq—he gave his voice to the place, and, most importantly, he let those people give their voices to it too.

The work of the Iraqi American artist Wafaa Bilal also influenced me. In his book, *Shoot an Iraqi: Art, Life, and Resistance Under the Gun*, Bilal remembers growing up in Iraq under Saddam Hussein, the Gulf War bombardment, Sunni-Shi'a violence, a refugee camp, and his life as an artist in the United States. When Bilal's brother was killed by an unmanned American drone, Bilal was prompted to create his 2007 interactive performance piece titled "Domestic Tension." For twenty-four hours every day for a month, Bilal lived in confinement, under constant fire from a chat room–controlled paint-ball gun. His chronicle of that time found its way into *While He Was Away*.

Acknowledgments

I never imagined I would write a novel about love and war. I never imagined I would have the courage. Now that I've given it my best attempt, I'm finding it almost as hard to find the right words to thank those who inspired and helped me along the way. My fiction pales in comparison to the reality of military service and to the experience of people who love soldiers and wait for them to come home.

I grew up hearing war stories, or hearing the resounding silence that served to muffle the trauma. My father served in multiple theaters during World War II. My mother lost her first husband there as well. So I'll begin at the beginning and thank my parents for sharing with me a glimpse of what they survived.

I am deeply indebted to the men and women who allowed me to interview them regarding their experience, serving and loving through wartime. They include Victor J. Garcia, an Iraq War veteran, Joan Halvorsen (who *always* gives), and also the incredible collective of Gold Star Wives who responded through their website to my questions. My friends Engineman First Class Horatio Chavez and Jen Chavez were exceedingly generous in their insights and in their affirmation of this project. Gail Schultz Ravitts allowed me to read her evocative memoir, *They're Playing Our Song*. It helped me not only remember the details of the 1940s but also brought me into the realities of a young woman at that time. In the last weeks of revision, Mr. Carl Francik and Captain Carl R. Weimer, United States Army, helped me by sharing details of their experiences in Iraq. And Master Sergeant Mark Hayes, Senior Military Science Instructor at Wheaton College, patiently answered all my phone calls and relayed the nuances of deployment. What I have written is the tip of the iceberg compared to what I have learned from these generous people.

This novel went through numerous drafts and great, gutting revisions. Laura Ruby, Cecelia Downs, and Gina Frangello asked the right questions at the right times. I am also grateful for the gentle scrutiny of Kathleen Leid, a true believer in books, who helped me see possibilities. Jennifer Grant blessed my efforts from the beginning and always asked for more of Penna and David. Thanks to the members of Redbud Writers Guild, champs at championing the soul's path. And to Lynn Wollstadt and Danna Gross, who really know their ink. And a special *grazie* to Carmela Martino, writer, teacher, collaborator, and friend, who met with me at a coffee shop over a period of months, hashing out the *what ifs* of *While He Was Away* and helping me discover the answers.

Without the support of the Van Kampen Boyer Molinari Charitable Foundation, I would not have had the time and resources I needed to finish the final draft. On a personal level, Randi and Mark Woodworth have been true and loyal friends all through this process. They loaned me a room of my own—one with a window that looked out onto a tree, which held a nest with a robin that brooded over her eggs as I brooded over the last pages of this book.

Many, many thanks to my agent, Sara Crowe, who waited with fortitude and sweet good humor for each evolving draft. She dexterously steered me along the circuitous path of publication and continues to gracefully support me along the way. And my heartfelt gratitude to my editor, Leah Hultenschmidt, and her colleagues at Sourcebooks, who chose this book, gave it a home, and helped it grow up and move out into the world. Along with Aubrey Poole, Kelly Barrales-Saylor, Kristin Zelazko, Lisa Novak, and Derry Wilkens, Leah has provided all the wisdom, insight, humor, and independent vision that I, as a writer, could ever want or need.

Finally, my husband, photographer Greg Halvorsen Schreck, was the first person reading and believing from the beginning through the middle to the end. Without him, and my children, Magdalena and Teo, I would not be who I am, and this book simply would not be. Thank you, dear family, for time, space, respect, comfort, and—forever and always—thank you for your love.

About the Author

Karen Schreck is the author of the young adult novel *Dream Journal* and the children's book *Lucy's Family Tree*, as well as various award-winning short stories, one of which earned a Pushcart Prize. She received her doctorate in creative writing and enjoys writing and teaching for a living. She also enjoys music, movies, cross-country skiing, yoga, traveling, and eating good food with friends. Karen once had lunch with the queen of Holland. There were many forks. Perhaps this inspired Karen's (failed) attempts at waitressing. She now lives outside Chicago with her husband and two children. You may visit her at karenschreck.com/blog, whilehewasaway.com, or on Facebook. If you'd like Karen to visit you (either virtually or in person) at your school, library, or gathering, please contact her. She'd be delighted to discuss the possibilities.